ALL THROUGH THE NIGHT

By the same author:

Who Goes Next?
The Bastard
Pool of Tears
A Nest of Rats
Do Nothin' Till You Hear From Me
The Day of the Peppercorn Kill
The Jury People
Thief of Time
A Ripple of Murders
Brainwash
Duty Elsewhere
Take Murder...
The Eye of the Beholder
The Venus Fly-Trap
Dominoes
Man of Law
All on a Summer's Day
Blayde R.I.P.
An Urge for Justice
Their Evil Ways
Spiral Staircase
Cul-de-Sac
The Forest
The Ride
Clouds of Guilt

JOHN WAINWRIGHT
ALL THROUGH THE NIGHT

St. Martin's Press
New York

Library of Congress Cataloging in Publication Data

Wainwright, John William, 1921-
    All through the night.
    I. Title.
PR6073.A354A794   1985   823'.914   85-11781
ISBN 0-312-02040-6

First published in Great Britain by Macmillan London Ltd.

First U.S. Edition

10 9 8 7 6 5 4 3 2 1

10 p.m. Radholme. Population, 25,000. A market town, not too far from the commercialised beauty of the Yorkshire Dales; not too far from the old Yorkshire/Lancashire border. A strictly functional town, without the gewgaws and guest houses which acne the better known tourist centres. A place where hard-headed sheep farmers and their wives buy and sell; where a few hundred moderately well off muck-and-brass Northerners have retired to solidly built cottages and bungalows of their own design. A town of basic values and no-nonsense opinions, where the effete Southerner – by which is meant anybody south of Nottingham – is looked upon with long-suffering tolerance as being a creature not yet quite dry behind the ears.

The four uniformed coppers descended the shallow steps of the police station. It was Tuesday, May the first and, by past reckoning, one of the quieter days of the week, followed by one of the quieter nights. Monday gave you the tail-end of the weekend. Friday saw the gradual build-up to the increased activity of Saturday. In spring, summer and autumn Sunday brought the traffic. Wednesday was market day and Thursday was half-day closing. Which left Tuesday; a something-and-nothing day when, as a general rule, the town relaxed, got its second wind and prepared itself for the surrounding hamlets and villages to shunt people in to mill around the stalls and open auctions of tomorrow. A something-and-nothing day, followed by a something-and-nothing night.

At the foot of the steps Kelly peeled off to the right.

Bell called a soft, 'Take care,' but Kelly didn't answer.

Kelly didn't even hear. Bell was his friend – a buddy, closer than most brothers – and, normally, Kelly would have raised a hand in a half-salute and come back with, 'And you.' But not tonight. Tonight Kelly's mind was filled with hurtful, and very personal, thoughts.

Next week, next month – some day in the vague and unknown future – the mental merry-go-round would slow down. The perpetual hint of headache would ease and friendship would resume. Indeed, friendship had never ceased; it had merely been given second place in priorities.

Meanwhile, thank God for small mercies.

Thank God (and Boothby) for 'A' Beat.

Kelly rounded a corner, crossed a road and, almost automatically, stretched out a hand to turn the knob of the first of the lock-up property.

Police Constable 1430 Bell – 'Dinger' Bell to his friends – was working 'D' Beat. D for Deadly. Deadly because 'D' Beat took in most of the high-class residential stuff. Flash houses and swish bungalows, occupied by an array of real gold-plated pillicocks. Not all, of course, but enough.

'I'm going away for a few days, constable. Will you keep an eye on my place, please?'

'Certainly, madam.'

'And Tiddles.'

'Tiddles?'

'He needs feeding, while I'm away.'

'Oh!'

'I'll arrange for milk to be delivered, and he can get in and out through the cat door. If I leave a supply of cat food in the out-house, you can . . . '

'I'm sorry, we can't do that, madam.'

'What?'

'We can't be responsible for domestic pets.'

Thereafter a prolonged argument with a woman who has never accepted 'No' for an answer in her life. Eventually, the suggestion that a slipped fiver might oil the wheels of non-officialdom. Then the counter-suggestion that the local cattery might be a better place to look after Tiddles.

'He'd fret.'

'They're very good, madam.'

'He'd be heartbroken.'

'One of the neighbours, perhaps.'

'I don't *trust* the neighbours.'

'I don't mean leave a key.'

'I trust *you*.'

'That's very good of you, madam, but . . . '

6

'Nobody else would feed him properly.' Then, petulantly, 'It's not asking a lot, officer.'

'I'm sorry.'

'I'm not asking you to go out of your way.'

'I'm sorry, madam. We're not allowed.'

'Rubbish.'

'I assure you. If we did it for you, we'd have to do it for everybody.'

'I'll have a word with Tommy.'

'Yes, madam.'

'Tommy' being the superintendent, and the remark being made to emphasise the fact that she was on first-name terms with *that* berk. Then, the next day, a call to Smeaton's office. A complaint of impudence, no less. Thereafter the superintendent's song-and-dance act. Sure, he wanted to keep in with the right people and, knowing these clowns, she might even have a direct line to the chief constable himself. But – hell's teeth! – not wet-nursing a bloody cat.

That was the sort of pantomime 'D' Beat could come up with.

Not that Dinger Bell cared too much. He wasn't sweating for promotion. A few years from now, they could all wave him a fond farewell. A steady number, a clean nose, a good salary, then a pension and a cottage somewhere near the coast. A spot of tax-free moonlighting and he and the old lady would be in clover.

He still had the brushes, he still had the touch and, despite the DIY crap, few men really *liked* decorating. Few men *could* decorate. But he could. He'd served his time before joining the force and he'd kept his hand in.

He opened the gate leading to the first of the 'unoccupied property' checks, and his mind continued its silent musings.

What the devil was wrong with Martha? Dammit, she was closing up to thirty, she wasn't *bad*-looking, but could she hell as get a man? Come to that, did she hell as seem to *want* a man? That wasn't normal. It wasn't natural. Her face wasn't the sort that had young bloods sniffing around, but there wasn't much wrong with her figure. All the hills and all the hollows in the right places. And she could cook. Her mother had taught her how to cook, and she'd been a willing learner.

On the debit side, she was a mite sloppy about the house. She couldn't make a decent bed if her life depended on it, and when it came to dusting and polishing, with her it was just a matter of stirring the dust around. But what the hell? Nobody was perfect.

And it was high time some other silly bugger took a hand at keeping her. Otherwise, this dream home of the future would have to have *three* bedrooms, and that would up the price considerably.

A quick check of the front door, a quick check of the rear door, a sweep of the windows with the torch beam, then a return to the gate. A careful closing of the gate, and the positioning of a used match on the lower hinge. Next time round, if the match was still there, no need to check further.

Dinger Bell's way of bobbying. Conscientious, but knowing all the tricks. Like decorating – easy when you knew how.

Boothby said, 'Contact Chatterton. Tell him I'll meet him outside Woolworth's at half-past.'

Morrison shambled into the alcove leading from the Charge Office and picked up the microphone which connected him with the patrol officers' walkie-talkies.

Boothby left the Charge Office and firmly closed the door of the Sergeants' Office.

Victor Boothby. One of the three sergeants who ran Radholme Section, and old enough to know better . . . and knew *that*, too. Or was he? Or, indeed, *did* he? In truth he had a nagging feeling of shame. Three kids – a daughter in her early twenties and two sons in their mid- and late-teens – yet when they'd raided Radholme's only sex shop last week, he'd slipped four of the pornographic publications under his tunic. Hard-porn stuff and surprisingly well produced. To gawp at in the privacy of the Sergeants' Office and, when he wasn't on duty, to keep locked away in the slim, steel wardrobe.

Sex Without Inhibition. Judas Christ! Good-looking lasses, too. Meet 'em in the street, see 'em neatly dressed, and you'd smile your pleasure and think the world wasn't such a bad place after all. Not the blowsy scrubbers, the *obvious* scrubbers, you'd expect. Not the bags you'd *think* went in for this sort of lark, much less allowed themselves to be photographed doing it.

An upside-down world. A can't-trust-anybody world. They looked decent, respectable daughters of decent respectable parents.

The truth was, Vic Boothby was a psychiatrist's dream boy and, in part, he was aware of that fact. Three years, a month over three years, since the brakes on the <u>bowser</u> had failed. *[handwritten: tank truck]* Since he'd taken the nine-nine-nine, attended the accident with the patrol constable, and seen Alice.

What had *once* been Alice.

He hadn't needed mucky books in those days. Not while Alice had been alive. Not while she'd shared his bed. Not that they had done *this* or anything like it. But normal, married people with normal, healthy appetites.

And then the bloody bowser . . .

He'd gone crazy. He'd howled like an injured animal when he'd first seen her. Then he'd had to be held back because he'd wanted to kill the driver. To kill him – to tear his throat out – to take his truncheon and smash his skull to pulp. The bloody brakes *should* have been working. The driver should have *checked* they were working.

Three months it had taken. Three long and weary months of dope and recuperation. Some of it he remembered. Much of it he would never remember. Nevertheless, three months, plus a head of hair with more white than brown.

Nor had the priest been much good.

In fairness, *he* had never been religious. Maybe? Maybe not? That had always been *his* outlook. Couldn't even call himself a Christian. Not really. Not like Alice. If anything, C. of E., but not really that. Alice had been R.C. Devout, without being painfully devout. With him as a husband she could have lapsed, but she hadn't. She'd kept it up, but despite a fair bit of

9

pressure had refused to let her church impose itself on the kids against their wills.

But *she'd* believed.

And the priest had come round and done damn-all. In all fairness, though, what could he do? Comfort? Boothby hadn't wanted comfort. He'd wanted his wife back again. He hadn't wanted assurance that she was in Heaven. He'd wanted her *here*, on earth, helping to bring up two sons and a daughter.

Selfish? Sure, selfish. Why not selfish? It was what Alice would have wanted. They'd been happy. Comfortable. Easing a way into the middle years, and content to enjoy what they had, without envy.

And then the bloody bowser . . .

It had taken three months and a lot of drugs to ease him from the heartbroken futility of asking only for what he couldn't have. Three months, and a transfer to Radholme.

And in the last three years – since he'd arrived at Radholme – he hadn't gone celibate. Not *quite* celibate. A couple of Annual Leaves; a couple of holidays, one at Bridlington, one at Filey. Each with a woman – different women, but both decent enough women – pushing the 'Mister-and-Missus-Smith' caper. Both women lived in Radholme. Both were widows of about his own age. Both knew the score. Both, if the truth be faced, with an eye on the main chance; hearing wedding bells while they coupled.

But no way!

It hadn't been Alice. Nor had it been anything likely to drive the memory of Alice from his mind.

And now this. God Almighty, he'd been reduced to *this*.

He closed the book, returned it to his locker, shut the door and turned the key. He lifted the telephone from its cradle and, when Morrison answered said, 'Make that ten-fifteen. Outside Woolworth's at ten-fifteen.'

Morrison muttered to himself as he shuffled around the Charge Office. The impression was that he'd been shuffling and muttering since the moment he'd taken his first breath.

10

Other men walked and breathed. Morrison shuffled and muttered.

Police Constable 1999 Edgar Morrison. Mid-fifties. Not much older than Boothby, but if he'd claimed to have been Sir Robert Peel's first recruit, outward appearances would have tended to back that claim.

All his police life he'd worked at Radholme, the last five years as permanent night-duty Office Reserve. He'd never been in trouble; he'd never once been on the mat for chancing his arm. On the other hand (and some said on principle) he *never* appeared in court and, even in the old days, he'd perfected the art of turning and walking away at the first sign of trouble. In short, Morrison was the complete and immaculate 'passenger'; known as such, recognised as such and universally scorned as such. Nobody asked him to help, because they knew he'd refuse. Nobody sought his advice, because everybody knew he had none to give. He answered the telephone, he passed messages to and from patrolling constables, he scrawled entries in the Telephone Message Book – and that's *all* he did. All he was prepared to do. Nobody complained; Morrison's wrinkled hide was impervious to complaints. Nobody expected more; his normal speed of movement and general demeanour suggested an immediate heart attack should he move from first gear.

The bell rang in the switchboard alcove. The direct line from Haggthorpe Divisional Headquarters.

'Radholme?'

'Aye.'

'Old Misery Guts?'

'Radholme,' breathed Morrison.

'A mugging at Haggthorpe. Two youths. One black, one white. Both wearing windcheaters and jeans. The white youth, long blond hair. The dark youth, black curly hair.'

'Is it worth it?' asked Morrison.

'What?'

'A poor description.'

'It's all we have for the moment.'

'Haggthorpe's a long way.'

'They've nicked a car.'

'Oh!'

'A Jag. That shortens the distance a bit.' He gave the colour and registration number, then added, 'It's an all-sections circulation. The bloke's in a bad way.'

'Ah!'

'Pass it round, eh?'

'I know my job.'

'Good. Don't break into a trot. Your toenails might drop off.'

Morrison sniffed and replaced the receiver.

The property on 'A' Beat was mainly lock-up shops and offices. A few pubs, a handful of restaurants and the town's only cinema. Actually, three cinemas; Odeon 1, Odeon 2 and Odeon 3. The modern way of making the motion picture pay its way.

Odeon 1 specialised in foreign films; Russian epics of ponderous solemnity, frothy Italian confections aimed at showing the Roman whore as an angel with a heart of gold, gesticulating French prints aimed at showing the Parisian whore as an angel with a heart of gold.

Odeon 2 tended towards the trendy, so-called 'adult' motion picture. Sometimes English, sometimes American, sometimes Continental. And always, safely hidden within the sweating skin and threshing thighs, the 'message'; the hint that somebody, somewhere, actually knew what the hell it was all about when the cameras started turning.

Odeon 3 catered for sanity; for those who yearned for the not-so-long-ago. It screened films which had earned themselves the name of 'classic'. Films like *Lawrence of Arabia, Butch Cassidy and the Sundance Kid, From Here to Eternity*. They were re-screening *From Russia with Love* and, after a passing nod to the woman in the ticket kiosk, Kelly strolled into the darkened auditorium.

The object of the visit was to check that yobs had not

infiltrated. That the back row hadn't been turned into a makeshift brothel. That flick knives weren't making the seats bleed their stuffing. It had happened in the past, and the manager liked patrolling coppers to call in and keep an eye on things. In return, and when they were off duty, coppers and their families watched films on the house. It was skin off nobody's nose, people didn't queue for the 'pictures' these days. Empty seats were always available.

The film was well under way; well into the second half. Robert Shaw was as cold-blooded as ever. Sean Connery – the best 'James Bond', by far – was at his laconic best. Tongue-in-the-cheek hooey, but served as top-line escapism.

Kelly watched, remembered and was sad.

He'd seen the film before. *They* had seen it before . . . they had seen it first time round. Seen it and enjoyed it. Laughed about it. Talked about it. Even argued about it. Who was the best film spy? James Bond or Harry Palmer? Sean Connery or Michael Caine? Julie had favoured Caine, but Julie tended to think it was for real, and she'd always had a soft spot for slim men with large spectacles.

A joke; one of those running gags that are part of every marriage.

'They set a face off. Like a good frame puts the finishing touch to a nice picture.'

'Unless there's something wrong with your eyes.'

'You'd look sweet.'

'There's nothing wrong with my eyesight.'

'Check and find out.'

'There's nothing wrong. Why should I see an optician?'

'You'd look dishy in glasses.'

'Oh, yes . . . very studious.'

'Plain lenses.'

'Oh, for God's sake! Like false boobs.'

Towards the end the joke had lost its real humour. It rankled. It brought an impatient – sometimes a very snappy – reply.

Well, James wore glasses. *The* James, not James Bond.

13

Bloody great glasses, like two headlights perched on each side of his nose. And that afternoon, when the judge had very formally droned the words 'decree nisi', it had been James, complete with horn-rims, who had taken her by the elbow and steered her out of court. James . . . when it should have been *him*.

A mistake?

Oh my word, yes, of course it had been a mistake. The mistake of his life. His mother and his sister had pushed like crazy, but they didn't *know*. Nobody knew. Nobody could understand. He could have forgiven her. He could have forgiven her anything. Anything! Forgiven her and never mentioned it again. Could have. And *still* could. Only let her stay his wife.

But, Christ, his mother. His mother, and that cold-eyed cow, his sister. All that prolonged crap about 'dignity' and 'manhood' and 'shame'. Well, now he *was* ashamed. Ashamed he hadn't told them both to mind their own damn business. Ashamed he hadn't told them to take a running jump. That he'd allowed himself to be persuaded. Ashamed he hadn't had the guts to take Julie to one side and say, 'Look, forget it, darling. It's important, sure it's important, but not when placed alongside our marriage. Let's both forget it and go back to square one. A new start. Let's not go *completely* crazy.'

It could have been said, and *should* have been said. That was all it had needed. But now, it *couldn't* be said. Not after today.

This afternoon had been like stepping off the edge of a cliff. After that, there was no choice of direction. The only way left was down.

The manager said, 'Like the film, constable?'

'Eh? What?'

Kelly jerked himself into the present. He had neither seen nor heard the manager come through the self-closing door and join him at the back of the seats.

'It's one of the best,' said the manager.

'Oh, sure. One of the best.'

'This one and *Goldfinger*.'

'A – er – a great character.' Kelly forced a smile to his lips. He spoke in a low voice. Little more than a whisper. 'Boy's blood stuff, blown up to adult size.'

'But entertaining.'

'Oh, yes.'

'Have you read the books?'

'Some of them.'

The manager chuckled. An all-lads-together chuckle. He murmured, 'All those birds. He never puts any of 'em in the family way.'

'No, well, he wouldn't, would he?'

'Leave 'em limp and helpless, eh?'

'I suppose so. Being James Bond.'

'Bring your wife along,' suggested the manager.

'Eh?'

'Your wife. Bring her along.'

'Well, er . . .'

'If she likes this sort of stuff.'

'Oh – er – sure.' The words almost choked him. 'I'll do that. Thanks.'

Chatterton scratched a match into flame and held it to the surface of the tobacco in the bowl of his much-used pipe. Chatterton was covering 'B' Beat, and if Chatterton had been covering every beat in the section – every beat in the force – it would not have stopped him from taking time off every so often for a pipe of tobacco.

Chatterton – Police Constable 1249 Ernest Chatterton – was respected as the definitive no-panic merchant. He didn't know what the word 'panic' meant. Come to that, he didn't seem to know what the word 'hurry' meant either. He had one speed – a steady, loping speed – but it never slowed and it never quickened and it went on for ever.

Not many people liked Chatterton, but on the face of things, nobody *dis*liked him. He wasn't like Morrison; he pulled his weight and, sometimes, more than his weight. It was just that he held people at arm's length. Everybody. He had this cold-fish quality which denied real friendship. He was prepared to go as far as first-name terms, but no further.

Four years ago, thereabouts, he had arrived at Radholme, and the local villains had eyed him with delight. This was no stop-at-nothing kid. This one was a right yo-yo. The age was right; well past wild enthusiasm, and content to let sleeping dogs claim their private patch of sunshine. He never shouted, he never bawled, he never so much as raised his voice. He never made a grab if he caught you on the hop. You just ran like hell, knowing *he* wasn't going to make a tap-dance routine out of it.

They learned the hard way. Basically, the only way they knew how to learn.

One had just come out, four were still doing time, and the rest had been hit in the pocket hard enough to stop their collective breath . . . and Chatterton hadn't even broken into a sweat. A yo-yo? In his own quiet, expressionless way this lad was Hades with the gates wide open.

Nobody tangled with Chatterton *these* days.

'No kids, y'see.' In a rare moment of conversational diarrhoea, Chatterton had once half-explained things to Boothby. 'Quiet. Peaceful. I need things that way. I've grown used to it. The missus is as deaf as a post, has been since birth, so there's not much mileage in raising your voice. She just switches the aid off, and that's you taken care of.'

'You don't like noise?'

'Noise . . . and other things.'

'It can be a noisy world.'

'I do what I can to quieten it.'

'Don't you ever lose your temper?'

'No. I daren't.'

And that had been that.

Ernie Chatterton. Thin as a rail. Topping the six-foot mark by more than an inch, but weighing less than ten stone, fully clothed and soaking wet. Chatterton and his pipe and his St Bruno.

And now he was in the loading bay behind Woolworth's,

16

puffing contentedly and waiting until it was time to go round the front to meet Boothby.

It was peaceful there. Quiet and shadowy in the back street. A mere echo of the noise from the road. Reflection rather than illumination. Directly overhead the clear sky was navy blue. Navy blue, confectioned with more stars than the eye could count. Navy blue, lightening to royal blue as the fluorescent street lighting washed skywards and transformed the rooftops into black silhouettes. Sharp-lined silhouettes, with the chimneys poking up like blunt pencils.

And one of the pencils was moving . . .

With a name like Riddle, plus the Christian name James, he had had to work doubly hard to win. But he'd made it to chief inspector and, with even a modicum of luck, he would eventually make superintendent or even chief superintendent. He had, perhaps, made a few enemies on the way up . . . but all things had to be paid for.

'One must try,' he would say and, if it sounded a little pompous, it was not meant to sound pompous. 'Try to reach beyond the immediate grasp. But, above all else, try.'

Big deal! Or so thought his father, and his father lived with them, and his father had been a desk sergeant, complete with stripes and a crown, when that rank had been in existence, and his father lived with the firm belief that authority – *real* authority – rested on respect tinged with more than a little fear, and had damn all to do with bits and pieces sewn to a tunic.

'Going out?' asked Riddle senior.

'For a few hours.' Riddle fastened the buckle of his tunic jacket, then stepped nearer to a wall mirror in order to check his tie. 'You should know. A chief inspector doesn't work an eight-hour day.'

'I've known some.'

'This isn't the Met.'

'More's the pity.'

'The Countryman people might not have agreed.'

17

'The Smoke?' Ben Riddle's lips moved into a slow and wicked grin. 'Some of the mobsters up there would have chewed you people up and spat you out before breakfast.'

'Possibly.'

'You wouldn't even have known it was happening.'

'If you say so.'

'I do say so. Up there in London . . . '

'*Down* there. It's south, therefore it's down.'

'You go *up* to the capital, lad.'

'Don't call me that.'

'What?'

'"Lad".'

'You want "Sir"? You want a salute? Like me to chop you one off?'

'Don't be silly.'

'That'll be the day.' The oldster chuckled quietly.

Riddle sighed, picked up his peaked cap and gloves from the sideboard, gave a quick smile of farewell to his wife and left the room.

Jenny Riddle gave the old man a sad-eyed look and slowly shook her head.

'You two,' she chided gently.

'A little man in big britches,' growled Ben Riddle.

'You tease him.'

'I goad him,' he corrected her. 'He needs it.'

'He hasn't much sense of humour.'

'He hasn't much sense . . . period.' He leaned forward a little in his chair. Gazed at the face of the woman he'd come to accept as a real, and fine, daughter. 'Jenny, my pet, I love him. He's my only child, so I love him. But I'm also ashamed of him. He's no fire in his belly.'

'He's not like you,' she admitted.

'When *I* was on duty . . .' He shook his head, slowly, at the memories. 'My God, when *I went* on duty.'

'It's different these days'.

'No.' The shaking head took on another meaning. 'When *I* went on duty, every time I went on duty, I kissed his mother.

18

She was my wife, and I had a job, and coppers sometimes get killed. It happens. Not often, thank God, but it does happen. Even chief inspectors. I always remembered that. *He* should remember it. He doesn't and that makes him that much bigger a fool.'

'He takes his responsibilities very seriously. You have to remember *that*, too.'

'Don't make excuses, Jenny. Not to me. I *know*. An inspector? A chief inspector? The best ranks in the force. Any mistakes, you play hell with the sergeants. Any wrong decisions, you blame the super for not being around to make the right decisions. Coming and going. I tell you . . .' The wicked grin touched his lips. 'I could have done *his* job in my spare time.'

10.30 p.m. What makes a Northerner tick? What makes him, or her, create a town like Radholme? A town unlike most northern urban areas; a town without grime and industry; a town with cosy estates but no slums; a town speckled with tiny gardens of rest, municipal lawns and flower beds, well-kept verges and tree-lined roads.

Few, if any, stockbrokers live in these places. Places like Ilkley or Settle. Places like Clitheroe or Longridge. Places like Radholme. They are neither 'stockbroker belts' nor 'dormitory towns'. They are uniquely 'home' to both Yorkshiremen and Lancastrians. The two rose counties which once fought each other to a standstill and, in the process thereof, ripped a nation to shreds but now share a common culture. A culture which, over the years, has conceived market towns tucked away in the folds of the Pennines.

Towns like Radholme.

'Boots the Chemists,' said Chatterton.

'Two?' Boothby stepped into Woolworth's doorway. Alongside Chatterton, and out of view of the roofs.

'I spotted two. Maybe more.'

'Reinforcements.'

Boothby raised a hand to unclip his walkie-talkie.

'Let 'em get inside,' advised Chatterton.

19

Boothby nodded.

'Front door, rear door covered. Then we go in.'

'Apple-Six to George. Apple-Six to George.' Boothby held the set close to his mouth as he spoke.

There was a moment or two of silence, then, 'George to Apple-Six.'

Despite the enclosed space, the reception was clear enough.

'Apple-Six to George. We have intruders in Boots the Chemists. We need the keyholder informed immediately. We also need urgent reinforcements.'

'Who do I send?' Morrison's whine killed the pleasant feel of rising excitement.

'For Christ's sake!' Boothby, too, threw radio procedure out of the window as he soft-snarled into the set. 'Use what little gumption you possess. Kelly, Bell, Wilture. Then get Adams out. Then yell up one of the nearest motor patrol units.'

'You'll leave the town bare.'

'Morrison, I'm not *asking*.'

'Something else might happen.'

'*Do* it!'

'Adams might not be at home.'

'Bloody well *try*.'

'I'll do what I can.'

'Morrison.' Boothby almost choked. 'Morrison. Make a cock-up of this, and I'll have your goolies on a plate.' He re-clipped the walkie-talkie, blew out his cheeks, and said, 'Talk about a happy little anchor-man.'

'He'll do it,' said Chatterton calmly.

'He's in for hell if he doesn't.'

'Now you've told him, he'll do it.' Chatterton edged himself nearer the pavement. 'I'll get back to the rear.'

'Fine. I'll keep an eye on the front door.'

'Stay well back. Let 'em know we're here when we've all arrived.'

To an onlooker, or an eavesdropper, it would have seemed that Chatterton had taken over. And perhaps he had. Boothby didn't view it from that angle. As far as Boothby was concerned, Chatterton was rock solid. No sweat. No flash. A man of cool determination who knew, almost instinctively, exactly what to do in any given situation.

Meanwhile, Ernie Chatterton hugged the walls of buildings as he moved silently towards the loading bays.

He concentrated his attention on two doors. The smooth, metal-faced door and the steel roller-door against which vans and lorries backed. Either might be capable of being opened from inside the premises. He wasn't sure; therefore, to be on the safe side, he took a pessimistic view.

Empty packing cases and cartons were available by the score, most of them neatly stacked against the walls of Boots and Woolworth's. Four plastic bins, holding rubbish, were also there. It was enough for Chatterton. Enough to hold up any rush for escape before other officers arrived.

He worked carefully. Slowly, deliberately and silently. He built a barrier of cartons, cases and bins around both doors. It wouldn't stop anybody, but it would temporarily halt any sudden dash for freedom. It would halt, it would surprise and it would kick up a din.

Then, having constructed the false walls, he stepped into one of the darker shadows and waited.

Wilture acknowledged the call with a voice which had glee bubbling beneath its surface. Glee tinged with a hint of apprehension. The excitement brought on a slight breathlessness he couldn't quite control.

Nevertheless, this was 'it'. This was what it was all about. For the first time, this was *real* bobbying.

Anthony Wilture, Police Constable 1428. He needed three more months to his twenty-first birthday, yet he was responsible for the 'life and property' of 'C' Beat. At that age the responsibility weighed lightly across his young shoulders. He almost scorned it. He was a cop on the first rung of a long and action-packed ladder.

He'd fed himself on a steady diet of *Kojak, Starsky and Hutch* and the like, and the boring reality of checking doors and

21

windows was a very poor substitute. The cathode-ray cops were for real. The endless procession of dolly birds, with never a carnal suggestion made, was how it should be. The shoot-outs and the fist fights were there to be had if you seized the opportunity.

Wilture yearned to mix it with the bad guys. He couldn't carry a hand-gun in a shoulder holster, and that saddened him a little. But, okay, he couldn't carry a hand-gun in a shoulder holster, but he *could* zip around in a high-powered motor car complete with flashing lights. Given time, of course . . . but, hopefully, not too long a time.

Thereafter, and given the right partner (because good cops always worked in pairs), he could make a name for himself. He could belt the ungodly into wincing submission. He could burn rubber from tyres he hadn't to replace. If necessary, he could even write off the occasional automobile in the name of law enforcement.

Therefore, there was a grin in his tone, as he snapped, 'I'm on my way.'

He re-clipped the walkie-talkie to the top pocket of his tunic and ran.

Kelly did not hear the call. He had lingered in the cinema and, as far as short-distance radio waves were concerned, that was 'dead ground'. In honesty, nobody could fault him. The night shift wasn't yet sixty-minutes old, the pubs hadn't yet shooed the last customers on to the streets and, as a general rule, wild happenings confined themselves to a few hours around midnight.

Needless to say, and eventually, everybody was monumentally wise after the event. The trio of breakers – three, no, as Chatterton had guessed, two – had chosen their time with what they'd thought to be care. Even cunning. Ten o'clock, thereabouts. Something everybody knew, but gave little thought to. Coppers work a shift system. The night shift starts at ten o'clock. To change shifts, they have to be at the nick. If they're at the nick, they aren't out dirtying the streets. Get in there, boy . . . fill your boots!

Somebody should have tumbled, but they hadn't. Nevertheless, not to bother; Chatterton had spotted them.

Meanwhile, Kelly was watching James Bond show the world exactly how it should be done. Kelly wasn't exactly enjoying the demonstration. It brought back too many memories for it to be enjoyable. But, dammit, he couldn't go hermit. With or without Julie the earth kept turning — well, more or less.

As he drove towards Radholme Sub-Divisional Headquarters, Riddle allowed his mind to probe the problem of his father. Riddle owed his father something. Much as he owed his wife, Jenny, something. But ever since his mother had died — ever since he'd extended the invitation to the old man to come north from Islington and make his home with them at Radholme — the old devil had made things uncomfortable.

Damn it all, *he* (Chief Inspector James Riddle) was the breadwinner. Jenny did the housework. All the old man did was potter around in the garden and help with a bit of shopping now and then. But the money — the wherewithal that kept things running smoothly — came from him.

That didn't matter too much. It didn't stretch resources; they had no kids to keep and what the old man ate wasn't going to move them into bankruptcy. But that wasn't the thing.

The thing was this job of his. A job that carried built-in dangers.

Dog sometimes ate dog in this job. In *this* force . . . what the devil it had been like at year dot in the Met. The golden-hearted Cockney image. The you-scratch-my-back-I'll-scratch-yours crap. Well, maybe . . . Riddle didn't know for sure, but he doubted it. He doubted it very much.

No matter. In this neck of the woods you didn't offer your back to be scratched too many times. Not if you had any sense. Not if you didn't want some hound one day to drive a knife in, hilt-deep.

Riddle had seen it. Not often, but too many times to be complacent. Often enough to keep self-preservation high on the list. Always to be on the look-out. Never to be too trusting. Subscribe to the belief of every man for himself, and make sure the lifeboat doesn't get punctured.

But the troublesome old devil couldn't see that. Couldn't, or wouldn't. Either way, he was trying to con Jenny into believing things she shouldn't believe.

He'd have to have a word with him. A serious talk. Out in the garden one day. Just the two of them. Then give it to him straight.

He mentally rehearsed what he might say.

'Look, father – don't take it the wrong way – but you have to be told. There's a saying. There's only room for one woman in any kitchen. In the same way, there's only room for one head of any family. You were head of *your* family. I'm head of *mine*. And now you're part of *my* family. You see what I'm getting at, don't you? I'm not enjoying saying this. I didn't think I'd have to say it. In fact, I'm surprised. I thought you had more sense. More feeling . . . '

It shouldn't be too difficult. It only needed the one telling. Firmly, but tactfully. No need to hurt the old man's feelings more than was strictly necessary. There'd be some sort of reaction, of course. Sulks, perhaps. Something. But it had to be done.

The traffic lights changed to green as he approached, and he steered the car round the corner and towards Woolworth's and Boots.

down spouts

Chatterton eyed the fire escape and wondered. That *must* have been the way up. That or fallpipes, and only a complete banana would risk a two-storey fallpipe climb. Especially when the fallpipes were old and dicey.

But they'd reached the roof via some hidden route, therefore it had to be the fire escape, then a hump up and a crawled journey across the tiles.

So, if they went *up* by the fire escape and in through the

24

roof, and if they were disturbed and made a run for it, the chances were they'd come out through the roof and *down* by the fire escape. Not for sure, of course. Nothing was ever sure when you were dealing with a bent mind. But the odds were in favour of that particular getaway.

Which added up to two doors and one fire escape, and only one pair of eyes. That, plus the added inconvenience of a good thirty yards which separated the doors from the fire escape.

The problem called for nice positioning.

Chatterton figured midway between the two. The cartons and the crates would create problems at the doors. The business of dropping from the roof, prior to the descent, would put the brakes on at the fire escape. Sure, the Seventh Cavalry was on its way and when it arrived there would be enough eyes, enough ears, enough legs and enough arms. But until then there was only Ernie Chatterton.

Therefore, midway between the two.

Fortunately there was a nice block of shadow in the right place. A gentle journey around the walls, a quick nip across a three-yard-wide spillage of illumination made by the back-wash of the street lighting, then an easing into the block of shadow.

Like a chess master contemplating the next half-dozen moves in the game, Chatterton weighed the pro's against the con's. He estimated distances and calculated times. Because he dealt only with realities, he discounted the arrival of colleagues and worked on the assumption that he would have to handle things himself.

Nor was he going to choke himself by being greedy. Just the one. The last one out and, as far as Chatterton was concerned, that meant the *second* one out.

In these capers the boss cat always led the way, both coming and going. The runt was left to tag along. Therefore it was wise to be satisfied with the runt. Grab the runt and hold. Because he was the runt, he'd cough under pressure. He'd name names and, as a result, somebody could knock on doors before the dew had left the roses.

Chatterton gave a tiny nod of satisfaction, then moved cautiously along the side of the wall.

John Adams stared at his newly born son and marvelled. Not because he was his son. Not because, by using great imagination backed by a wealth of wishful thinking, he could kid himself that the child already carried the Adams eyes, nose and mouth. Not even because the infant was a ten-day-old human being. But merely because he *was*. Bald as a billiard ball but, other than that, quite perfect. A living, gurgling miracle.

Adams had a sneaking suspicion that it had never happened before. All the others had been lead-ups to this. This little chap would end up in *The Guinness Book of Records*. But definitely!

Very tentatively, very carefully, Adams stretched out a hand, cupped the chubby foot and thumbed a gentle journey along the miniature toes. All present and correct. Each the right length. Each with its full quota of joints. Each with its ridiculously tiny nail.

Bloody *miraculous*.

The babe widened his half-open eyes, gurgled his pleasure, blew bubbles of spit and dribbled slightly.

'See?' Adam's face split into a half-moon grin. 'He knows me. He knows me already.'

'Darling, he can't even *see* properly.'

Rosemary Adams smiled the smile of new motherhood. She realised that she now had *two* babies to guide and advise.

'What?' The grin left Adams's face. 'You mean there's something wrong with his eyes?'

'No.'

'Has the doctor told you . . . '

'Babies can't focus properly.'

'Oh!'

'Not for the first few weeks.' She used a soft tissue in a clean-up job around the dribbling mouth.

'*All* babies?'

'All babies,' she assured him.

'He still knows me,' he insisted. 'He knows it's me.'

'Of course, dear,' she soothed.

Which was when the telephone bell rang and a tiny, personal paradise was shattered.

The heavily built youth's name was Chambers. He was of a sub-culture. It was not his fault; the fault was in the accident of his birth. His upbringing, his friends and his surroundings fed that sub-culture and denied what finer emotions he might have felt. He was the perfect product of an environment, and there was no escape clause.

Nobody called him 'Chambers'. He answered to the name of 'Potty'. It was a play upon his real name. It was also a measure of his slight slow-wittedness.

He lowered the girl through the hole in the ceiling plaster. He lay across the joists, gripped her wrists and allowed her the full length of his arms. She was no weight at all. A skinny bint with a bit too much mouth, swallowing pills like so many Smarties, more than a little cock-happy, but officially Nicco's personal screw. So what was all this careful-you-don't-hurt-her crap he was feeling?

'You got her?' he grunted.

'Yeah.'

Nicco was standing on the perfume counter. His boots were firmly planted among the lipsticks, powders and scent bottles. He reached upwards, slid one hand up the inside of her thigh, fingers exploring the crotch of the skin-tight jeans.

The girl gave a high-pitched giggle of delight.

Potty growled, 'Don't arse around.'

Nicco said, 'Okay. Let her come.'

The girl squealed, 'I'm sodding well *coming*.'

'For Christ's sake!'

'Okay, Potty. Let go.'

Potty released his hold on her and Nicco staggered slightly, before regaining a footing among the broken plaster, trampled glass and thin metal across the counter's top.

✳ ✳ ✳

27

Vic Boothby was a patient man. This by nature and of necessity. Little more than three years back, the shock of suddenly seeing the mangled body of his wife had almost driven him over the edge. Indeed, temporarily, it *had* driven him over the edge, but with the help of dope and funny farmers he had clawed a painful way back.

Nevertheless . . .

'Understand me, Sergeant Boothby. You must take things at a very steady rate of knots.' The psychiatrist had belied all snide remarks made about his profession. He'd been a very honest man, a very down-to-earth man and, most importantly, a man capable of communicating the terms of art peculiar to his chosen calling. 'Up there, under your scalp. I'm not talking about your brain, I'm talking about your *mind*. Think of a clock – a very expensive, very beautiful, very finely made clock – and imagine what would happen if somebody swung a sledgehammer and smashed it into that clock. In effect, that's what's happened. That's what *did* happen.

'A century ago, half a century ago, that clock would have been finished. But we've learned a lot since then. We've repaired the clock, and it's back to keeping perfect time. It will continue to keep perfect time, but it has certain weaknesses.

'It can't take the strains it once could. Therefore no worry. *Force* yourself not to worry. Don't get uptight. Ever. If you do, you'll be back on drugs and you might need them for the rest of your life. Concentrate on the fact that you have two sons and a daughter. That you have responsibilities, and that the first of those responsibilities is to ensure that your children aren't saddled with a mental invalid for a father . . .'

Very heavy stuff, and at first it had scared Boothby. He'd found himself concentrating like crazy on *not* worrying. Which, of itself, was a form of worry. Thinking about what he *hadn't* to think about. It had been a new angle on the old gag when somebody tells you not to think about elephants . . . and, immediately, you start thinking about elephants.

But it had come. Very gradually, he had developed the habit of strolling through life. Day at a time. Hour at a time. He could even remember Alice, and not get an immediate vision of a smashed and broken body.

Nevertheless, his hand trembled, ever so slightly, as he unclipped the walkie-talkie.

'Apple-Six to George. Come in, George.'

'Hello. George here.'

'Where the hell are those men, Morrison?'

'I can't get Kelly.'

'Try again.'

'He won't answer.'

'What about the others?'

'I've told them.'

'For God's sake!'

'That's all I *can* do.'

'Motor Patrol?'

'I was just going to get them when you called.'

'Get them, Morrison.'

'Look, I can't . . .'

'*Get them.*'

'I'm just going to telephone DHQ.'

'Do it, Morrison. Do it . . . *now!*'

Dinger Bell took his time. The call had not suggested any urgency.

'George to Apple-Two. Boothby wants to see you outside Woolworth's. He's there with Chatterton.'

The slightly tremulous tone of Morrison's message had been made a little metallic by the walkie-talkie set. Nothing unusual. A meeting with the section sergeant. A signing of Bell's pocket book. It happened twice, sometimes three times, in each shift. A company stroll around the streets; Boothby leaving Chatterton and continuing his patrol with Bell. An exchange of small-talk and, as far as Boothby was concerned, a few lungsful of fresh air prior to starting the night's paperwork.

Therefore, Bell took his time. Which was why he never made Woolworth's.

Instead, he virtually caught the drunk in his arms as that

29

drunk was thrown, neck and crop, from the Horse And Jockey and on to the pavement.

'What the bloody hell!' Bell grabbed the drunk, and they performed an awkward waltz around the kerb before Bell regained his balance. Then Bell recognised the drunk and said, 'Sammy . . . not you again?'

'You wanna make summat . . . '

'And stay out,' bawled the landlord from the pub doorway. Then in disgust and to Bell, 'He wants putting away. He hasn't the muscles of a sparrow and all he does is pick fights.'

'Warra you mean. I'll bloody well . . . '

The drunk wriggled free of Bell's grasp and rushed, headdown, at the angry landlord. It was a silly thing to do. A thing on a par with hara-kiri. The landlord was built like a house, complete with beer-belly bay window. He pushed out a fist at the end of a girder-stiff arm, and that was all it needed. A billiard ball could not have rebounded faster from the balk cushion.

Bell caught the drunk a second time and lowered him gently on to the pavement.

'You've seen it all,' he said wearily, and the gathering knot of onlookers began to move off. To the landlord he said, 'Why do you feed it to him? You know he gets like this at the sniff of a barmaid's apron.'

'It's a pub. It's my living.'

'This clown causes trouble.'

'So?'

'You *know* he causes trouble.'

'Only to himself. He isn't big enough to cause anybody else trouble.'

'Bar him,' suggested Bell.

'He likes his booze.'

'Maybe, but the booze doesn't like *him*.'

'He's barred from half the pubs in town.'

'Why be different? Make this one more.'

'If that's the way you want it.' The landlord shrugged. 'Tell him when he comes round.'

The landlord returned into the Horse And Jockey. Bell straightened his helmet, then bent down to assist the sobering drunk to his feet.

'Come on, Sammy. You're nicked.'

'Who? Me?'

'That's who I'm talking to.'

'What for?'

'Drunk and dizzy . . . What else?'

'Me? Drunk?'

'Pissed as a newt, mate.'

'Who says I'm drunk?' The man put on an expression of outraged innocence.

'*I* do.' Bell's fingers tightened on the drunk's elbow. 'I'll say it again, on oath, tomorrow. Let's get you into a cell before somebody kills you.'

Riddle spotted Boothby in Woolworth's doorway and jumped to a wrong conclusion.

Coppers skive. Even sergeants skive. As far as Riddle was concerned he'd come across a skiving sergeant.

Riddle stamped on the brake pedal. It was an instantaneous reaction, without thought of anything other than hoiking Boothby from his hiding place and giving him an on-the-spot ballocking. Which is why the wheels stopped revolving before the car stopped its forward motion which, in turn, brought the sound of protesting rubber. Which – again in turn – resulted in the car following Riddle's car being unable to stop in time.

As an accident, it wasn't much. Nobody was injured. The boot of one car and the bonnet of another car were crumpled a little and the bumpers were locked and slightly twisted.

A nothing, but it made an uncommon amount of noise.

Chambers jerked his head and said, 'What's that?'

'Check.'

Nicco was in charge, so Nicco gave the orders. Short, one-word orders, in a manner of which Humphrey Bogart or Edward G. Robinson would have been proud.

Chambers limped to the window. He limped, because that sodding ceiling had been a very high ceiling. Even with his arms outstretched, it had been a long drop. And Nicco had been too bloody busy groping his bint to lend a hand. So he'd dropped, half-missed the counter and sprawled. And that had been one big belly laugh. He'd gone arse over tit while the other two had almost pissed themselves.

Which was why he limped.

At the window, he turned, winced as the pain caught his ankle, then pressed himself with his back to the wall.

'The sodding law,' he gasped.

'Where?'

'Out there.'

'How many?'

'Some top jerk's arrived in a car. Another flat's pounding round the corner.'

'Cool it, Potty.'

'Cool it! The bleeding place is stiff with the bastards.'

Then Nicco made everything ten thousand times worse by fishing the shooter from inside his windcheater.

The patrol car was five miles from Radholme when the speaker crackled and the message came over the air waves.

'Foxtrot to Lima-Ten. Foxtrot to Lima-Ten.'

Hindley was doing a spell as observer. He lifted the mike from its rest. 'Lima-Ten here.'

'Foxtrot to Lima-Ten. Assistance required at Radholme. Sergeant Boothby requires immediate assistance outside Woolworth's Stores.'

'Lima-Ten to Foxtrot. Understood. Over and out.'

Hindley replaced the microphone. Bulmer pulled the squad car to the kerb and braked. He did a neat reverse into a side lane then accelerated back the way they had come.

Hindley flicked the switch and the blue, revolving light on the roof of the car sent its winking warning into the darkness.

Hindley said, 'I have this feeling. It's going to be one of those nights.'

'You could be so right.'

The 'flat pounding round the corner' was Police Constable Wilture. He was really pumping it. Genuine four-minute-mile stuff. He heard the squeal of tryes, followed by the crash, before he recognised the front car. Then, as Riddle bounded from the driving seat, Wilture skidded to a halt.

'I got the message, sir,' he panted.

'What message?'

'The message to . . . '

'Just a minute, Wilture. Can't you see . . . '

'What the devil sort of driving do you call *that*?' The bearded man was very angry. His beloved automobile had had its nose pushed in.

' . . . some fool's collided with the back of my car.'

'*I've* collided with the back of *your* car!'

'Oh. So you're the driver are you?'

'Sir, the message was to . . . '

'Leave both cars just as they are. Don't move them.' The bearded man swung his head from left to right. 'Let's have some witnesses. Let's have somebody who . . . '

' . . . meet Sergeant Boothby outside Woolworth's.'

' . . . saw the crazy way you suddenly . . . '

'Obviously, you were far too close.'

' . . . dropped every anchor on board, and damn who might be coming up behind.'

'Much too close.'

'Of all the . . . '

'Why . . . ' Boothby made the trio into a quartet. He was visibly trembling, and his voice had a choked quality. 'Why don't we send for the Brighouse and Rastrick Band. That's all we need. Two quick choruses of 'Blaze Away' should go down very well indeed.'

'Sergeant, I don't know why you're . . . '

Wilture did not actually scream, but it was a very loud yelp. He staggered sideways, caught his shoe on the pavement edge, then sprawled on the ground behind Riddle's car.

Then, or so it seemed, they heard the crash of glass and the sound of the shot.

11 p.m. The ballistic experts, who have a way with words, call it a semi-automatic, Parabellum Pistole '38, calibre 9mm, blade foresight, fixed-V rearsight. Which is rather a mouthful. Therefore, to the man in the street, it is a Luger.

Accepting the proposition that, in this wicked world, even shooting irons can be good-looking, it is a very handsome gun.

There is, moreover, a curious mystique about this most famous of semi-automatic pistols. Give the wrong man a Luger and, immediately, that man assumes he is ten feet tall. Other killing tools are as efficient. Some are even better. But none are better known.

The Luger has, perhaps, a certain appeal to the eye. It looks very capable and, from the blunt end, quite safe. It is certainly a very comfortable gun to handle; it fits in the grip with perfect balance, the barrel becomes a fifth finger and one merely points that extra finger, then squeezes the trigger.

Which is what Nicco had done. He had seen the uniform, smashed the glass with the butt, then pointed and squeezed. Fortunately, he was no Dead-eyed Dick. He had aimed at Wilture's head and had hit Wilture's bum . . . but at least he had not *missed*.

'Bloody champion,' said Chambers with feeling. 'Now you've really shit the holeful.'

Radholme was a police section. It was also a police sub-division and, because it was a sub-division, Riddle carried the rank of chief inspector and, for a moment and for the first time in his life, he wished he didn't. The sudden responsibility smacked him in the teeth and frightened him.

In the road outside Woolworth's pedestrians scattered; like iron filings subjected to a negative force, they dived in all directions. Even the bearded man forgot his anger, gasped, 'Hell's teeth!' and ran for it.

Riddle's immediate urge was to join him, but Riddle was not

allowed to. Riddle wore a uniform and, once upon a time, Riddle had taken an oath.

He therefore had to be content with shouting, 'Boothby! Get down,' before ducking behind the shelter of his car. Wilture was already there, groaning from behind clenched teeth.

Boothby joined them.

'Of all the bloody stupid things . . .' began Boothby.

'Shut up, sergeant.' Riddle peeped from behind the rear of the car. 'Where are they, anyway?'

'In Boots.'

'Oh.'

'That's why I was keeping a low profile.'

'I see.'

'I've already sent for more men.'

'Good.'

'Chatterton spotted them on the roof.'

'Where's Chatterton?'

'Round the back. If he's any sense, he'll stay there.'

'How many?'

'Chatterton counted two.'

'Oh.' Riddle turned his attention to Wilture. 'What about you, son? How do you feel?'

'It hurts like Joe Fury.'

'Of course. But I don't think it's too serious . . . is it?'

The pause, followed by the two-word question, told its own tale. The addendum was heavy with uncertainty.

'If,' moaned Wilture, 'having half the right cheek of your backside blown away isn't serious . . . '

'He's losing blood, sir.'

'I appreciate that. But there's nothing vital down there.'

'If you say so.'

'Look!' Wilture was scared. He was losing blood and it was *his* blood. All right, a bullet through the backside. Very funny . . . but not too funny if it happens to be *your* backside. He was also in a state of shock. He rasped, 'I think somebody should send for an ambulance.'

Riddle reached out a hand, and said, 'I'll use your personal radio, sergeant. Leave it to me, Wilture. I'll have an ambulance here. And some men to surround the place.'

Chatterton heard the noise – the shunt-up, the breaking glass, the pistol shot, the soft roar of people shouting and running for cover – and in his mind he built up a fairly accurate picture. Guns, plus something of a flap. Somebody howling therefore somebody hurt. Hopefully nobody dead. Just the one shot. Therefore, chances were, nobody dead.

No police sirens yet, but they'd arrive soon.

Meanwhile, sit tight, Ernie. Sit tight, keep hidden and watch those doors and that fire escape. Watch, but take care. No chances. Not even half a chance.

Guns are not jokey things. The ball game has changed. When you grab, if you *have* to grab, remember that. No chances.

You are no longer playing around with pussy cats. Tigers, boy, tigers!

Very gently, very calmly, he loosened the truncheon in its pocket down the outside of his right leg.

It was light enough to see things. Gloomy – like being inside a cave – but light enough to see. To see Nicco, for example. To see Nicco's bint.

Fleming, that was her name. Patricia, some fancy handle like that, but nobody ever called her that. She was Nicco's bint, and a little crazy. Something of a nympho, and hooked on benzedrines. A crazy man, a crazy woman and he, Potty, needed a brain transplant for being part of this cock-eyed caper.

The hint of burning cordite gave a slight tang to the stink of scent from the smashed bottles on the perfume counter. That stink came across in waves. In clouds. The bloody stuff almost choked him.

Choked him with scent. Choked him with memories.

What was it? Californian Poppy? They all stank the same to Chambers. They all stank of Californian Poppy.

36

That's what the old lady had used. What she'd once used. Drenched herself in the sodding stuff. Stank like a Turkish wrestler's crotch. The silly old cow had seemed to think it killed the other stench. The stench of *her*.

Why for Christ's sake?

The old man hadn't been such a bad old bugger. He hadn't knocked her about. He hadn't been tailing other women. Okay, he'd got himself pissed sometimes. Pissed legless. But only *sometimes*. Not every night. About once a week, no more. No more than once a week.

And it hadn't been 'nasty' beer. Not with the old man. Just legless, but not nasty. Laughing a lot and shouting a lot. Singing at the top of his voice. Maybe you could say he'd been noisy. But that's all you could say.

And, by hell, he'd had cause. The old lady had been a right old tease. With other men, of course, and at *her* bloody age.

Jesus Christ, he'd had cause!

The bint, Fleming, said, 'You gonna shoot your way out, Nicco? That what you're gonna do? You gonna shoot your way out?'

She seemed to fancy this idea. She seemed to think it was possible. She was bloody light-headed.

'Yeah.' Nicco, too. Out of his stupid skull. 'Stick with me, kid. I just might.'

Chambers growled, 'You two have rocks between your ears.'

Too true, the old man had had cause. What the hell had he ever done wrong? Getting stoned now and again . . . but who doesn't? He hadn't left the old lady short.

Not bad furniture. Not *bad*. All on pledge-and-promise, but so what? Who doesn't?

And, bloody hell, he hadn't had a job for years. Unskilled labour. That's how the pricks behind the desks always put it.

'I'm sorry, Mr Chambers, but you're unskilled labour.'

First to the old man, now to him.

'I'm sorry, Chambers, you're unskilled labour.'

Whose fault? Whose bloody *fault*? Nobody wanted to be unskilled labour. The old man hadn't. But he'd kept the gelt

37

coming in. An odd job here, lifting a bit there, nicking a bit somewhere else. The poor old bugger had tried, and the silly old cow had had enough coming in.

Enough to drown herself in Californian Poppy before going out on the bash.

The Fleming bint asked, 'Where's the stuff, Nicco?'

'What stuff?'

'The bennies.'

'Cool it, kid.'

'Hey, before you start shooting a way out we want the bennies.'

Chambers said, 'Downstairs. Where they make up the medicines.'

'That's where,' agreed Nicco.

'Let's get 'em, eh?'

'Sure, kid. Sure.'

'They'll be locked away,' grunted Chambers. 'They're always locked away.'

Nicco waved the gun, and said, 'We got this. We can shoot the sodding lock off.'

'Maybe.' Chambers didn't sound too sure.

A couple of stretches inside, see? The poor old bugger *had* to be caught. Chance your arm enough times, you have to be caught. So he'd been caught a couple of times.

So what? No skin off *her* nose. Other women managed. *She* could have managed. But, no, *she* had to go on the game. *She* had to be different. *She* didn't give a toss. About anybody.

The lousy bitch!

Then, when he'd come out, when he'd come out the last time, all that crap about how she'd *suffered*. My Christ, suffered! She hadn't been in her own bed long enough to get it warm. Then meeting him with all that crap. How she'd suffered.

So he'd belted her. Belted her but good. Her and her sodding Californian Poppy.

Maybe he'd heard. Some right crawling bastards get put inside, so maybe he'd heard. About all this cross-shafting.

Chances were he had heard. Slinging her snatch around like that, then going on a bucketful about how she'd suffered.

Of course he'd belted her. About time, too.

Chambers came back to the present, and muttered, 'Forget the bennies.'

'Are you crazy?' The Fleming bint almost screamed the question.

'*Shut it!*' Nicco spun round on her and, for a split second, it looked as if he might squeeze the trigger a second time. He spoke to Chambers. 'What's with you now, Potty?'

'How many coppers?'

'Who knows? One less.'

'Dozens? Scores?'

'Who cares?'

'Yeah . . . who *cares?*' echoed the Fleming bint.

'That ground floor,' said Chambers, heavily. 'If they heave a brick, they're in. They're all over us.'

'They get shot if they . . . '

'*All* of 'em?'

'They keep down. They give us some space.'

'For ever, Nicco? For ever?'

Adams braked his car to a halt.

Riddle crouched, waved and shouted.

'Keep down. Keep well down, they have guns.'

Adams did not like this one little bit. A deserted street, Riddle and Boothby squatting behind cars, a copper flat on his stomach and obviously in a bad way, and now Jimmy Riddle flapping his arms and yelling a warning about guns.

Guns! Guns meant trouble. Trouble, with a capital T. As a newly made father Adams could live without guns. Indeed, as a detective constable, he could live without them 'any time, any place, anywhere' – as the TV commercial insisted.

He had stopped on the offside of the road in front of Riddle's car, therefore he could open the door and roll out, rather than take the chance of standing upright. He scurried towards the chief inspector and the sergeant.

'What's happening?'

'In there.' Boothby pointed. 'Boots. Breakers. They have guns. Wilture's been shot.'

'Badly?' Adams craned his neck.

'In the back.'

'The backside,' corrected Riddle.

'Christ!'

Boothby said, 'The ambulance is on its way.'

'I think it's only a flesh wound,' contributed Boothby.

'What about the guns?'

'Guns?'

'Guns,' repeated Adams.

'The sergeant's already told you. They're in Boots, and they have guns.'

'No . . . I mean *us.*'

'Oh!'

'If anybody's taking pot shots at *me*, I want somebody taking pot shots at *them*.'

'Ah.'

'And men,' continued Adams. 'Three and a wounded soldier doesn't add up to much.'

'Chatterton's round the back.'

'All right. *Four* and a wounded soldier.'

'They've – er – they've already been sent for. We . . . ' Riddle scowled his worry. 'I suppose we could use more.'

'The more the merrier,' agreed Adams.

'And guns, of course.'

'Definitely guns. And a loudhailer.'

Riddle sighed, then said, 'Give me your personal radio again, sergeant. We'd better notify the superintendent . . . and everybody.'

Jenny Riddle listened and, sadly, knew it was no more and no less than what Ben Riddle believed to be the truth. The old man was still musing; still re-living his own police service in the Met. The memories were rose-tinted with the passing of years, but they had a basic honesty that could not be denied.

Nor could anybody argue that Ben Riddle did not love his son. Indeed, he loved him enough to want to show him the way to a better life.

'It's so easy,' he said. 'So *easy*. Coppers are a lot of things, like everybody else. Strong, weak, loud-mouthed, introvert, extrovert. Like everybody else, but by and large they can all be trusted. They wouldn't be coppers otherwise. See a bloke in uniform . . . trust him. You'll rarely go wrong. Don't listen to what the madmen say. Trust him!'

'Agreed,' she smiled.

'So, coppers should trust each other. Do that and it's easy. Do it James's way and it's difficult.'

'He's very conscientious.' She was Riddle's wife and, in his absence, she fought his corner.

'Maybe.' Ben Riddle shrugged. 'Maybe he is. But y'see, pet, that's not enough. It's more than being just conscientious. It's not even *being* conscientious. Not all of it. Not what I'm talking about. Not the part that James won't see. It's working with people. Being part of the whole set-up.

'Every copper chances his arm. James included. Every copper. He *has* to. It's part of the job. He chances his arm, or he cops out. And you can't cop out every day of your life.

'To get the law working, you have to chance your arm . . . so you chance your arm. If you come unstuck you try to cover. If you cover you keep your mouth shut. If you can't cover, and you're a working copper, you tell your sergeant, because you trust your sergeant. Then the sergeant tries to cover for you. If the sergeant can't *he* tells the inspector, and the inspector tries.

'I'm not talking about covering-*up*. Not that. Not being on the twist. Conning the public. Not being bent, not being on the take . . . not *that*. I'm talking about practical bobbying. Working with each other. Dammit, trusting each other. Playing the wide-boys at their own game. Jenny, pet, it's necessary. Otherwise, they'd *always* win.' He sighed. 'Why the devil can't James see that?'

'He doesn't make friends too readily,' she said gently.

'Does he make friends at all?'

41

'Not easily.'

'Why? He's only got one life.'

'He finds it difficult.'

'Being friendly with fellow-coppers?'

'He can't do it, Ben.'

'For God's sake, why not?'

'He's been hurt.'

'No.' Ben Riddle shook his head. 'He *fancies* he's been hurt. He's too touchy. He isn't pushy enough.'

'It's the sort of man he is,' she said softly.

'It beats me . . .' He rubbed the nape of his neck and allowed himself a slow grin. 'How the devil did he find *you*?'

'*I* found *him*.' The smile was shaded with sadness. It carried a hint of accusation. 'I felt sorry for him. Very gradually I fell in love with him. A little boy – he's still a little boy – shy beyond belief.'

'That's what I mean. He won't . . .'

'No.' The interruption was soft-spoken but firm. 'Ben, you had a high old time in the police force. I don't doubt for a moment that you loved James's mother. But I've grown to know you. And, remember this, you've mellowed with age. You've become more reasonable. You weren't always like you are today.'

Ben Riddle's face became expressionless as he waited.

She seemed to gain courage, and in a stronger voice continued, 'If a boy, or a youth, can't trust his father – if he can't rely upon his father to back him right or wrong – who *can* he turn to? Who *can* he rely upon?'

'Has *he* told you that?'

'No.' She shook her head. 'I've seen it. I've witnessed the result of it, scores of times. You love him. I don't deny that. But it's the love of the strong father for an unsure son. He is unsure. As long as I've known him he's been unsure.

'You set yourself up as a templet, Ben. As far as James is concerned, an impossible templet. Because, however much you wish he was, he's not *like* you. I've seen you criticise him – goad him, to use your own expression – not because he wasn't

42

doing something, but because he wasn't doing it the way *you'd* have done it. His has always been the wrong way. By that I mean not *your* way. But to him the *right* way.' Again she shook her head. 'Goading him. Year after year. All his life. The man who should have been encouraging him. The man he should have looked to for guidance. But instead . . . goading him.' She paused, then added, 'He's what you made him, Ben. He's *exactly* what you made him.'

'Guns!'

Police Constable 1999 Morrison's eyes widened into orbs of disbelief. He gaped at the loudspeaker as he gasped the word into the microphone.

'*Guns!*'

'Guns.' Riddle's voice was recognisable despite the distortion. 'Guns and range-trained officers. And men. As many as you can contact. Oh yes, and a loudhailer.' The distinct sound of a quiet gulp came over the air waves. 'And notify the superintendent.' There was another pause then, in a slightly choked voice, 'And Detective Chief Superintendent Barstow. Tell him what's happened, and that I thought he should be notified.'

Morrison pressed the transmit button and said, 'What – y'know – what *has* happened?'

'For God's sake, man.'

'No. What I mean is . . . '

'Sergeant Boothby has already passed the information.'

'Just that he wanted somebody out there.'

'As many men as possible.'

'At Woolworth's.'

'*Boots*.' Riddle's voice threatened to crack the loudspeaker. 'Intruders at Boots.'

'Oh!'

'For heaven's sake, get it right, Morrison. Armed intruders at Boots.'

'Nobody said anything about . . . '

'One man's already been shot, so *we* need firearms. We also need officers to keep the public clear of the place.'

'Oh!'

'Get it right, Morrison.'

'I'll – er – I'll jot it down.'

'What?'

'Then I'll be sure.'

'For God's sake!'

'Men. Guns.' Morrison muttered at slow dictation speed. 'Loudhailer. The super. Detective Chief Superintendent Barstow.'

'You're wasting time, Morrison.'

'I'm sorry, sir, but . . .'

'It's urgent.'

'I'll do it, sir. I'll do it now.'

'Please. *Please.*'

'How – er – how many men do you think, sir?'

'I don't give a no-good damn.' At last Riddle exploded. 'Get the whole bloody force out. Everybody! *Just get them.*'

Like Riddle, Bulmer came from a 'police family'. His grandfather and two uncles had been coppers. His niece was married to a sergeant in the North Yorkshire force. His brother had hit a personal jackpot, in that he had emigrated to Canada and was now making a name for himself in the Mounties.

Bulmer, therefore, had grown up amid the clipped phraseology and the dry humour of bobby-talk. As far as the actions of the ungodly were concerned, Bulmer was fireproof, waterproof, dustproof and airtight.

Nothing – but *nothing* – surprised him.

'Fun and games,' he grunted, as they came within sight of Woolworth's and Boots, and saw the two cars, the huddle of uniformed figures and the otherwise deserted street. 'Jimmy Riddle's on the job. The three-ring circus seems to have come to town.'

He leaned forward, switched off the roof lamp, then braked the squad car to a halt behind Adams's vehicle.

Riddle and Adams shouted a warning and Bulmer, followed

44

by Hindley, left the squad car on the driver's side and made a crouched dash to join the others.

'They're armed,' gasped Riddle.

'Wilture's stopped one in the backside,' added Boothby.

Hindley scrambled nearer to the fallen constable and asked, 'How are you, mate?'

'It hurts.' Wilture was almost in tears.

'We've sent for an ambulance,' said Boothby.

'You'll live.' Hindley grinned make-believe confidence down at the frightened Wilture. 'You'll be a hero, old son. Big headlines tomorrow morning.'

'For Christ's sake, *do* something.'

'In Boots?' asked Bulmer.

Riddle nodded, and said, 'We think they went in through the roof.'

'They'll come out through the roof.'

'Possibly. Chatterton's at the rear.'

'Behind a thick wall, I hope.'

'Oh – er – yes. If he has any sense.'

'We've sent for men and guns,' contributed Adams.

'How soon they get here depends upon Morrison,' murmured Riddle heavily.

'I'll notify control.' Hindley scuttled away from Wilture and made for the open door of the squad car. 'I'll get things moving.'

'Please,' sighed Riddle.

'How many in there?' asked Bulmer.

'Two. Chatterton saw two.'

'Chatterton spotted them?'

'It seems so. Then they must have heard the noise. Some fool drove into the back of my car; that's when they started shooting.'

'So, they know we're here.' Bulmer was quietly weighing up the situation. 'They also know we know they're there. We already outnumber them. The first job is to convince them they aren't going anywhere.'

'Quite.'

45

'*Then* they might start seeing sense.'

Riddle nodded.

Bulmer frowned and continued, 'Chatterton's the weak point. Four in front, one behind. I'd better get to Chatterton.'

'I – er – I can't make it an order. Guns, and so forth.'

'Just don't order me *not* to. I might not hear.'

'Ah.' A nervous smile touched Riddle's lips. 'Er – good luck. I'll – er – I'll make sure it's mentioned.'

11.30 p.m. Every copper, from chief constable to cadet, knows the jigsaw structure of a force; knows the ranks and designations, the insignias and the authorities. Knows, for example, that a force area – be it a city force, a county constabulary or a metropolitan district sprawl – equates with a local authority area.

There is the geographical area, be it ancient or one of the more modern brainchildren of government non-thinking, and the police area is imposed upon that geographical area.

Then comes a head-count.

The force is divided into divisions, and a division's size is governed by the density of population. Divisions are, in turn, split up into sub-divisions – sometimes two, sometimes three, occasionally four – and the sub-divisions are carved up into sections.

Each section is sliced into beats and, in an urban community, where the PBI travel around on shoe leather, the size is once again determined by acreage; a night-duty copper being expected to tramp the beat and try doors twice, in an eight-hour shift, plodding along at a steady four miles per hour.

All clever stuff, but relatively easy if you happen to be a Chinese mathematician. The tricky bit comes when it is realised that divisions and sub-divisions can also be sections, and that specialised sections of the whole force are, themselves, divisions . . .

Having relieved him of shoes, jacket, tie and belt, Bell locked Sammy Sutcliffe away in a cell and strolled into the Charge Office. In the background from the alcove Morrison droned away into the telephone, but Bell took no notice.

A Drunk and Disorderly was small beer; less than thirty

minutes to jot down a few notes, dictate a report for the morning typist, then leave the forms to be completed. Then out on the street again, knowing that the bumph would be ready for signature at 10 a.m., in time for court.

Bell casually flipped the required forms from their slots in the stationery cupboard, then made to leave the Charge Office for the room where the dictaphones were housed.

'What's happening, then?'

Bell turned as Morrison asked the question.

'What's all the heat about?' asked Morrison.

'Heat?' Bell scowled incomprehension.

'All the sweat and panic?'

'No panic, mate.'

'Eh!'

'Sammy Sutcliffe. Pissed as a newt. I've just tucked him away.'

'Bloody hell!'

'What's to do?'

'Is that *all*?'

Bell returned the stare and said, 'Your trolley's loose, Morrison. You're getting worse by the hour.'

Bell left the Charge Office. In the room at the back he fed a new cassette into the recording machine and pondered upon more important, more personal things.

His daughter, Martha, for example.

What the hell was *wrong* with her?

Was she . . .

For Christ's sake, she *couldn't* be . . .

Well, she *could*, but she'd better *not* be . . .

But *was* she a bloody lesbian?

Before switching on the recorder, he muttered, 'My cup runneth over, by hell it does.'

Kelly had taken a chance. It was not a hanging job, it had been done hundreds of times before, but had he been caught he would have faced the chief constable across a desk top within days. To that extent, it was a chance.

He had left 'A' Beat without radioing in and, worse than that, hurried along a few streets and visited his mother. It was a spur-of-the-moment decision, and it was prompted by the knowledge that his sister would be on her fortnightly, overnight visit, and that the two women would not yet have gone to bed.

It was a neat little bungalow, but one of many; part of a fairly large privately built estate of moderately well-constructed dwellings; the sort of estate that sits there, with its nose in the air, pretending to be more select than it is; a place of shopkeepers and white collar workers, with a good sprinkling of well-corseted, blue-rinsed widows.

The bungalow (like its fellows) kidded people along a bit.

It was 'detached', just. To get to the side door – which was always euphemistically referred to as the 'rear entrance' – you had to walk sideways or risk brushing against walls.

Nevertheless, Mrs Kelly was a good and efficient housekeeper. She had been an above-average wife and as good a mother as she had known how, and today she dutifully thought nice thoughts about her dead husband (when she had a moment to spare), was the secretary of the local WI, an active member of the TWG, addressed envelopes, when necessary, at the local Conservative headquarters and, if she was feeling particularly charitable, asked housebound neighbours whether they wanted anything brought back from the shops.

'Freddie!' She raised her eyes from the copy of *Vogue* and greeted him as if he'd returned from an outer-space mission. 'What a very pleasant surprise. You'll be able to do this more often now, dear, won't you.'

The younger woman asked, 'Are you just coming off duty?'

The younger woman might have been Christine Kelly's young sister. Cynthia Maitland (née Kelly) was rolling smoothly along in her mother's life-wake, as surely as a linked-up railway carriage following an engine. Already she had that brittle, plastic sheen which was the identification mark of her kind; the fibreglass-like hair-do, the carefully applied make-up which made her as non-individual as a garden gnome, the pastel shades and careful cut of the dress which suggested that the area between the knees and the neck had long been designated 'Forbidden Territory'.

'I'm *on* duty.' Kelly closed the lounge door. 'I came on at ten. I knew you'd both be here.'

'Oh!'

'How did things go today, dear?' asked his mother. 'Quite smoothly, I'm sure.'

'Smoothly.' He nodded, then dropped the keys on to the surface of the coffee table. 'I won't need these any more.'

'I'm sorry. I don't . . . '

'Tomorrow . . . ' He took a deeper than usual breath. 'Tomorrow I'm going to see Julie.'

'Really? I don't see what . . . '

'I'm going to ask her to come back.'

'You idiot!' Cynthia's nostrils actually quivered. 'You poor, miserable . . . '

'That's enough!'

' . . . weak-willed idiot.'

'That's enough.' This time it was more of a warning than an exclamation.

'Haven't you enough pride to . . . '

'*No.*' Even as the rage welled up he marvelled that a dislike amounting almost to naked hatred could exist between brother and sister. 'Pride has damn-all to do with it.'

'To you pride isn't important, of course, but to anybody with a sense of decency . . . '

'What the devil has *pride* to do with it?'

'You, of course, can't see that.'

'I'm talking about happiness. *Happiness.*'

'Freddie, my dear, she hasn't given you a day's happiness since you married her.'

'Fornication.' The younger woman's mouth twisted into a sneer. 'That's all she thinks about. That's her sole idea of . . . '

'*Shut up!*'

'Children,' soothed the mother. 'Freddie. Cynthia. You really mustn't . . . '

49

'We are not children.' Kelly almost choked on the words then, in a calmer voice, 'We are not "Freddie" and "Cynthia" any more, mother. We are Mr Kelly – Police Constable Kelly – and Mrs Maitland.'

'You're *my* children.'

'What about *us*?' demanded the sister.

'You?' Kelly's expression showed complete non-understanding.

'Us. The family. People will laugh at us. They'll all snigger.'

'Don't be stupid.'

'Everybody *knows*, you know.'

'No, I don't "know".'

'Well, take it from me. The whole town knows what a little trollop she is.'

'Cynthia.' Her mother read the signs, and tried to step in and prevent a blazing row.

'No. Let her say her piece.'

'Well, surely you're not *so* besotted.'

'Let's assume I am,' he said grimly. 'Get what you have to say off your chest.'

'People talk. People gossip. Julian hears things in the shop . . .'

'Julian.'

'He hears things in the shop. People drop hints. Good heavens, she's the talk of the whole town.'

'Julian?' repeated Kelly and, this time, he made it into a question, shot with sarcasm.

'It embarrasses him. And now you're even thinking . . .'

'Not "thinking". I'm *going* to.'

'You'll rue it. My God, you'll rue it.'

'Another assumption. You're very free with your assumptions. Has anyone ever told you?'

'Where's your manhood? Where's your pride?'

'Little sister. Dear, darling little sister.' The tone was as hard as tungsten. Yet quiet and very deliberate. It was meant to hurt. It was meant to savage and wound beyond repair. 'We've talked about *my* wife. Now, let us talk about *your* husband. Let us talk about Julian. That watered-down man who shares your bed.

'Julian wouldn't do what I'm going to do. And why? Do you know why, sweet little sister? Because if he could rid himself of *you* he wouldn't move an inch to get you back. That's what's getting up your pretty little skirt. That nobody, not even Julian, would raise a finger to get you back.'

'Freddie!'

'No, mother. It needs saying. It's needed saying for a long time. To both of you.'

Then, still pinning the younger woman into silence with tone and expression, 'And why? Why is Julie so different? So much better than you'll ever be? *Fun.* That's why I lost her. You two. You've made me as miserable as yourselves. As miserable as Julian. As miserable as father was. I honestly don't *blame* her for leaving me. I don't blame her. But I'll change. If she gives me another chance, I'll change.

'I won't be like you. Like the damn "Kelly" family. I'll be different. I won't give a damn what other people think. What you two think. What anybody else thinks. I'll get drunk occasionally. I'll spend money on outrageous things. Not always on "sensible" things. Dammit, I'll *laugh.*

'When did *you* laugh last, dear sister? Mother, when was the last time *you* laughed? I don't mean bitchy laughter. Snide laughter. What you two think is worth a behind-the-hand snigger. I mean *laughter.* A belly laugh. A bawdy laugh. A laugh linked with what you call "fornication". And that's a prissy word, if ever there was one.

'Do you ever laugh when Julian's on the job, sweet little sister? Do you ever actually *enjoy* yourself? You're supposed to, you know. It's supposed to be a joyful experience . . . '

'Of all the disgusting . . . '

'That's what I mean. It *disgusts* you. Everything – anything you can't do with your little finger crooked – it *disgusts* you.

'It doesn't disgust Julie. That's something I've learned the hard way. Something you'll *never* learn. She enjoys life, every aspect of life, and she's so right. So wise. So . . . '

The steam seemed to leave him. Quite suddenly, he quietened.

He became less angry, and in a much gentler tone ended, 'That's it, mother. I've shocked you, but it needed saying. I've returned the keys. I won't be visiting you any more. And, both of you, when you see me – if you pass me in the street – from now on, don't stop. Don't acknowledge me. I won't answer. I'll – I'll ignore you. I want rid.'

There was nothing else to say. The two women were white-faced and speechless. For a moment Kelly looked as if he wanted to add something but could not find the words. Instead he gave a quick nod then left them.

When he reached the street, and as he made his way back to 'A' Beat, he found himself panting a little. Sweating a little.

Nicco stood by the smashed window, raised the Luger and squinted along the sights. He closed one eye, tilted the barrel and grinned. His finger was not on the trigger. He was simply 'lining-up'. Enjoying the possibility of what he *might* do. What he *could* do. What he *would* do . . . if it became necessary.

Nicco was bloody crazy. He must have been dropped on his skull when he was a kid. Him and the Fleming bint, both. Two crazy characters, a gun and that sodding scent. He (Chambers) must have been dropped, too.

Why? That was the question. *The* question. Why the hell had the wicked old cow done it? Come to that, why had the old man done it? Couldn't he have held on to his temper just one more time? Y'know, just one more time? Jesus, he'd taken enough hammer in the past. It wasn't as if he hadn't known. He *must* have known.

So why had he gone for her like that?

Straight out of the bloody slammer and he goes for her. Not just a slap-down. A fist and boot job. A sodding hospital job. Bones gone, a right going over.

She hadn't expected it – she hadn't enjoyed it – but when it was all over she'd gloried in it. Made a right bloody meal of it.

'Yes, officer, I think he *was* trying to kill me.'

'Yes, officer, I think he *would* have killed me if my son hadn't dragged him off.'

'Yes, officer, of *course* I'll give evidence.'

Then, in court, the clown in the wig and gown.

'My lord, I ask the court's permission to treat this man as a hostile witness.'

Her fault. Who else, if not *her*? Of course he hadn't wanted to go into that bleeding witness box against the old man! The poor old bugger hadn't done *him* any harm. But, by Christ, when that tricky bastard in the wig and gown had finished . . .

Ten years. Ten years – *attempted murder* – for giving the silly cow what she'd been asking for for years. And his own son standing there, telling the world. Not being able to say what he *wanted* to say. What *should* have been said. Only being allowed to tell the unimportant bits *they* wanted to hear.

Then in the corridor outside the court. Waiting. Screwed up. Wondering what the hell was going to happen. Bust up inside. Not understanding things. Not wanting to remember. And the crazy old bitch standing next to him, stinking to high heaven of Californian Poppy.

Jesus!

And now this.

He muttered, 'Attempted murder, my arse.'

'What?' Nicco turned from the window.

'We should move,' growled Chambers. 'We should *do* something.'

Fleming gave one of her quick laughs, and said, 'Yeah. Let's find the bennies.'

'Forget the bloody bennies.'

'The bennies,' she whimpered. 'That's what we *came* for.'

'Nicco's shot a copper since then.'

'You promised . . . '

'Shut it!' Nicco spun on her. This man was crazy, for starters, and the Luger fuelled his already roaring fire. He waved the pistol. 'Help yourself to some time.'

'Eh?'

'Time. Watches. Help yourself.'

53

The counter showed a display of clocks and watches, and her eyes widened as she focused in on them. Her lips puckered into a silent whistle as she bent closer and saw the array of wrist watches beneath the glass surface of the counter. She almost ran behind the counter, bent down and pushed a sliding door open . . . and the alarm bell fixed on the outer wall of the building ripped the silence to shreds.

'Bloody sparkling!' Chambers lost his temper. 'Bloody marvellous! Send a sodding postcard to Armley. Tell the bleeding screws to get a cell ready.'

The noise of the bell hit Bulmer as he dashed, in a crouched run, across the road. At that moment, he was completely exposed, and the clamour smashed into him with a near-physical impact. It sent the adrenalin surging, and he covered the last few yards in a combined dive-and-roll.

He held himself close to the wall in the narrow street leading to the rear, pulled himself upright, then allowed himself a few seconds in which to regain his breath. He soft-footed his way to where the street broadened out at the loading bays, paused, then called in a voice which was little more than a whisper.

'Ernie. Ernie.'

'Who is it?'

'Bulmer. Charlie Bulmer.'

'Take it easy, Charlie. They're armed.'

'I know.'

'Who the hell set the alarm off?'

'It must have been them.'

'Are you the only one who's arrived?'

'No. Ben Hindley. And Adams is here. So is Boothby . . . '

'I know about Boothby.'

'And Wilture. Wilture's been shot.'

'Oh, my Christ!'

'And Riddle's here.'

'It helps to fill the box,' observed Chatterton drily.

Bulmer risked poking his head around the corner, then said, 'They went in this way, you reckon?'

'The fire escape, then across the tiles. Chances are they'll come out that way.'

'Chances,' agreed Bulmer. Then, 'Maybe the back door.'

'It's boxed up.'

'Great. Where do you want me?'

'Where you are. It bottles one bolt hole.'

The keyholder arrived. He arrived by car, parked the car primly at the rear of the squad car and, quite calmly, strolled towards the sheltering group of officers.

'That infernal alarm.' He began speaking quite cheerfully, before he was within talking distance, before he had sized up the situation. 'We really must get it fixed. Every time a bird lands on . . . '

'GET DOWN!' Riddle howled the warning and flapped his arms. 'They're inside. They're armed.' Then, almost as an afterthought, 'Have you the keys?'

'Yes. My name's Hanbury. Your man tele . . . ' Riddle's words registered, and he gasped, 'Good God!' dropped to his hands and knees and crawled the rest of the way on all fours. 'They're inside? There's somebody *inside*?' He seemed to have difficulty in believing what had been said. 'You mean they're actually *inside*?'

'And armed.'

'Good God!' Then he saw the bleeding Wilture, and repeated, 'Good God!'

'The alarm?' asked Boothby. 'They've smashed a window, but the alarm didn't go off.'

'Oh?' Hanbury could not take his eyes from Wilture. 'Oh, er . . . yes. You have to *open* a window. Or an outside door.'

'In that . . . '

'Or a show case. Some of the show cases are wired.' He dragged his eyes from the injured constable, and breathed, 'What are you going to do?'

'They've opened a show case,' murmured Adams.

'Cool types.' Hindley rubbed his mouth meditatively. 'They know we're here, but they're still nicking.'

'What are you going to *do*?' repeated Hanbury.

'What we are *not* going to do,' said Adams, 'is try for posthumous medals.'

The ambulance rounded a corner. Its light flashed and its bell tongued noisy counter-melody to the alarm bell.

'Not long now, old son.' Hindley stretched out a hand and gripped Wilture's hand. The hold tightened and held, and it meant something. 'Hang on, mate. The beds are comfortable and the sheets are cool.'

Wilture worked to squash the panic. *Kojak, Starsky and Hutch* did not mean anything any more. Cathode-ray cops trading cathode-ray bullets no longer dominated his thoughts. In less than an hour he had attained complete manhood. His backside – it was one hell of a place to carry a scar – but if either he, or the bullet, had been a foot to one side . . .

That close!

The pain had spread, and it was now a throbbing ache. An ache, the like of which he had never before suffered. It hammered in time with his heart and wrapped itself around his pelvic region. From just above the knee the leg was useless. Not dead, not paralysed – some instinct told him it was not *paralysed* – but for the moment useless. He could not move it, nor dare he try too hard.

But everything was okay, now. He could fight the panic and fight the desire to slip into unconsciousness. All that was necessary was that he fight long enough to reach hospital and hand himself over to the experts. Meanwhile, everything was okay. The ambulance had arrived. He was not going to bleed to death after all. The indignity was *not* going to be fatal.

A tear spilled from the outer corner of one eye and ran towards his ear.

'I'll pop in and check, when we've put these hounds where they belong.'

Wilture whispered, 'Thanks.'

And the damnedest thing. He suddenly felt proud. He had done nothing. He had stuck his rump in the way of a hooligan's bullet. He had panicked like the very clappers because he had thought he was bleeding to death, but he had gripped that panic as tightly as he was gripping Hindley's hand and, for that, Hindley was treating him as an equal. And Hindley was a man-and-a-half.

The ambulance boys did not duck. Nor did they seek cover. Not because they counted themselves either armour-plated or immortal, but because that was the way they worked. The only way they *could* work.

Accidents, street battles, terrorism, open warfare. Fools maimed each other, then allowed ambulance men the freedom to save life. There was no law – no written and signed agreement – merely an understanding, built firmly upon the knowledge that ambulances and their attendants arrived, collected shattered flesh then left. No guns, no bombs, no smuggling in of necessities. Only stretchers, blankets and plasma . . . and that to be used upon *anybody*.

They eased Wilture on to a stretcher, folded him into a scarlet blanket then lifted him into the ambulance. The alarm bell roared its clamour, but other than that the suspension was complete. No shooting, no shouting, no movement. The police watched in silence. Nor did sound or shot come from Boots.

Introducing Detective Chief Superintendent Harry Barstow . . . people loathed him or people loved him. There was no halfway. Those who loved him held him as the definitive police officer; the definitive detective and the definitive chief superintendent. Those who loathed him were at a loss for words.

Barstow was never at a loss for words.

His tongue was his weapon. It was as swift and as merciless as a cobra's tongue, and his words dripped venom. Gentle venom. Soft-spoken venom. And he truly did not care, or even think he *should* care, who heard those words.

Yet he never raised his voice and rarely used raw language.

On the other hand few people had seen him laugh, and those who had hurriedly explained (if asked) that the cause of Barstow's merriment had been the extreme discomfort of some smarter-than-average law-breaker; some cunning villain who, thanks to Barstow's monumental and everlasting hatred of criminals, had come unstuck at a rare rate of knots. *Then*, and for a moment, Barstow laughed.

'Guns?' he said, and his tone carried mild disapproval.

'At Radholme, sir.' The duty clerk at headquarters switchboard smiled to himself. He could visualise the slightly cocked eyebrow which accompanied the question. 'Somebody holed up in Boots. An officer's already been shot.'

'Riddle, I trust,' murmured Barstow.

'No, sir.'

'Make my evening, constable. Tell me it's Smeaton.'

'No, sir. One of the foot patrol men. Chief Inspector Riddle has taken over control, pending the arrival of Superintendent Smeaton and yourself.'

'In that case I'd better get there, before there's wholesale slaughter.'

'Yes, sir. I've already arranged for marksmen and reinforcements.'

'Check it.'

'Sir?'

'Check it, constable. Take nothing for granted.'

'Yes, sir.'

'And get word to Riddle. If anybody else – other than himself – gets shot before I arrive I hold him personally responsible.'

'Yes, sir.'

Barstow replaced the receiver. He was vaguely annoyed; as annoyed as any man who holds the rest of the human race in mild contempt can *be* annoyed. It was a peculiar Barstownian annoyance. He was not annoyed because he had been called out just as he was thinking of bed. He was not even annoyed because somebody had shot a copper. He was annoyed because he had not been there; because, however fast he drove, he would not be there as things developed. Ergo, the impudent tykes might get away. The ungracious slobs might put a bullet into another copper and make a successful run for it. With a character like Riddle running things, anything was possible.

Not just Riddle, of course. *Anybody* . . . other than Chief Superintendent Barstow.

Nor was Barstow even slightly concerned that he had voiced his cynicism to the constable clerk. Barstow said whatever he felt like saying, whenever he felt like saying it. He was a power unto himself, not limited by normal standards of behaviour. Indeed, the chief constable hesitated long (and usually changed his mind) when Harry Barstow seemed deserving of either criticism or contradiction.

Barstow left the house without bothering to tell his wife where he was going. She heard him leave and sighed. Age had, perhaps, matured him, but in no way had it mellowed him.

Kelly heard the alarm bell as he resumed patrol on 'A' Beat. It was in the distance and far enough away to be beyond his immediate responsibility. Nevertheless, he heard the alarm bell and wondered.

A break-in?

One of the regular malfunctions of almost all burglar alarm systems?

The questions were, for the moment, of academic interest as far as Kelly was concerned, therefore he dismissed them from his mind and continued checking lock-up property.

Morrison did not hear the alarm bell. Had he deliberately listened he might have heard it, but deliberate acts which might lead to extra work were never a part of Morrison's lifestyle.

Police Constable Edgar Morrison lived within his own tight cocoon of personal, non-identifiable misery. Years ago he had opted out of the world. To be charitable, it had not been a deliberate decision; merely that his gutlessness had made it the only choice. Life, and its problems and responsibilities, had become too tiresome and not worth the trouble. Thenceforth he had been happy to be miserable. Nobody expected anything. Nobody got anything. Nobody was disappointed. Morrison did not handle hills and troughs. He preferred a steady plateau of vague despair, otherwise life was full of pot holes and, for no good reason, you might fall down one and break your stupid neck.

And yet . . .

Years ago, when he had first joined the force, he had been quite a lad. He had built up a reputation as a parochial Lothario. Without actually queuing up, the local young ladies had been eagerly waiting. And young Constable Morrison had happily obliged. He had been *too* obliging. The outcome had been two unmarried females, each in the family way and each anxious to become Mrs Morrison.

Instead, he had married a third admirer; a good cook who, at the time, had shown uncommonly broadminded tolerance.

The tolerance had soon worn off.

Come to that, the cooking had not turned out as good as he had anticipated.

For years she had needled him and made snide remarks about the cash he had had to find for the two growing children. Officially, it was the money required to cover two paternity orders. Shirley insisted upon calling it 'Penis Money' and blamed it for just about everything short of chilblains.

'It's years since I had a new coat. Years! We can't afford decent clothes *and* Penis Money.'

'You're getting a good wage, now. Other people can go abroad for their holidays. We can't. It's all that Penis Money you have to pay out.'

At first he had retaliated, but that had not got him far. Then he had learned to ignore the taunt, to go 'deaf' whenever she spat her ill-tempered remarks at him, and that had driven her into a frenzy of even wilder accusations.

For years now he had not even *heard* the nagging and, of late, Shirley had realised that she was whipping a long-dead donkey; the money had ceased years ago, but in truth they did not seem a penny the richer.

So . . . what the hell?

Freewheel through life. Float along, making as few waves as possible. Screw the whole rotten world – all bar two, and let them find a nice quiet corner and get busy screwing each other.

Which is why Morrison did not know, or *want* to know, about the all-singing-all-dancing production being enacted inside and outside Boots the Chemists.

A lot of loose talk about guns and such. But Bell (whom Morrison thought had come from the incident) had just bounced Sammy Sutcliffe inside for being plastered. A strange way of policing. They apparently needed guns and gold braid even for drunks these days.

Morrison no longer cared about such matters.

Morrison no longer *cared* . . . period.

Midnight. Force areas, divisions, sub-divisions, sections and beats. Ignoring exotica like 'regions' – which encompass the districts covered by crime squads, and widen out to envelop all other boundaries – the jigsaw of law-enforcement remains complicated enough. And each piece equates with its own rank.

A beat is the responsibility of a patrol constable. A multiple of beats form a section, and a section is the responsibility of a uniformed sergeant. A plurality of sections make up a sub-division and, depending upon the number of men required to police that sub-division, the man in charge is either an inspector or a chief inspector. Sub-divisions fuse to become a division and, again depending upon how many officers come under his immediate control, the divisional officer is either a superintendent or a chief superintendent.

This, of course, discounting odd sergeants, inspectors and chief inspectors, who float around as if in outer space, ready to step in when one of their kind is on holiday, on sick leave or in any other way indisposed. These are the 'swingers'; the pigeons who have yet to find a permanent roost.

At the top of the heap chaos rides pure farce.

The chief constable is undisputed master. Thereafter come assistant chief constables, deputy chief constables, assistant deputy chief constables and deputy assistant chief constables. The permutations are endless, love or even basic respect is at a premium, and all think themselves but one place removed from the golden throne.

And in this forensic dog's dinner sat Radholme. Radholme was a sub-division. It was also a section. As a sub-division, it encompassed five sections, including itself, each of which had its quota of constables and sergeants. As a section – in effect, one of its own sections – its boundaries were limited by the boundaries of the old Municipal Borough of Radholme. Nevertheless, and because it was also a sub-division, it could call upon far more officers, in an emergency, than any of its fellow-sections.

Bully for Radholme Sub-division. Bully for Radholme Section.

Bully, also, for the Motor Patrol Division which, and in order to complicate matters, had a boundary which coincided with the boundary of the force area.

Smeaton – Superintendent Thomas Andrew Worburton Smeaton – drove his Rover at a very moderate speed and, while he did so, exercised his mind by working out the various angles to buckpassing via which he could duck even the hint of personal responsibility, should this copper, this unknown and utterly unimportant Police Constable Wilture, have the monumental bad taste to snuff it. The obvious can-carrier was, of course, Riddle. Riddle should not have let it happen. Riddle had been at the scene – he had actually been *there* – when some clown had started shooting. It followed, therefore, that Riddle had some very awkward questions to answer.

A lot of questions.

'Why did you allow an officer to stand in the line of fire?'

'Did you not, at the very least, *consider* the possibility that the intruders might be armed?'

'Riddle, are you not aware that violence, even armed violence, is now part of everyday street crime?'

And plenty more where they came from.

And, of course, Barstow had been called out. Indeed, and with any luck, Barstow would be on the scene before he (Smeaton) arrived.

Given care and an ear for timing, Barstow could be used to excellent effect. A subtle, throwaway remark, a carefully worded criticism, a few cunningly inserted asides. Barstow would undoubtedly bite and, having bitten, he would quietly devour Riddle with the ease and enjoyment of a mid-morning snack.

With luck Barstow might go too far. Admittedly he had not *yet* gone too far, but it had to happen one day.

It was a nice and comforting thought. It was high time Barstow was shown that he was a long way from being non-inflamable. The lesson was long overdue. A stormy session with a chief constable who subscribed to the all-pals -together theory of policing would do Harry Barstow the world of good, and clip his claws as a bonus.

Smeaton felt a warm glow of satisfaction. All was not lost, a good thing out of a bad, the darkness before the dawn . . . and all the rest of it. It was hard lines about the Wilture chap. Being shot could not be a pleasant experience. Nor was it the sort of thing a superintendent would wish to happen to a man under his command. Indeed, one hoped that it was nothing fatal. But if it *was* – if, after all this, the palaver of a police funeral became necessary – the man had not quite died in vain, had he? To make Riddle squirm, and at the same time put a snaffle on Barstow . . .

The thing was to be ruthlessly objective. To be very 'professional'. Above all, not to take these things too personally.

Smeaton slowed down as the Rover approached the traffic lights. They were at green, but they had been at green since Smeaton had first seen them. They would turn to red very soon. He really had not time to cross unless he put his foot down, and it was a built-up area.

It would not do for a police superintendent to break the law. That would not do at all.

Bevis Hanbury, MPS, rather wished he was *not* the keyholder.

Hanbury was a peace-loving individual with a happy disposition and (until this moment) he had had a weakness for the old-fashioned, Warner Brothers' gangster movies. In the past he had rarely missed them when they had been shown on TV – usually as a near-art-form on BBC 2 or Channel 4 – but from now on he would be viewing them from a new angle.

Guns, it would seem, did more than go 'bang'. Of *course* they did – he had known that, too – but he had not fully realised exactly what *else* they did.

For example they caused great panic.

For example they cleared a street of pedestrians quicker than any thunderstorm.

For example they made everybody who even *might* be in the line of fire come out in a rash of sweaty apprehension.

Being something of a well-read type, Hanbury was aware that, theoretically, the gun was the ultimate in phallic symbolism. The hell it was! The phallus created, but the gun destroyed. One gave life, while the other took life. So that was one more beautiful theory up the spout.

Nor were coppers all he had been led to believe them to be.

No heroes were squatting behind these cars. Only ordinary men who, despite their fancy uniforms, were as scared as *he* was. And, what is more, made no pretence not to be.

Strange . . . Hanbury found himself liking them for their weaknesses. It was as if a wall had been pulled down, or a curtain drawn aside. In the future (assuming he had a future) he would see more than a uniform with a humanoid inside it. He would see a man, complete with bowels, bladder and sweat glands. Like old Shylock, that man would bleed, he would hurt and he would laugh.

It came as a bit of a shock – and, indeed, that it came as a shock was itself something of a shock – because Hanbury was a television fanatic and his mental image of coppers had, until now, included riot shields, linked arms and even baton charges. And that image was as false as the old-time gangster films.

This was the real world. The normal world. At the moment, a very uncomfortable world, but in the long term a very *comforting* world.

Vic Boothby hung on to himself and forced himself to follow each thought to its own logical conclusion. It was not easy.

That hint of an ache behind his eyes worried him and, for the moment, his brain seemed to have the consistency of wet cottonwool. It was soggy; too slow, and unable to cope with the build-up of worry. To think – to push hindering emotions to one side, and concentrate – required a deliberate effort.

Dammit, he was *not* ill. He was *not* mad.

Or was he?

He had picked one hell of a time to resolve *that* particular argument, but at the same time it was the incident itself which had forced the final mental showdown. This was the tester. This was more than writing in books, patrolling the streets with constables, making up the section diary. This was none of those things, nor anything like those things. This, dear doctor, was the cracker, and it had to come.

So. Was he still fit to be a section sergeant?

Was he even still fit to be a copper?

That he asked himself the questions more than hinted at a negative answer.

Therefore he spoke to her in his mind, but the words were as real as if they had been mouthed past his lips.

Alice, old darling, give me a hand. I need you. Maybe there's a God – maybe there isn't – but there's always you. You were always there. You're still there. Be there, Alice. Advise me. Help me. Help me, Alice. Please.'

Somebody said something.

'What's that?' Boothby forced himself to listen.

'The Fire Service,' repeated Adams. 'They'll have a loudhailer. It might be quicker.'

'Get on to them.' Riddle acknowledged his agreement by giving instructions to Hindley. 'Use the car radio. Make it urgent . . . but be careful.'

Hindley nodded and made a stooped run for the squad car. He, Boothby, should have heard Adams's suggestion when it was first made. He hadn't, which meant he was slower then Riddle. Slower, and less useful, than any of them.

The ache behind his eyes became more real. It moved from the shadowy hint of something not yet there. And, frighteningly, the harder he tried to ignore it the less shadowy it became.

To acknowledge it was to assist in its creation. To think about it was to induce it.

Help me, Alice. Please, Alice! For God's sake, help me. If you can't think of me, think of the kids. But help me. I don't blame you. I swear I don't blame you. What I once said – about you not having any road sense – I didn't mean it. I never really meant it. I didn't want it to happen, old darling. I didn't want it to happen. I wasn't criticising. I was frightened, and it happened, but I was not criticising. You know that now. You know everything now. You know what I'm going through. For God's sake, help me. Straighten me out, like you always have done.

Boothby blinked his way back to the present and immediately saw the stain on the pavement where Wilture had been. It was the same colour. There was not as much, and it was not the same blood, but it was the same colour. And for the same reason. It was there because of violence and because of pain.

'Why?' he muttered.

'What?' Riddle could not understand the question.

'The waste.'

'I don't follow what you're . . . '

'The stupidity.'

'They're louts, sergeant,' sighed Riddle.

'That's no answer.'

'What?'

'That doesn't explain things.'

'Explain things?' Riddle frowned puzzlement. 'You can't "explain" this sort of situation. People who shoot police officers are beyond the scope of any "explanation".

They don't understand. Alice, old darling, they do not even understand. Nobody. But you and I understand, don't we? You and I, but nobody else. You and I could always understand each other. We still can. Not to talk to each other, as people talk to each other. But our way. I can talk to you, and I can hear you. Help me, Alice. Help me to do the right things.

It was a little like tearing his arm from a vice, but Boothby clenched his teeth and forced his wavering mind to steady itself.

In a tone which carried a slight tremor, he said, 'We can out-wait them.'

'Till the guns arrive,' added Adams.

'We can . . . if necessary.' Riddle did not sound happy at the prospect. 'It seems to be a very negative approach.'

'Sir, there isn't much we *can* do.'

'Sergeant, as I see things, we have to regain the initiative. I don't know how we'll do it, but that's our first priority. To regain the initiative, and let them *know* we've regained the initiative.'

Adams grunted, 'While they have the only guns around, I don't see how.'

Hindley joined them, and said, 'The loudhailer's on its way. They're making it a rush job.'

Bell squashed out what was left of the cigarette, dropped the tape and the forms into the tray to await the typist, then picked up his helmet. The prospect of returning to the streets worried him not at all. Six hours or so of knob-twisting, followed by a few hours in a comfortable bed before being awakened in time for court, was no hardship these days . . . which was odd.

Time was when a mere three hours of sleep had not even *started* to compensate for a night on the pavements; when next-morning court hearings had been a damn nuisance. But not any more. Even without the court, he would be up and about by ten; pottering around in the greenhouse; chatting to neighbours. He would be wide awake and, other than a catnap after the main meal of the day, ready for another night shift.

Maybe the pundits were right after all. He had read it somewhere – or heard it on TV perhaps – that everybody had a different sleep requirement; that the eight hours a day bit was all moonshine; that, with youth disappearing into the middle distance, the number of hours of sleep needed gradually became less.

Which was all bullshit, of course, because some of the old biddies and old codgers in homes and institutions seemed to spend half their lives asleep. They were like kids; like babies

. . . geriatric babies.

Well, he had not reached *that* stage, yet.

Martha might. Indeed, the chances were that Martha *would*.

God Almighty, if anybody was born to be a toothless old maid, it was Martha. Born to be a nagging old crone. Born to be frustrated; gnashing her ancient gums in frustration.

Without too much of an effort he could picture her.

Buggering about with *petit point*. All nose and jaw. Moaning like a drain about rising prices; moaning like a drain about the winters being too cold and the summers being too hot; moaning like a drain because kids lacked good manners. All the usual dreary crap.

For Christ's sake, Martha! Move your arse a bit. Don't *get* like that.

Bell turned into the cell corridor to have a last word with Sammy Sutcliffe.

The cell was lined with white tiles. It had a concrete floor, a concrete ceiling, a single-bed-sized wooden staging upon which to sleep and a tiny-paned window with half-inch-thick glass. The only movable objects were two army blankets and a hessian-covered pillow. However ashamed he might feel, a would-be-suicide was guaranteed a thin time with that little lot.

Sutcliffe was sitting on the staging, elbows on knees and head in his hands.

Bell said, 'Are you fit to understand things?'

'Eh?' Sutcliffe raised his head and screwed up his face in quick pain.

'You're barred from the Horse And Jockey.'

'Who says?'

'I say. The landlord says. Nobody else matters.'

'Why?'

'Don't act dumb, Sammy. One quick sniff at the barmaid's apron and you're a mobile disaster area.'

'People start things.'

'Lots of people. You're one of 'em.'

Sutcliffe rubbed his mouth with the back of a hand, and mumbled, 'Am I nicked?'

'You're not waiting for the last train, mate. I'll let your missus know.'

'Don't bother.'

'All part of the room service.'

'She couldn't care less.'

'Who can blame her?'

'What about bail?'

'Not tonight, Josephine.'

'That's a bit rough.'

'My heart bleeds for you, but I'll live. Court at ten. You'll be fed, groomed and watered before then.'

'That's a day's pay gone.'

'I know. Think of all the booze that might have bought.'

'D'you think that's fair?' Sutcliffe's outrage was not a put-on.

'I think it's fair,' said Bell solemnly. 'Since you ask, I think it's just, right and proper.' As he turned to leave the cell, and just before he slammed the door, he added, 'Sleep well, Sammy. Don't do anything you wouldn't like photographed.'

The man from the Fire Service raced round the corner, dropped to his haunches alongside Boothby, and gasped, 'Here. I've left the van in the other street.'

Boothby took the proffered loudhailer.

'Just press the trigger,' explained the man. 'Then talk. They'll hear you. The batteries are new.'

'Should *I*?' Riddle held out a hand.

'No, sir. I'll do it.'

Stay with me, Alice. You've brought me this far. For God's sake, don't let me down now.

'Be careful,' warned Riddle.

Boothby ignored the warning. He straightened to his full height and walked slowly and stiff-legged from the cover of the cars. When he reached the crown of the road, he stopped. He steadied the slight tremble of his leg muscles, then tilted his head to look up at the broken window.

Then he raised the loudhailer.

Kelly saw the backwash of the street lighting reflected in the switched-off headlamps.

Kelly knew 'A' Beat; he had worked it more times than he had worked any other beat in the section. He knew the dimly lit car parks, the cul-de-sacs and the other private places where a car might stand while its occupants enjoyed a kiss-and-cuddle session. Very often he knew the cars – their makes, their registration numbers and their owners – and knew that on a certain night a certain car would be parked secretively in a certain place.

Behind the town's main Indian restaurant, for example, on the patch of waste land to one side of the concrete area where the proprietor of the restaurant parked *his* car. The same Volvo was there every Friday and every Sunday and, with it, the young, ginger-haired chap – the young blood who worked in the council offices – with what Kelly assumed to be his regular girl friend on a Friday and some other woman, who was invariably older than himself, on a Sunday. They were doing nobody any harm and, although they did not realise it, they were keeping villains clear of the vulnerable spots at the back of the premises. The trick was to spot the car, recognise it, then continue the patrol with an easy mind.

But to see a strange car parked where a car should *not* be, called for a certain amount of nosing around.

It was not voyeurism, neither with Kelly nor with most other conscientious police officers. Cars were used as passion wagons, but that was not illegal, as long as the age was right and everybody was a willing party. That was where the rub came in. Rape was a very nasty crime, and some schoolgirl scrubbers took perverse delight in playing jail bait to horny clowns who should have had more sense.

Therefore Kelly 'investigated'.

He cleared his throat, he flashed his torch and he stamped

70

his feet. He made quite a production number out of it. Youth must have its fling, and every dog must have its day, nor was Kelly anxious to spoil a good thing, but the car *had* to be checked. For a moment he even thought of whistling to announce his approach, but that seemed to be going overboard a bit.

Then he swung the beam of his torch to inside the car and, for a moment, he was speechless.

The car contained one man and one woman. They were sitting on the rear seat and there was at least a foot clearance between them. She was immaculately dressed; summer two-piece, neat-fitting hat, complete with light veil; even gloves with a matching handbag on the seat alongside her. By contrast, he was as naked as nature had made him; he wore not a stitch, his hair was a little ruffled, he was sitting with his hands grasping his knees, and at his crotch was a rapidly melting hard.

Both of them were so prim; so correct; so quietly composed.

Bell moved the torch beam and there, on the front passenger seat, were the man's clothes; undergarments, socks, shoes and, in plain view, the khaki tunic with a second lieutenant's pip on each epaulet. They were all neatly folded and deliberately placed, as if for formal inspection.

Bell kept the beam on the clothes. He could see everything from the overspill of light.

'Police,' he choked.

'Are we parked where we shouldn't park, officer?'

The man had a gentle, educated voice. It carried not a hint of embarrassment, and the manner of asking made the question both polite and reasonable.

'Er, no, sir. Just that – y'know – I wondered.'

'Quite.' The smile complemented the tone. Then, as if the two words explained everything, 'She's French.'

'Oh! I see.'

The truth was, Kelly did not 'see'. His police experience stopped well short of this. It looked wrong. It even looked illegal . . . but as far as Kelly knew it was not illegal. They were both well beyond the age of consent. Nobody had made, or was making, any complaint. Nobody was being 'offended'.

Kelly hesitated, then took a deep breath and murmured, 'Goodnight, sir,' and left them to it.

And yet . . .

As he continued his patrol, Kelly knew something was not quite on the up-and-up. Something was wrong. The woman had not spoken. She had not even moved. She had just sat there, her face masked by the veil.

He turned the door knobs automatically and worried. There was *something*. Something he had not spotted, but should have spotted. Something he had seen, but still did not realise he had seen. It was like a melody he could not quite place or a quotation he could not quite remember.

'I,' said Chambers with some feeling, 'have been on this bloody cake walk long enough. We worked our way into this bloody place for a nice, quiet lift. Risked our stupid necks. So far all we've done is shoot sodding coppers and get the bells of hell cracking. We're inside, Nicco. Look at it how you like, there's a bleeding cell waiting. I say cut our losses and walk out.'

'I say get stuffed.' Nicco stood in the approved manner – the way cornered tough guys always stand – with his back to the wall, peeping round the window opening and down on to the street. 'I say we have the bastards by the balls.'

'Steaming Christ!'

'All they have is sticks. We have the shooter.'

'Nicco, that's arse-hole talk.'

'We have the bleeding shooter,' insisted Nicco.

Chambers sighed. The Fleming bint was not listening. She was still busy choosing watches.

Nicco continued his scanning of the street and said, 'Just because your old man's a pick-a-penny tea leaf . . . '

'Leave him out of it, Nicco.'

' . . . that makes you two-bit. You even think two-bit.'

'All right. Drop the bloody subject.'

'He's inside. The useless git. You'll be inside, Potty. Bet on it. You old man's dumb, so that makes *you* dumb.' The voice had a low, sing-song quality. It was a dirge of utter contempt. 'He lets the cops crap all over him, Potty. That's how dumb he is. You, too . . .'

'Drop it, Nicco.' Chambers's voice had lowered a few semi-tones. It was brittle and tight.

'Me? I ain't like that stupid old sod . . . '

Chambers felt the Californian Poppy stench touch the back of his throat, and it threatened to choke him.

'I'm not moving behind granite because I'm bloody dumb. As dumb as you. As dumb as your old man . . . '

'Knock it off, Nicco.'

Chambers's words were little more than a whisper, but they were a whispered warning.

Nicco did not even hear them. He was peeping around the side of the window, watching his *known* enemies. He was so sure. He was so sure, and so stupid.

'You'll be like that crazy old coot, Potty. Be like your old man. You'll know every screw in the world. So why not be like me, kid? Why not . . . '

The carriage clock was too handy. Without truly realising it, Chambers gripped it. His fingers seemed to close around the heavy metal case of their own volition. The Fleming bint glanced up and grinned; she thought the big man was taking the clock for himself. Then she saw how wrong she was and tried to scream a warning, but it was too late. Much too late.

There was nothing half-hearted about the swing. Chambers was a violent animal, reared in violent surroundings, and as the carriage clock landed on the side of Nicco's skull it, in turn, was the high-point of an upsurge of violent rage as uncontrolled and as terrifying as a volcanic explosion.

'You've killed him!' The Fleming bint breathed her sudden panic.

'Maybe.'

Then from the street came the words, mutilated by the amplification of the loudhailer.

* * *

73

Ben Riddle was taking the dog for a walk. It was not his dog. Neither was it his son's dog. It belonged to Harry Barnes's widow. It had originally belonged to Harry Barnes and the three of them, Ben Riddle, Harry Barnes and the dog, had walked miles. On decent days they had tramped the surrounding countryside. They had even taken bus trips to explore new ground. And always the dog made up the trio.

Bozo . . . a damn stupid name for a dog, but a nice old dog nevertheless.

It was late, but that did not matter. A lifetime of shift work had taken the sting from living by the clock. And with Harry, too. An ex-miner, he had worked shifts and, when he had been at work, he had been God knows how far underground where it was always night.

He had tended to puff a bit.

'The dust, mate.' That was what he had said. He had said it scores of times, and always in a breathless voice. 'The dust. But I've licked the bugger. I'll live for ever, now I can breathe clean air.'

But he had not lived for ever. In the end the dust had killed him.

The dog moved as if to cross the road, then stopped when Ben Riddle slapped the side of his shoe with the walking stick. The perky spaniel bitch on the opposite pavement seemed to give the canine equivalent of a 'come on' sign, and Bozo opened his mouth and panted a little.

'Heel, boy.' And when the dog reluctantly obeyed, 'Forget it, lad. You're like me. Too old for amorous thoughts.'

Too old for it? Or, maybe, just too old – period – for *anything*.

He talked quietly to the dog, and the dog kept lifting its muzzle and looking up at him, as if listening, understanding and sympathising.

'Bozo, old mate, it's a pity they can't do to us what they do to you. A quick jab with a needle, and that's it. No more aggro. Get us out of the way. Put us out of our misery.

'We're a bloody nuisance, but we can't alter. We're always opening our mouths too wide. We think we're saying the right things, but we're not. We're hurting people we don't want to hurt, and not meaning to. That's the hell of it, Bozo. We don't *mean* to hurt.'

Ben Riddle was talking to himself, quietly and seriously, even sadly but, as always, self-conversation brought no answers. The questions were asked a dozen different ways, but the answers were already known and already there, and nobody was around to suggest that they might be wrong answers, or even that there might be other answers.

'I should have stayed in the Smoke, old son. That's where I belong. I have friends down there. Friends, not family. They're more important than family, but you don't learn the truth till it's too late. It's always the same, isn't it? Always the bloody same. You value what you once had when it isn't there any more.

'Then your boss went and died on me. That was a stinker of a trick, mate. The one bloke I'd got close to. The only bloke up here on my wavelength. And the rotten devil dies on me. Dies on both of us. Dies on all three of us. I reckon your old lady feels more than a bit lonely these days. All right, he was a grumpy old sod, and maybe a bit awkward to live with . . . but I bet she misses him.'

For a few minutes Bozo found a lamp-post of more interest and Ben Riddle paused and eyed the animal quizzically.

'Be told, dog. You have prostate trouble. That or hollow legs.'

Then they continued their stroll and Ben Riddle continued his musings.

'Do you have a son, Bozo? You wouldn't know, would you? Dozens, very likely. An old ram like you. Sons all over the place. But none like mine, eh? As if you cared. None of 'em a ponced up ninny who needs a bloody woman to justify his existence. *And* playing at being a copper.

'What the hell did I do to deserve him? To deserve a son like that?

'I left him to his mother too much. That's what. I didn't take enough interest. But that's not right, Bozo, is it? That's not a fair whack. I gave 'em both a good home. Good grub. All they asked for. All I was able to give 'em. What more can a man do?

'Y'know the trouble, Bozo? He won't accept the responsibilities. Not at home. Not at work. That's his trouble. Too soft. Not enough vinegar and ginger. That's his mother coming out. He won't spit in people's eyes. Won't heft the big stick when it's necessary. So, things go wrong and he gets scared. He won't take aggro in his stride. Jenny knows that. That's why she argues the way she does. He's only half a man, see? My God! If I thought his mother had made empty excuses for me . . . '

The dog stopped, arched its back and defecated.

'Whoever you are, you haven't a chance. Don't make things worse. The officer you shot only has a flesh wound. You're surrounded. You can't get away. Take good advice. Throw out your guns, then come out with your hands on your heads.'

Chambers heard the words. He understood them and took them not as advice but as a challenge. They voiced his own earlier opinion, but that meant nothing because that had been *his* opinion.

The crap-arsed cops thought they had all the answers. They were like Nicco. They only *thought* they had all the answers.

His logic was immaculate in its illogicality.

He turned on the Fleming bint, and snarled, 'There's a ladder. To reach the top shelves. Shove it under the hole. We're getting out of here.' Then when she stood, open-mouthed and terrified, '*Move your bloody self!*'

He limped towards the unconscious Nicco, picked up the fallen gun and rammed it into the waistband of Nicco's jeans. Then he stooped, grunted as he hefted the unconscious man to shoulder height, and growled, 'Take the bleeding gun. And the stupid sod who used it.'

12.30 a.m. Take a war or an uprising, a railway disaster or an aeroplane crash, take an assassination or a multiple murder – take extreme and unnecessary violence, a swill of blood and a mindless degree of pain –

then search for a common denominator.

You will find it in ordinary people; in the man who lives next door; in the housewife standing alongside you at the supermarket check-out.

Later they blamed the alarm bell, but that was only because they needed an excuse. To have acknowledged the truth would have been a shameful admission. It would have put modern man on a par with the howling mob screaming for carnage at a Roman amphitheatre. Therefore they blamed the alarm bell.

But they were gathering long before the alarm bell was triggered. They had deviated from their journeys. They had left their homes to watch. They remained at what they thought was a safe distance, but they craned their necks.

The bullets were real. The blood was still warm. The fascination was complete.

Boothby froze as he saw the window and frame shatter. He stood motionless as glass showered down on him and as the figure turned and tumbled towards him. Had he had his wits about him, he might have ducked, or even stepped aside.

He did neither.

More than nine stone of deadweight human flesh landed first on Boothby's suffering head, then on his shoulders, then, as he sprawled, across his back.

The world – specifically *his* world – collapsed around his ears, and nothing was worth a damn any more.

A handful of men, some of them off-duty special constables, did stand-in crowd control pending the arrival of more officers.

They tried to keep the crazier rubber-neckers out of the firing line, and give that small knot of coppers at the scene some sort of chance to contain the situation, without having the additional worry of protecting men, women and even children who should have known better.

But still the gawpers came, and still the press of onlookers grew.

Bulmer gasped, 'What the hell was that?'

'Leave it!' Chatterton called the warning softly from the

shadows. 'Stay put. It could be a diversion. There's enough of 'em at the front.'

Bulmer grunted his agreement.

Bulmer was glad Ernie Chatterton was there. It was nice. It was comforting. If he could not have his colleague, Hindley, he was happy to have Chatterton. Chatterton was a quiet type, but he could count beans. Chatterton was not likely to be conned, or flurried, by *anything*.

Nevertheless something was happening at the front of the shops.

Bulmer sensed it, and was sure he was right. This little lot was not going to spin itself out into a Spaghetti House Siege. This was going to be a quick, bish-bash-wallop job. Bulmer was ready to bet money on it. And there had been Bulmers at others like this in the past. Two police medals had been earned by the family – one by his uncle and one by the husband of his niece – and both of them had been earned at this sort of caper, with villains airing their muscles and having to be slapped down.

Certain basics had to be understood. Those crap-hats inside the shop were scared. They were like penned wild cats, and as vicious as wild cats. They would fight for their freedom. They would not *get* their freedom, that was out of the question, but they would certainly fight for it. They were animals, and they thought like animals. They could not be coaxed out. They had to be tamed. All that garbage about coming out with their hands on their heads was empty blather. Boothby had to say it, but nobody really *believed* it. Those bastards would come out swinging. And maybe that was what the noise was about.

In a carrying whisper Bulmer called, 'I reckon a chair.'

'Eh?'

'A chair.'

'Oh!'

'Smashing a window with a chair.'

'Could be.'

'Then coming out after it.'

'Maybe.'

'If that's it . . . '

'Hold your water.'

'What?'

'Maybe you're right. If you are, we'll hear. We'll nip round and help.'

'What I'm getting at . . . '

'It could be a diversion.'

'Oh!'

'To get everybody up front while they nip out at the back.'

'Just – y'know – we want to be where it's all happening.'

'Let it happen . . . then we'll know.'

Rosemary Adams was a proud young woman. A wife of less than two years, with a new baby son and a loving husband who was already a valued member of the Radholme police fraternity. He was one of the youngest detective constables in the force, but Chief Inspector Riddle (whom Rosemary respected as one of the most 'human' policemen she had ever met) had hinted that older men, with more experience, rarely detected crime more swiftly or more efficiently.

John Adams was going places.

And yet . . .

There was a puzzle which did not admit of a ready solution, and that puzzle caused her secret worries. Was it a certain sort of man who was drawn to this profession of policing? Or did policing create that sort of man?

John, her husband, was different. At least, she *hoped* he was different and was almost *sure* he was different, but from what little she had seen . . .

She had met some of the men her husband worked alongside, at a couple of police dances. They had been with their wives, and they should have been relaxing. Indeed, and on the face of things, they *were* relaxing. They had been officers from Radholme and officers from other sections which made up the division; they were policemen and, because of that and if the propaganda was to be believed, they were 'men apart'. And, indeed, when she had met them they had been men apart.

They had been so much apart they had frightened her a little.

Some could not unbend. Others unbent too far.

The stupidity and childishness had sickened her.

The lick-spittle types had, perhaps, been worst; the inspectors, chief inspectors, superintendents and chief superintendents who had (supposedly) been off duty – who had (supposedly) been enjoying themselves – each with his tiny cortège of simpering attendants, offering them seats, lighting their cigarettes and obediently laughing at their jokes. It had been a nauseous sight, emphasised by the fact that those buttered up had taken it for granted and as their due, and those doing the buttering up had been blind to any argument suggesting that they might be cheapening themselves.

John was not one of those. God willing, he would never become one of those.

But the ones who had not been able to relax had been as pathetic. They had tried. They had so obviously tried so hard, but had found it to be an impossibility, and that had been the sad part of it. Small talk and chit-chat had embarrassed them. Normal conversation had left them mumbling. They had had an inner sullenness, a deep-rooted frigidity, which had robbed their polite smiles of humour. Their jackets had all been buttoned correctly, their ties neatly knotted and their hair-styles an almost obligatory short-back-and-sides. They had given the impression of for ever being on parade; of doing everything, including dancing and drinking, strictly by num-bers. They had had a po-faced solemnity which, in their minds, went with the business of policing.

But if those who could not bend worried her, the few who bent too far disgusted her. She had seen that, too.

Example, the sergeant from a neighbouring section, whose father had served in the Scots Guards in World War II. He was not even from north of the border, but the kilt and the bagpipes had become symbolic of a family highlight; a tartan-tinged peak in a life of dry-plain monotony.

He had boozed himself into a state of noisy and awkward drunkenness on whisky and, towards the end of the dance when the band had struck up The Gay Gordons he had gone mad.

He had whooped with delight. He had charged across the dance floor. He had scattered moderates left and right. It had been a disgraceful exhibition, and he had ruined what might have been a pleasant evening.

John told her of the outcome.

There had been Misconduct Sheets all round for the sergeant and his foul-mouthed, drunken colleagues whose antics at the bar she had only heard about. The explosion of ill-mannered irresponsibility, the running amok of men incapable of understanding what the word 'moderation' meant, had demanded nothing less.

But that was John's job, and these were the people he worked alongside.

Which, of course, begged the question – did the man find the profession, or did the profession make the man?

She leaned across, smiled at the babe sleeping in the carrycot tucked away in a corner of the sofa. She eased a corner of the tiny pillow away from the dribbling mouth as she spoke.

'We mustn't let him, darling. We mustn't allow it to happen. We must make sure he stays exactly as he is.'

Superintendent Smeaton parked his car behind the Fire Service van and walked. He knew the lay-out of Radholme. He knew where all the excitement was, and the gathering of onlookers merely verified that knowledge. The object of his slow-fuse arrival was to give himself time to assess the situation before his presence was known, to spot any mistakes – and there would be mistakes, because mistakes were always made, and thereafter have a firm platform upon which he could erect his complaints and criticisms.

He was there to stir things up and get things moving.

He elbowed his way through the crowd, ignoring the protests of those he pushed aside. He recognised a man trying to perform some degree of crowd control as a special constable sergeant, in plain clothes.

As Smeaton stepped from the front of the crush, the man hurried towards him, and said, 'I'm sorry, but you can't . . . ' He stopped then added, 'I'm sorry, sir. I didn't recognise you.'

'Who's keeping them back?' demanded Smeaton.

'I'm doing my best.'

'Just you?'

'I'm being helped, of course.'

'What about beat constables?'

'They seem to have their hands full.'

'Do what you can, sergeant. I'll soon have men to assist.'

Smeaton turned the corner, saw the huddle of men in the road and, figuratively speaking, licked his chops in anticipation. Here was a whole bagful of goolies. They were all squatting there, like a gaggle of old women discussing the latest in knitting patterns, with one man – obviously a detective constable – cowering down in the shelter given by cars.

'You there.' The man looked up and Smeaton snapped, 'What do you think you're doing?'

The full arrogance of superintendentship went into the question.

Hanbury looked nonplussed.

'Answer me, man. What are you doing?'

'Why?' Hanbury stared. 'Who wants to know?'

'*I* want to know.'

'And who the deuce are *you*, when you're at home?'

'I,' barked Smeaton with growing exasperation, 'am your divisional officer.'

'Oh?'

'Now, answer the question. What the devil are you doing, skulking behind motor cars?'

'I'm keeping my head down,' said Hanbury grimly. 'And, if it's of any interest to you, you are *not* my divisional officer, nor are ever likely to be.'

'What?'

'I was called out by the police.'

'Why the devil should they . . . '

'I'm the keyholder.'

'Oh!'

'And if you're who I think you are . . . '

'Smeaton. Superintendent Smeaton.'

'Well, *Superintendent* Smeaton, I think you should know that, until this moment, I've admired the way the police have behaved. Now you're here I'm beginning to entertain serious doubts.'

Which put the skids under T.A.W. Smeaton and, when the Volvo raced up the street and made a Grand Prix halt within feet of the grouped officers, Smeaton felt a very hard-done-by uniformed superintendent.

Barstow had arrived and, as he dived from the Volvo as if propelled by catapult, nobody was left in doubt about the incident moving into another and more rarified dimension.

'Who's handling this ridiculous fracas?'

'I am.' Riddle straightened.

'Not too successfully by the look of things.'

'A constable's been shot.'

'So I'm told.'

'And now there's a sergeant been injured by a man jumping from an upstairs window.'

'That's a rather droll way of assaulting a police officer.'

Riddle continued, *sotto voce*, 'With any luck the next one will be a detective chief superintendent.' Smeaton joined them and Riddle added, 'Or perhaps a divisional officer.'

'What's going on?' demanded Smeaton. 'Why haven't you men handling the crowd?'

'Where do I get men?' sighed Riddle. 'So far only the chiefs have arrived. I'm short on redskins.'

'Oh, very droll.'

Hindley stood up and half-ran towards the squad car.

'Where's that man going?' barked Smeaton.

'To radio for an ambulance. We have two badly injured men here, and one of them is a police sergeant.'

'Any advance on two?' murmured Barstow.

'I demand to know . . . '

'Smeaton . . .' Riddle interrupted. Beyond the superintendent's shoulder he saw two more patrol cars arrive and brake behind the car which had bumped his own vehicle. Both Smeaton and Barstow had their backs to the minor road accident, and the din from the alarm bell killed any likelihood of anybody else hearing what was being said. A tight, grim smile touched Riddle's lips, as he continued, 'Smeaton – and you, too, Barstow – each man to his own priority. If you have a fetish about crowd control, if you get pleasure from making ill-mannered remarks, go ahead. Don't let me stop you. But *my* priority is to get two badly injured men to hospital as soon as possible. I see other officers have now arrived. They're at your disposal, Smeaton. Meanwhile be advised, both of you, somebody else is still inside those premises. He may or may not be armed. Which means you may or may not be shot.'

Kelly returned to the cinema.

It was a gamble, in that the programme had ended more than an hour previously. He was lucky; he caught the manager as that worthy was leaving the cinema and on his way to drop the takings into the bank night safe.

'10p pieces.' Kelly felt in his hip pocket. 'Can you let me have a quid's worth?'

'Sure.'

The manager unlocked the door of the cinema, they returned to the foyer and the manager counted out ten 10p pieces. He exchanged them for a note.

The weight of the coins bumped against Kelly's hip as he made his way to the kiosk. They seemed to nudge him; to hurry him along before it was too late. The decision had been made. He had broken with his mother and his sister, and he was prepared to crawl. Julie could set the pace; she could decide upon the conditions; she could demand as many provisos as she wished.

Only let her agree.

Only let her be there, at the other end of a telephone wire.

✳ ✳ ✳

In minor roads between Haggthorpe and Radholme two young tearaways – one white, one coloured – enjoyed themselves playing tag in a stolen vehicle.

The coloured youth could drive. He had a natural flair. He handled the wheel with the skill and panache of his compatriot West Indians wielding a cricket bat.

Twice already they had out-foxed pursuing squad cars; zipped along side roads – once into and out of a field – doubled back, raced through gaps with inches to spare, and already they were beginning to monopolise the police air waves.

They were no longer skulking behind squad cars. Barstow skulked for no man, and Barstow set the pace. The ambulance gave a measure of protection but, when Boothby and Nicco had been loaded, even that slight shelter would have gone.

It mattered not. Barstow's manner dismissed bullets as being as unimportant as annoying gnats.

'You've sent for the Dog Section?'

It was phrased as a question, but the emphasis suggested that, of course, Riddle had sent for the Dog Section; the question was merely a verification that the world was not, perhaps, peopled exclusively by idiots.

'No.'

'You surprise me.'

'I rather thought I might.'

Riddle found it easy enough to counter Barstow's caustic contempt, knowing, as he did, that the contempt was universal rather than personal. Nevertheless, it was tiresome. The detective chief superintendent accepted that sarcasm might be met with sarcasm, and seemed not to mind. Perhaps his hide was too thick to allow the barbs to penetrate. The trick – as Riddle knew from previous experience – was to indulge in gentle insolence, and return some of what was being received.

Nor did circumstances nor time prevent Barstow from acting like one half of a burlesque double-act. He said, 'You should know by this time, Riddle. Misbegotten germs who break into shops have a great fear of doggies.'

'Even when they're armed?'

'We have more dogs than they have bullets.'

'The RSPCA might not like it.'

'Good God! You're not serious.'

'Having shot a police officer,' said Riddle, pointedly.

'I don't follow.'

'They may go completely beyond the pale, and shoot a dog.'

'Riddle, you're not of this world.'

'If you say so, chief superintendent.'

The attendants slammed the rear doors of the ambulance, and hurried towards the cab.

Hindley and Adams moved to within earshot of Barstow and Riddle, and Adams voiced his concern.

'Should we get under cover, sir?'

In a very deadpan voice, Riddle said, 'Detective Chief Superintendent has now arrived, Adams.'

'What, exactly, does that mean?' demanded Barstow.

'I now *take* orders.'

Barstow sniffed. It was a very expressive sniff. It carried, in equal parts, disgust for chief inspectors who lacked the simple gumption to send for Dog Sections, a poor opinion of detective constables who wanted to hide behind corners and an airy dismissal of addle-brained law breakers who thought guns made a scrap of difference.

With obvious reluctance, Barstow growled, 'I suppose we'd better get somewhere where they'll have to actually *aim*. Not that they'll hit us. These lunatics couldn't hit a pig in a ginnel.'

'Constable Wilture might not agree.'

'Rubbish, Riddle. Whatever else they were aiming at, they weren't aiming at Wilture's arse.'

Julie answered, and Kelly pushed the first 10p into the slot.

'Julie. It's me.'

'What?'

'Don't ring off. Please don't ring off.'

'Who *is* that?' There was surprise and non-recognition in her voice.

86

'It's Freddie.'

'Oh!'

'Please, don't ring off.'

'What on earth . . . '

'*Please*, don't ring off.' Kelly's voice had a groaning quality. 'Listen to me, Julie. Listen to me.' He swallowed, then blurted, 'Today . . . I didn't mean it. Honestly. I didn't mean it.'

'Freddie, I don't know what . . . '

'*Please* don't ring off.'

'All right. I won't ring off. Although why you've telephoned is beyond me.'

'I'm sorry.'

'Sorry?'

'About today. About everything.'

'Look, I was in bed. You've got me out of bed . . . '

'I'm sorry. Truly, I'm sorry.'

'Are you drunk?'

'What?'

'Drunk? Are you drunk?'

'No. I'm not drunk. I'm . . . '

'Are you sure? Have you been drinking?'

'I'm on duty. Of course I'm not . . . '

'How on earth can you be ringing me if you're on duty?'

'I'm using a kiosk. I had to speak to you.'

'What about?'

'About today. It mustn't happen, Julie. We mustn't let it happen.'

'Freddie, if this is a joke . . . '

'Oh, my God!'

'If it isn't a joke . . . '

'It isn't a joke. I swear it isn't a joke.'

'. . . I don't understand.'

'I don't want you to leave me.'

'It's too late.'

'No, it's not. It's not!'

'After today it's too late.'

'Julie – please, listen.'

87

'It won't do any good.'

'It's *not* too late.'

'Freddie, we aren't married any more.'

'Yes. Yes, we are.'

'We're divorced.'

'No . . . we're *not.*'

'Freddie, it wasn't a charade today. It wasn't just quarrelling.'

'I know. I'm sorry.'

'We aren't married any more.'

'We are. Yes, we *are.*'

'You're behaving like a child, Freddie.'

'No.'

'Telephoning me out of the blue like this.'

'Please! Don't ring off.'

'All right. I won't ring off, but . . . '

'It's not final, you see.'

'What?'

'The decree. The divorce.'

'You're being very silly.'

'No. It's not final. Only *nisi*. Not absolute.'

'I don't know what you're talking about.'

'*Nisi.* We're only divorced, unless something happens.'

'Nothing's going to happen, Freddie.'

'Unless we make it up. We're only divorced if we *want* to be divorced.'

'We're divorced, Freddie.'

'No.'

'We aren't married any more.'

'Yes. Yes, we *are.*'

'Freddie!'

'I don't *want* to be divorced. I *never* wanted to be divorced.'

'You've left it too late.'

Chatterton saw the two shapeless figures moving cautiously and, occasionally, breaking the straight line of the ridge tiles.

'They're coming.'

'Which way?' Bulmer's question was as whispered as Chatterton's warning.

'The fire escape.'

'Now?'

'Not yet. Let 'em get down here.'

'How many?'

'I count two.'

'I'll take the first. You take the second.'

'Fair enough.' Chatterton paused. 'Don't argue. Hit first.'

'You bet.'

Sutcliffe's wife, Maggie, had long ago ceased to dream about turning men's heads.

Once upon a time she had read cheap romantic novels and speculated upon the possibility of some slim, dark-haired, masculine creature sweeping her off her feet and rushing her off to some secluded country inn where, prior to the asterisks at the end of the chapter, undying love would be sworn and her bosom (what little she had) would rise and fall with mounting passion. Once upon a time, she had dreamed.

Now she sighed, 'Pissed again?'

'I'm afraid so, luv.'

Bell stood at the doorstep of the tiny terraced house and, not for the first time, wondered what the hell two people like Sammy and Maggie Sutcliffe had ever seen in each other. He was a slob, she was a slut and, granted that each deserved the other, that did nothing to explain what must have been some sort of hope for the future.

'Keep him in, Mr Bell.' She hugged the light overcoat which did duty as a dressing gown tighter around her skinny frame. Beneath it a few inches of grubby, cotton nightgown flapped above caricatures of feet. 'Last time you let him out at three o'clock in the morning.'

'He won't come out tonight,' promised Bell.

'Three o'clock, and he had me brewing tea and making him bacon sandwiches.'

'Court at ten.'

'Serve the silly old devil right. I hope he gets time. It's what he deserves.'

'He'll not go down, luv.'

'It's what he deserves,' she repeated.

'Anyway, that's it. You know where he is. Go back to bed with an easy mind.'

Bell wished Maggie Sutcliffe goodnight, then returned to the sweeter atmosphere of 'D' Beat; to where a man skilled in the decorator's craft was not offended by the peeling paint; to where a complete re-paint job was a five-yearly necessary inconvenience.

Bell approved of 'D' Beat and could not fathom the mentality of the Sutcliffe way of life. Muck bred muck, but muck was not obligatory. Soap and water was cheap enough, and a damn sight cheaper than booze. Nor was good paint too expensive.

Nobody was suggesting an *Ideal Home* standard, but to get beyond a certain degree of sheer filth demanded years of work. It demanded the conscious and deliberate collecting of filth.

And another thing . . .

Why the hell didn't somebody switch off that alarm bell? It was somewhere at the other end of the town, and it was bad enough hearing it as a background noise. It must be blue murder for those living nearer to it.

They came down the fire escape. The girl came first, followed by Chambers. Owing to his limp, Chambers missed his footing slightly when he was about two-thirds of the way down, and Bulmer heard the noise, tensed, then relaxed when there was no movement from Chatterton.

Chatterton waited until they had left the fire escape; until they were moving cautiously towards the narrow passage leading from the yard of the loading bays. Then he slipped the truncheon from its pocket and raced from his hiding place.

He called, 'Now!' and Bulmer joined him.

Bulmer grabbed the first figure, and the first figure was the girl, Fleming. The realisation that it was a girl only came when he wrapped his arms around the body, and he silently cursed his luck.

Where the hell do you grab a struggling female? Where do you take a grip that will quieten her without some defending solicitor hinting at indecent assault? Wherever he touched was wrong. She was twisting and screaming and, unless he did something drastic, she would be away.

He dodged clawing fingers, gasped, 'Oh, bugger it,' then swung a full-blooded backhander which smashed across her mouth and sent her sprawling.

As he bent to haul her upright, he pulled handcuffs from his hip pocket.

'Take it easy, girl,' he warned. 'You're nicked. Take it easy or I'll have to carry you to the station.'

1 a.m. It has been said, by people who profess to understand these things, that love and power, as exemplified by sex and violence, are the natural urges of the twentieth century; that self-preservation and an inborn desire to perpetuate the species have been pared down, stripped of all fine excuses and made naked and shameful.

Certainly, and in the so-called 'civilised world', hunger based on poverty has been eliminated. Fear has become too universal; it is now an international terror, personified by a mushroom cloud of slow extermination, which stalks the nightmares of all mankind.

Were he alive today, Freud would have to re-think some of his basic theories.

The argument goes that there is no God, with the escape clause which adds that, if there is He is not worthy of the name. But if God created life, man created the contraceptive; if God approves of righteous anger, man has fouled that anger by turning it into terrorism.

This, then, is the age of pornography; the pornography of sex and the pornography of violence. Coppers spend a small lifetime trying to control that hydra-headed pornography – but fail.

Like an incoming tide across ridged sand it crawls into every community . . . even a community like that of Radholme.

Chatterton killed Chambers.

The turned hickory of the truncheon landed on the youth's

skull with all the whipcord-and-whalebone strength Chatterton could muster. No attempt was made to grab. Chatterton spoke no word after that first, 'Now!'

For one terrible moment he allowed his temper to surface.

That was all it needed.

Chatterton murdered . . . and Chatterton *knew* he had murdered.

Kelly fed another 10p into the slot.

'Are you still there?'

'Of course. Although why you've telephoned me . . . '

'I've broken with mother.'

'What?'

'And Cynthia. I've broken with both of them.'

'I don't know what you mean.'

'Julie. You never liked them. So, I've broken with them.'

'They – they . . . ' Her voice trailed off into silence.

'Come back to me, Julie.'

'Freddie, you can't be serious.' He heard the sigh quite distinctly. 'You can't be *serious*.'

'I am. Honestly.'

'Look, you can't just . . . '

'I've never been more serious.'

'Freddie.' She spoke as a mother might speak to a naughty child. 'I didn't ask you to break with your family. I never wanted *that*.'

'You've often said . . . '

'Not to quarrel with them, Freddie. To face them.'

'That's what I . . . '

'No. Not to be under their thumb. That's all I ever asked.'

'I've done it, now.'

'You've done far more than you should have done.'

'Julie. I . . . '

'Now you've nobody.'

'You. I have you.'

'Freddie . . . '

'Please, Julie. I love you.'

'I don't want that sort of love.'

'Any sort. Any sort of love you like.'

'Freddie . . . '

'Just stay my wife, Julie. Anything at all.'

'Freddie, you . . . '

'Just stay my wife.'

'Freddie, don't be . . . '

'I'll come over.'

'What?'

'Now. Now, I'll come over.'

'At *this* time?'

'What does it matter? That's what I'll do. I'll come over, then we can talk.'

'You're on duty.'

'That doesn't matter.'

'Of course it matters.'

'No. I'll leave the beat. It's not important. I'll get the car, then I'll . . . '

'Freddie!'

' . . . drive over, and we can settle things. I can't go through another . . . '

'Freddie!' She shouted the name.

'Julie, I love you,' he groaned.

'All right. All right.' She paused, then said, 'Tomorrow. Come over tomorrow. We'll talk.'

'As soon as I come off duty.'

'No. That's too early.'

'Julie, you're . . . '

'In the evening. I have to go to work.'

'Look, I mean it. If you . . . '

'I'll be home by six. Come then.'

'You're not just putting me off?'

'No, of course not.'

'Truly?'

'I'll be here, at six o'clock.'

'I mean, if you're . . . '

'I don't have to lie, Freddie.'

93

'No . . . of course not.'

'We'll talk. No promises . . . but we'll talk.'

'You'll come back to me.'

'We'll *talk*.'

'I love you, Julie. Anything – anything at all – just that I love you.'

'Tomorrow.'

'You'll *be* there?'

'Of course I'll be here.'

'Goodnight, darling.'

'Goodnight, Freddie.'

'You truly will be . . . '

'Good*night*, Freddie.'

Kelly held the dead receiver to his ear for a moment. He watched the ghost reflection of his face in the tiny panes of the kiosk, then replaced the receiver on to its prongs. He laid his forearm across the receiver, then lowered his head on to his forearm.

She would come back. He was sure she would come back. He had broken the hard husk with which she had surrounded herself; that emotional incrustation which, earlier in the day, had seemed rock solid and incapable of being cracked.

He had cracked it, and the James character could look around for somebody else. He could not have Julie.

Nevertheless, it had been hard and exhausting work.

Kelly straightened, pocketed the remaining 10p pieces and left the kiosk.

'How many left in there?'

Man or woman, Barstow did not care where *he* grabbed. He jerked the fistful of blouse higher and the girl, Fleming, stretched her neck but still gazed, orb-eyed, at the bleeding Chambers.

'He's – he's . . . '

'Never mind him, you miserable little madam.' The fist pushed her chin higher, and he shook her into listening to his question. '*How many left in there?*'

'None – none,' she gasped. 'He threw Nicco through the window . . . '

'That's a novelty.'

' . . . and now he's – he's . . . '

'Shove her in a cell.' The impression was that Barstow tossed the girl, almost offhandedly, into the arms of Bulmer. Then, to the chief inspector, 'Your job, Riddle. Search the place and make sure.'

Riddle took a deep breath.

As an afterthought, Barstow asked, 'Have the Wild West fraternity arrived yet?'

'I think some marksmen have arrived,' said Riddle.

'In case she's lying, arrange to be able to shoot back, if necessary.'

'Thank you, chief superintendent.'

'Where's Smeaton?'

'Crowd control, sir.' Adams answered the question.

'Get word to him, Riddle. My compliments and would he mind breaking the habit of disappearing into the middle distance when things start happening.'

'My pleasure.'

'And, unless he has obscure religious objections, would he please keep an eye on things round the front, while I tie the loose ends up at the back here.'

'And an ambulance?' suggested Riddle.

'Of course. And hint that if we send for them any more times tonight we'll go Dutch on the price of the petrol.' Then, turning to Adams and Chatterton, 'Does anybody recognise this comedian?'

'Chambers,' said Chatterton quietly. 'Answers to the name of "Potty".'

'*Answered,*' corrected Adams gently.

'You're not a medical practitioner, Adams,' said Barstow. 'You know the rules. If he's had his arms and legs torn off – even if he's been decapitated – he's officially *alive* as far as ignorant policemen are concerned.'

'Yes, sir.' Adams was squatting alongside the fallen

Chambers. He looked sad as he added very softly, 'But I wouldn't bet the weight of my next breath on it.'

'What happened, Chatterton?'

'He made a run for it,' lied Chatterton, and his voice was quite steady. 'I tried for the collar bone, but he turned.'

'It goes that way sometimes.' Barstow stared down at the man they all three knew was dead. 'People tell me life is precious, even priceless . . . just don't try to dun me into a contribution towards a wreath.'

'No, sir.'

'Go with him. Listen to some acne-faced young medic tell you something we already know. Then get back to the station. I'll see you there.'

'Yes, sir.'

'You too, Adams. Oh, and Adams . . . '

'Yes, sir.'

'Find a squad car. Radio in to headquarters. I want the complete West End production. A homicide, resultant upon a break-in. That's all. No details.'

'Next year would have been our Golden Wedding.'

Mary Barnes (Harry's widow) made the observation quite calmly. She made it as she re-filled Ben Riddle's teacup, and there was no sadness in her tone. Nor was there relief. Had she said, 'Tomorrow is Wednesday,' the same tone of voice would have been used.

Ben Riddle sat in Harry's old chair alongside the near-dead fire. His left hand hung down the side of the chair and the fingers scratched behind the dog's ears.

It was a crazy o'clock and most of the surrounding world was abed, but coppers and ex-coppers make no concession to time and the woman had been a night owl all her life.

She replaced the cosied teapot on its stand on the tiled hearth and, for a moment, the stretch of her dress outlined her bodily contours. She was a very handsome woman for her age. She was neither skinny nor run to fat. Indeed, in Ben Riddle's considered opinion, she was *very* handsome – for her age.

He said, 'I miss him.'

She returned to her chair across the hearthrug from where Ben Riddle was sitting. She did not answer.

'*You'll* miss him,' he added.

'I find it a quieter life,' she said gently.

'A bit empty.'

'I didn't say that.'

'Quieter, then,' he corrected himself.

'Fewer quarrels. I don't have to fight for every little luxury.'

'Oh!'

Her response had not been quite what he had expected. He sipped his tea, and watched her without obviously watching her. Harry had not mentioned any quarrels. He had not been that sort of man. No heart-on-the-sleeve stuff for Harry Barnes. He had been a good chap; straight talking and a man quite capable of keeping his own house in order.

'You don't feel lonely?' probed Ben Riddle, cautiously.

'Sometimes, but it passes.'

'I liked Harry.' He sipped the tea, again. 'I liked him a lot.'

'You were very similar to each other.'

'That's why we got on.' He stared at the surface of the tea, then spoke awkwardly. It was a strange awkwardness; as if he was offering something, even *giving* something, but embarrassed at the possibility of thanks. 'Like you say, we were like each other. We – er – y'know, we had the same principles. Didn't mince words. That's why . . . ' He paused to take a deeper than usual breath. 'We – er – y'know, neither of us are getting any younger. Us two, I mean. And – all right, it's a bit soon yet – but . . . '

'Don't go any further, Ben.'

'Eh?'

'Don't say what you're trying to say.'

'I could make you happy,' he muttered.

'That I doubt. You're too much like Harry.' She smiled at the shock in his expression then, in a quiet voice, continued, 'He wasn't a good husband, you know. Oh, he *thought* he was. In his own way he *tried* to be. But he wasn't.'

'I never saw him look at another woman.'

'He never did,' she agreed.

'In that case . . . '

'That's not everything, Ben. It's not even the most important thing.'

'Some people might not . . . '

'*You* think it is. *He* thought it was. He was for ever reminding me.' She shook her head. 'Marriage is more than that, Ben. It should be. That part should be taken for granted.

'The important things.' A sad, dreamy expression touched her eyes. 'Not being able to live without each other. That means sharing. Really sharing. Sharing a life. Not just what *you* want. Sharing what the other one wants – even if you don't want it. I shared what Harry wanted. What I wanted wasn't important enough to share.'

'He's not here to defend himself,' he said gruffly.

'He defended himself well enough when he *was* here.' There was no acrimony in the words; they were, if anything, a solemn explanation and a negative answer before he had even asked his question. 'He was head of the house. The breadwinner. The most important member of the family . . . and, all right, he was. But he never let anybody forget it. He wasn't mean, but we all had to ask. We received, of course we received, but we always had to *ask*, and then be grateful. That was his way, you see. That's not sharing. That's on a par with charity.

'The children grew to hate him. I can't really blame them. You can only make so many excuses when you're young, even if you're excusing people you're expected to love. They all three left home before it was necessary. One ended up with a broken marriage . . . '

'You can't blame Harry for *that*!'

Ben Riddle found himself defending the memory of his friend against the accusations of the friend's widow. At least, that is what he *thought* he was doing.

'Ben,' she said, simply, 'I blame him. It wasn't deliberate, but it was *his* fault. She grabbed a husband to get away from a father.' Her lips moved into a slow, sad smile. 'Nobody cried at his funeral, Ben. Nobody! That's a terrible indictment. Even *you* didn't cry. Remember?'

'Grown men don't cry.'

'Some do. The weak ones, perhaps. Also the truly strong ones. Men who aren't *afraid* of tears.'

'I don't know what you mean.'

'No . . . of course you don't. Harry wouldn't have understood, either.' She moved a hand. 'Finish your tea, Ben. Don't ask the question you were trying to ask. That way we'll stay friends.'

'C' Beat was not covered. Kelly and Bell were covering 'A' and 'D' Beats. The police presence on 'B' Beat was increasing by the minute. But 'C' Beat remained Wilture's pigeon, pending some other officer taking over, and Wilture was in hospital and, thanks to Morrison's unique brand of mental stagnation, nobody really knew who the hell was where and who the hell was somewhere else.

And, as always, when a crowd gathers, when attention is diverted elsewhere and when police activity is concentrated upon one specific incident, troublemakers with a kinky turn of mind tend to take advantage.

The two lunatics called it 'having a good time'. Moderate people would have called it 'vandalism'. The local Parks Department gardeners, who had coaxed the cuttings and bulbs into glorious life, would have viewed it as a minor form of homicidal madness.

Julie threw her dressing gown over a chair and climbed back into bed. She was quite naked.

'Who was it? asked James.

'Freddie.'

'Good God!'

It was voiced as an exclamation, but it was *not* an exclamation. It was a cool-voiced drawl of the required reaction. James – James Wover – was a very cool-voiced customer. He was very 'with it'. He had a naturally fine physique, and knew it. In a slightly offbeat way he was quite handsome . . . and knew it. His dark hair and brown eyes gave him a distinctly Latin appearance; he knew that, too.

Indeed, there was not much about himself that James Wover did *not* know and, moreover, approve of.

He would quite cheerfully have accepted the expression 'stud', because that was what he was and that was all he wished to be. He had slept in some very good beds, very comfortable beds, none of them his own. He always slept in the buff and expected his women to do likewise, because the motion pictures he favoured all had the near-obligatory bedroom scene, and 'they' always slept in the buff, and whatever 'they' did was great, because 'they', too, were expert spring-interior gymnasts. He collected women much as a philatelist collects postage stamps. The Americanism he favoured for the act of fornication was 'balling a dame' because he was inordinately proud of his equipment and viewed any partner he happened to be coupling as a highly favoured female.

Thus James Wover, and for the moment he was rather enjoying himself leading Julie Kelly up the primrose path.

He reached out a bare arm and collected cigarettes and a lighter from the bedside table. He flicked the packet, threaded a cigarette between his lips, thumbed the lighter, blew smoke then replaced the cigarettes and lighter. He removed the cigarette from his mouth and allowed tobacco smoke to trickle from his mouth and nostrils.

'A real fink,' he murmured.

'A child.' She ran her finger through his chest hair.

'Okay, a childish fink.'

'Pathetic.'

'Who cares?'

'When it's through – the divorce, I mean . . . '

'Uhuh'.

'We *will* get married?'

'Honey, what do you think I am?'

It was his standard evasive answer and she sighed. She

knew *exactly* what he was, but for the moment it did not matter. Freddie was the safety net. Freddie would come running whenever she crooked her little finger.

Meanwhile . . .

'He interrupted something,' she whispered.

'Yeah. I'll finish this drag, then we'll start at the beginning again.'

Barstow was round at the front of the shops needling people. He had arranged for spare coppers to keep an eye on the rear, and he met Superintendent Smeaton as that officer approached from where he had been organising crowd control.

By this time officers, and to spare, were on hand. Squad cars had arrived, along with vehicles which disgorged stern-faced men carrying cased rifles, and other men holding holstered hand-guns. Both weight and fire power were available, but that did not prevent Smeaton from aiming his petty criticism, and at the same time nudging the door open ready for possible future excuses.

'I can't find Constable Kelly or Constable Bell.'

Barstow cocked a sardonic eye.

'They obviously aren't where they should be,' complained Smeaton.

'You haven't enough?' murmured Barstow.

'What?'

'You need Kelly and Bell for a full house?'

'They should be here.'

'They're in good company. I can name a superintendent who should have been here for some time.'

'I've been . . . '

'A job for you,' interrupted Barstow. 'There's a character called Chambers. For obvious reasons known to his intimates as 'Potty'. He is now taking harp lessons from the angels. His next-of-kin need informing. The same with the lunatic who jumped. The same with Sergeant Boothby's wife.'

'Boothby's a widower.'

'Whoever needs telling.'

'He has a daughter and two sons.'

'They might have more than passing interest. At a guess, he'll live. So, unfortunately, will the idiot who landed on him.'

'Right. I'll get Riddle to . . . '

'Smeaton, we are not playing Pass the Parcel.'

'What?'

'You tell Riddle, Riddle tells a sergeant, the sergeant tells a copper, the copper tells the nearest stray tom cat. *Not* Pass the Parcel. Not even The House that Jack Built. *You.*'

'I'll instruct Riddle . . .'

'Superintendent Smeaton, don't be tiresome. At the moment Riddle is busy praying that nobody is going to shoot holes in him. He's busy. You are not. Take a copper to hold your hand by all means – if, that is, you feel particularly lonely. But *you* do it.'

'Really, Barstow, I don't think . . . '

'A homicide, resultant upon a break-in,' purred Barstow. 'Big stuff, Smeaton. Trouble by the vanload if even a slight mistake is made.'

'Oh!'

'If you're sure you can handle it, give me a nod. I have a very comfortable bed waiting.'

'Oh, no – I – er . . . '

'If, on the other hand, you think it's well out of your own puny little league, start doing what you're told.'

'Yes, of course. I just . . . '

'And what about Wilture?'

'Wilture?'

'The wounded soldier.'

'Well, I . . . er.'

'His next-of-kin have been notified, have they?'

'Well, no. Not yet, but . . . '

'It's a fair assumption that somebody might be mildly interested to know he's stopped a bullet with his tail end.'

'I was – I was . . . '

'Don't let me keep you.'

'No. I'll – er . . . '

'Suggest they buy cushions by the job lot.'

Despite what Barstow had said behind Boots the Chemists, he was no acne-faced medic. Among other things he could slip FRCS *and* FRCP behind his signature, and it was an open question as to whether he was a better surgeon or a better physician. Certainly he was one of the top diagnosticians in the country, and he was at Radholme for a very humane reason. He had been born there. His mother still lived there, and he had journeyed north to visit her at Radholme Cottage Hospital where she was recovering from a hip operation resultant upon rheumatoid arthritis.

His name was Martin, and he looked and dressed like a prosperous and well-fed farmer. He was also a born raconteur. That was why he was still there. He had been sipping hospital tea and jawing with the duty medic when Wilture had been brought in, and he had ambled down to Emergency with his new-found friend. He was still there when Boothby and Nicco were placed on the examination couches.

Surprisingly slim fingers for such a stout man gently explored the region around, above and below the nape of Boothby's neck.

'Traction, squire.' Martin's eyes had a faraway look; as if every ounce of concentration was being focused into the tips of his fingers. 'Third and fourth vertebrae. I make them slightly out of plumb. See if you agree.'

Martin stepped back, and the duty medic went through the motions. It was pure protocol. No duty medical officer would have seriously considered arguing with Martin about that sort of diagnosis. Nevertheless, the medic took over and repeated the gentle examination.

'They're there.' The medic nodded. 'I'll arrange for a bed and traction.'

The medic hurried to where nurses stood waiting.

Martin smiled down at the terrified Boothby, chuckled, then

said, 'Not to worry, squire. People break their necks on the rugby field all the time. You'll have some very sexy nurses waiting on you hand and foot for a few weeks. That can't be bad.'

'Is it – is it . . . ' Boothby tried to talk without moving his jaw.

'Easy, squire.' Martin touched Boothby's upper arm, comfortingly. 'You'll live to dandle your grandchildren on your knee.' He turned to the second couch and, as the duty medic returned, said, 'What about this chap?'

'Concussion. From what I gather he jumped from an upstairs window and landed on the sergeant. I think he might be out for an hour or two.'

'Nothing obviously broken?'

'Nothing obvious.'

'The sergeant here made a soft landing spot?'

'Exactly. I think a wash down, then bed and keep an eye on him to see how things develop.'

'When in doubt.' Martin nodded sagely. 'Do nothing until something *needs* doing. For what it's worth, I like your approach, squire. You're not a plumber, you're not a butcher – you're a doctor. You need the patient's help to know what's wrong.' He glanced at Boothby. 'I'll lend a hand, if you like. I'll see to the traction side of things, while you keep an eye on Sleeping Beauty.'

'That's very good of you, sir.'

The language might have made a bargee blush. The mindless damage was beyond all reason. Nevertheless, the two teenagers, homeward bound after a boozing party which had followed a disco, laughed, yelled and cursed as they ripped plants from the soil and hurled them at each other in makebelieve battle.

The half-acre or so of lawn and flower beds was one of the show spots of the Parks Department. It, and its fellows, had put Radholme in the running for an award in last year's Britain in Bloom contest.

It was not likely to happen this year. The two young hooligans were destroying all hope of that.

The man was called Blackburn. He turned a corner and there was enough starlight and diffuse street lighting for him to see the vandalism being committed, and he went crazy with anger.

'We'll need a policewoman out,' whimpered Morrison.

'Uhuh.'

Bulmer grunted agreement to a very obvious remark. Bulmer was making entries in his notebook; entries about the call to Radholme, entries about the situation when they arrived, entries about his own participation at the rear of the attacked premises, entries about his arrest of the girl and, most important and most carefully worded of all, entries about Chatterton's arrest and killing of Chambers.

So many things had to be considered.

The report itself, of course, but also the inquest, the court case and the near-certainty of an enquiry. It was likely to be one hell of an enquiry, because Chatterton had brought his staff down with real force. There had been no warning and no struggle. There had been that one bone-breaking smack on the back of the skull . . . thereafter, telephone the funeral parlour.

'Where do I get the authority?'

'Eh?' Bulmer looked up.

'To call out a policewoman.'

'There's a female prisoner.' Bulmer stared. 'She has to be searched. *We* can't search her.'

'I know. What I mean is . . .'

'Look, mate.' Bulmer jerked his head. 'Out there, it was hell on roller-skates for a few minutes. Men injured. Young Wilture shot. One of the bastards killed. And that little cow is part of it . . .'

'Oh! I didn't . . .'

'. . . the super's out, arsing everybody about. Barstow's there, buggering things up generally. We've enough coppers to man a bloody picket line. And you're getting your long johns in a twist because we need one little policewoman.'

'Nobody tells *me* anything,' moaned Morrison.

'Oh, for Christ's sake!' Bulmer lost his temper. 'Get a policewoman out, you miserable git. *Do* something for a change. Don't just stand around like a spare prick at a wedding.'

Having delivered the broadside, Bulmer returned to his note-making and his very private worry.

Ernie Chatterton was up the proverbial creek and, much as he loathed the idea, he (Bulmer) was going to be one of the people called upon to scuttle the canoe. It was small compensation to know that it was not self-preservation. It was not a Chatterton-or-Bulmer set-up. Nor did it help to know that few people would mourn the passing of the Chambers character.

It was just that . . .

Dammit, nobody was allowed to *kill* people. That was what it boiled down to. It was as basic as that. Because, if that was allowed, the loud mouths were justified in yelling 'Gestapo'.

But that knowledge did not make things any easier for Bulmer.

Blackburn moved into energetic action.

Blackburn was in his mid-twenties and in superb physical condition. In fact he was on his way home after a late night workout at the local gym. As an employee of the Parks Department, he had planted many of those young plants. He had carefully spaced the bulbs. He had cut and edged the tiny lawns. It was a spot he walked past regularly and, every time he passed, he viewed it with personal pride. It was his contribution towards giving Radholme its own individual character.

And now a duo of young vandals was tearing it apart.

Blackburn dived in and did his stuff. Blackburn was a gardener – he had been a gardener all his working life – therefore he had the patience peculiar to men who work the soil. Equally, he had the deep-rooted outrage towards morons who deliberately destroyed natural beauty.

He also had the muscle to augment that outrage.

From behind, he whipped an arm around the first teenager's neck, grabbed a handful of the material at the teenager's backside, then heaved, grunted and threw. The young tearaway landed, face first, in a nearby rose bed, and the thorns on the pruned roses tore the skin of his cheeks and forehead and, for the moment, that was *him* taken care of.

The second teenager saw the danger and turned to run . . . but it was too late.

Blackburn's swinging fist landed, like a hammer, on the side of his neck and he, too, went down.

Then they were dragged, panting and cursing, across the grass and, literally, hurled at the wooden bench placed there for oldsters to sit and take the sun. They hit the seasoned oak with enough violence to bruise them for days, and they were suddenly very frightened.

Blackburn stood over them, and the impression was that he seriously contemplated annihilation.

'You horrible, *horrible* people,' he choked. 'I could – I could . . . '

He was unable to finish the sentence, but both teenagers caught the gist and one of them allowed his face to crumple and the tears to come.

'I want your names,' rasped Blackburn. 'I want your names and I want your addresses. And I want proof they *are* your names and addresses. If there was a policeman handy ...' Disgust touched the furious harshness of his tone. 'There never *is* a policeman around when you want one. But you'll be seeing one. One will visit you. *I'll* see to that. By gum, I'll make you rue this little lot.'

1.30a.m. Radholme stretched its arms, stifled a yawn and prepared to sink into delayed slumber. Its moment of excitement was passing, the crowds were dispersing, the law officers still at the scene were performing mundane, albeit very necessary, tasks and, now the alarm bell had been switched off, the lack of noise seemed to accentuate the growing stillness

107

of a country town as the long seconds ticked their way towards a new dawn.

Radholme was no city. Radholme was no metropolis. Radholme was no gaudy tart, eager to kick her heels until milk was delivered to doorsteps. Radholme was a rural lady who enjoyed her high points of passion, but was wise enough to value the peace of sleep.

It had become Wednesday, May the second . . . and nobody seemed to have noticed the birth of another day.

Martin pronounced life extinct. He examined the corpse of Chambers, then asked Chatterton a few questions. Chatterton answered the questions, and some of the answers were lies.

'The mortuary,' said Martin tonelessly. Then, as the attendant made to wheel the trolley from the Examination Room, 'Get him cleaned up a bit, please. I'll have another look at him later.'

Ben Riddle closed the door behind him and, from upstairs, his daughter-in-law's voice called, 'Is that you, Ben?'

'I'm going to have a drink, pet,' he called from the foot of the stairs. Then, on an impulse, 'Come down and join me.'

He was almost surprised when she accepted the invitation; when she walked into the living room with the dressing gown over her nightdress; when she smiled her thanks as he handed her a tumbler of well watered down whisky, and sat in the armchair across the hearth from him. Jenny Riddle was no small-hours drinker.

He leaned forward and snapped on a bar of the electric fire before he spoke.

Then he moistened his lips, and said, 'I'm leaving here, Jenny.'

She waited. She looked neither surprised nor disappointed.

In a lower voice, he growled, 'If I stay, you'll come to hate me. Not James – he hasn't it in him – but *you* . . . and I wouldn't want that.'

'Did Bozo do this to you?' she smiled.

'Not Bozo.' Then, petulantly, 'Don't laugh at me, pet. I'm serious.'

108

'Of course you're serious, Ben.' The words were a gentle apology. 'And I'm taking you seriously.'

Ben Riddle felt an irritating disappointment. He had not counted upon such an easy acceptance of his decision. Nobody was pushing him out of a door but, at the same time, nobody was making any real effort to hold him back.

'I have friends where I came from,' he said gruffly.

'Here, too . . . surely?'

'Since Harry Barnes died?' The counter-question held bitterness.

She raised her glass to her lips and eyed him above the top of its rim.

'You're feeling sorry for yourself,' she accused.

'Maybe.'

'Why?' She sipped at her drink.

'Nobody's busting a bloody gut to keep me here,' he blurted.

'*Really* sorry for yourself,' she teased, quietly.

'Well . . . are they?'

'Ben.' Her solemnity was genuine. 'When a man like you makes up his mind, that is *it*.'

He had no means of denying the observation without denying his whole life. He scowled and took a quick swig of his drink.

'Not Bozo,' she mused, quietly. 'Mary?'

'I made a fool of myself.' He sighed heavily. 'You know what they say: there's no fool like an old fool.'

She waited, expecting the remark to be expanded, but he sipped his whisky and water again, then stared at its surface.

'You – er – you asked her to marry you?' she ventured in a gentle, sympathetic voice.

'I didn't even have to ask her.' He moved his shoulders. 'She saw it coming and refused before I got that far.'

'Too much like Harry?'

'That was the gist of it.' Then in a stronger, angrier tone, 'What's so wrong with that? I liked Harry.'

'You weren't married to him.'

'No.' He bit off the word, then raised his eyes and his

109

expression was as near to pleading as he was capable of. 'What's wrong with me, pet?'

'You're lonely,' she fenced.

'I'm also pig-headed . . . that it?'

'That, too,' she agreed gently.

'Whereas – what is it? – the meek shall inherit the earth.'

'Something like that.'

'It's not my belief.'

'Of course not.'

'The meek shall be crapped on, from a dizzy height. That's more like the truth.'

Very deliberately, very softly, she said, 'I wouldn't call *you* meek.'

'Dammit, I'm not a bad man.'

'Of course you're not.'

'I'm not an evil man.'

'Ben, you asked me down here,' she retaliated. 'If you're fishing for compliments, you're wasting your time. You're a hard man, perhaps that's why you were a good policeman, but that can't be denied. You're a hard man.

'You're of a generation, and that generation doesn't belong any more. Harry Barnes was of the same generation . . . and he wouldn't change either. Your women, your wives, *expected* it. These days, they wouldn't even tolerate it.'

'James loves you, Ben. I love you. But we love you *despite* . . . not *because*. You – men like you, men like Harry Barnes – you're not the minor gods you once were, but you won't change. You won't accept it. You won't alter your beliefs or your behaviour.' She paused, then, in a very gentle voice, ended, 'I'm sorry, Ben. I'm sorry for *you*. I'm sorry for James, because he can't get close to you, and you won't let him. I'm so very sorry. Because James won't change . . . nor would I want him to. And, however much it's explained, you *can't* understand.'

Policewoman Fanny Nash was built like a tank. Or, if you wish, like a barrage balloon. Or if you favour non-military

110

comparisons, like a gasometer. She was *huge* . . . in all directions.

It had something to do with her glands. It certainly had nothing to do with her appetite; she nibbled, rather than scoffed. And, like so many gargantuan women, she had a delightful disposition. She never complained, she had compassion by the ton and, on top of all this, she had a bubbling sense of humour.

She lived within a five minutes' walk of the sub-divisional office and, as she walked, she proved herself to be surprisingly light on her feet. She was not in uniform, and she wore a lightweight, raglan-type coat as a sop to the slight night chill.

She bustled into the station and into the Charge Office.

Morrison greeted her with, 'Bulmer told me to send for you,' and thus washed his hands of all further responsibility.

Adams, who was also there, said, 'There's a female prisoner.'

'That's my beauty sleep gone,' said Miss Nash cheerfully.

'A young lass,' added Adams. 'There's been a break-in and some shooting. She was with the villains.'

'Anybody hurt?'

'Young Wilture stopped one.'

'Oh, my God!'

'Nothing too serious.' Adams grinned. 'He'll have to take his meals standing up for a few weeks. That's all.'

'That's *all*?'

'One of the breakers copped it.' Adams switched to sudden seriousness. 'Ernie Chatterton belted him with his peg.'

'*Killed him*?'

Adams nodded.

'Oh, my God! Poor old Ernie.'

Morrison whimpered, '*I* didn't know about all this.'

'You mean you . . . '

'Nobody tells *me* anything.'

Adams snapped, 'Shut up, you miserable old sod.' Then, in a gentler tone to Nash, 'The girl was there. I think she saw it.'

'How old is she?'

111

'Late teens. Very early twenties at the most. One of the lunatic fringe, I'm afraid.'

'They're around,' sighed Nash.

'And we collect 'em.'

'Do her parents know?'

'Not yet. We haven't had time to get her address.'

'What's her name?'

'Fleming . . . so Bulmer says. Patricia Fleming.'

'Thanks.' Nash unbuttoned her coat and let it swing loose. 'Leave it to Aunty Fanny. Let Charlie know I'm in with her.'

Policewoman Nash waddled from the Charge Office, collected the keys, continued along the corridor and into the cell area, then unlocked the cell door.

The girl was huddled on the bed sobbing.

'Come on, pet. It's not as bad as that. Nothing's as bad as that.'

Nash sat on the side of the bed and, like a child, the girl buried her face in the huge bosom and wept uncontrollably. Nash cooed and comforted her. Nor was it makebelieve. That bulky frame could not hold the limitless humanity and sympathy within Nash's personality. She suffered for and with this silly young woman and, for the first time in her life, Fleming knew unqualified love and absolute understanding.

It was an all-night filling station; self-service, with the oldster in the kiosk tucked safely away behind reinforced glass. He had firm instructions. During the dark hours he must stay put. He must check the price on the machine, take the cash through the narrow slot but, above all else, he must keep the door closed and locked. No heroics were expected. Petrol was not *that* valuable.

The coloured youth was still at the wheel of the Jag. His white companion held the nozzle in the neck of the tank. The lighted digits flicked, and the oldster divided his attention between the numbers and the car.

It was a flash car; a not too old, high-priced Jag. Dammit, they were not old enough to have that brand of car. Or if they *were* old enough, and rich enough, they did not dress the part.

112

They wore tough-guy outfits – tearaway outfits – and the outfits went with the don't-give-a-damn curl of the lips.

The white youth replaced the pump nozzle.

They had taken ten gallons, just over ten gallons. The tank was full and the cut-out had operated.

The oldster rested a hand on the telephone receiver and watched.

The white youth returned the cap to the car's petrol tank, then strolled as if he was making his way to the kiosk. At the last moment he opened the front passenger door of the Jag and dived inside. The Jag started up and raced away.

Before the car was clear of the forecourt the oldster had dialled the first 'nine'.

'A' and 'D' Beats abutted each other. Along one stretch the dividing line was Crown Street; one of the main shopping centres, with varying sizes of emporiums lining both sides of an arrow-straight, well-lighted thoroughfare. Whenever Bell and Kelly worked these two beats it was their practice to share Crown Street and patrol in unofficial tandem, each leaving his own area of responsibility by a few yards, cross the road and chat with each other while they checked shops.

It was a very minor infringement of the rules. It did no harm and, for a time, it broke the monotony of solitary knob-trying. They were friends – they shared small secrets – but it was even more than that. Bell was Kelly's matrix. In the older man, Kelly recognised a solid, down-to-earth copper, nearing the end of his service. Kelly was willing to learn, and Bell was ready to teach.

A force is run that way. Its success depends, in no small degree, on the willingness of older men to pass on the experience of their years; to explain and demonstrate how 'book law' can be translated into practical bobbying; to make what, at first glance, seems impossible into something moderately easy.

As they strolled, they talked.

'Let's have five.'

Bell turned into the shelter of a shallow arcade as he made

the suggestion. Kelly followed, then, when they were both resting their rumps upon the narrow sill of a shop window, cigarettes were produced and a few moments of complete relaxation set in.

'I telephoned Julie,' confessed Kelly.

'Oh, aye?' It was a deliberately non-committal reaction.

'I asked her to come back to me.'

'And?'

'She will.'

'Did she say so?'

'As good as.'

'What's that mean?'

'I'm seeing her tomorrow.'

'Is that a fact?'

'Six o'clock tomorrow evening.'

'And she'll come back?'

'I'll make her see sense.'

Bell enjoyed a long draw on the cigarette, then said, 'What's your old lady think?'

'I've broken with her.'

'Feeling your feet a bit?'

'And with Cynthia.'

'Oh, aye?'

'She's a frigid-faced bitch.'

'Who?'

'Cynthia.'

'Happen.'

'Mother's not much better.'

There was another long pull on the cigarette, then Bell observed, 'It's been a hell of a waste. Money. Time. Worry. Everything.'

'What?'

'This divorce lark.'

'It was a mistake.'

'Aye, you don't want many of *them* to the pound.'

Morrison, Bulmer, Adams and (a recent addition) Hindley were all in the Charge Office. And now Barstow, accompanied

114

by Riddle, arrived.

'Are we interrupting a sit-in?' Barstow's tone was reminiscent of the smooth, gentle stalk of a big cat moving to within springing distance of its kill. 'Or is it an attempted takeover? A meeting of high intelligences, perhaps?' Then to Riddle, 'These fine, upstanding examples of the local constabulary, chief inspector. Do they suffer agonies from bunions? Are the pavements too hard for their tender little feet?'

'Adams?' said Riddle, wearily.

'Detective Chief Superintendent Barstow instructed me to meet him, here,' said Adams in a very straight-faced voice.

'You have an office . . . or has nobody yet bothered to mention that small fact to you?' Barstow was not going to let a little thing like obeying orders put him off . . . not even when *he* had issued those orders. 'It is a special room, Adams. It is sanctified and kept apart for the use of tired little CID creatures, seeking somewhere to allow their over-worked brains to cool.'

'Wait in the CID Office, Adams,' droned Riddle.

'Yes, sir.'

'Bulmer?'

'I arrested the girl . . . '

'Oh, my word! That must have made you old before your time.'

' . . . then I made up my notebook . . . '

'A Tolstoyian epic, no doubt.'

' . . . then I arranged with Morrison for a policewoman to come on duty . . .'

'I wonder you've had time to breathe.'

' . . . and *now* I'm going to dictate my report.'

'Have you energy enough left? Don't you feel a little light-headed after all that exertion?'

'Go dictate your report, Bulmer,' sighed Riddle.

'And what about *you*?' demanded Barstow.

'I dropped in to pick Constable Bulmer up,' said Hindley calmly.

'That's very understandable,' mocked Barstow. 'You were feeling very lonely, is that it?'

'No, sir. I was feeling like a smoke.'

'Oh!'

'I was just going to have one when you arrived.'

'What's your name, constable?'

The question was asked in a gentle, stone-wall voice. There was no bluster and no noise. There was only menace, contempt and, perhaps, a hint of reluctant approval.

'Hindley, sir. I partner Bulmer in the squad car.'

'Work at it, Hindley,' said Barstow. 'Given time and a decent cross-wind you'll make chief constable. You have the nerve. You have the gall. I hope, for your sake, you know exactly how long the rope is . . . before you hang yourself.'

'Yes, sir. Thank you sir.'

'Wait for Bulmer in the canteen, Hindley,' murmured Riddle.

Hindley left, and Morrison remained. Secretly, Riddle was rather looking forward to Morrison receiving his quota of Barstowisms. Indeed, Riddle started the ball rolling.

He said, 'Morrison, I'm puzzled and certainly Superintendent Smeaton will want to know; why didn't Constables Bell and Kelly show up at the scene?'

Morrison bared his skinny breast for the bullets by asking, 'Which scene, sir?'

'*Which scene?*' Barstow's eyes widened, then narrowed. He turned to Riddle, and asked, 'Did this clown ask that question or did I misinterpret the word?' Then without waiting for a reply, he returned his attention to Morrison. 'You geriatric numbskull . . . '

'Nobody tells me . . . '

' . . . You miserable, misbegotten apology for a police constable. This one-horse town has, for the last few hours, been like Chicago on Capone's birthday . . . '

'Sir, nobody ever . . . '

' . . . Any more characters stopping stray bullets and they'll have to build an extension to the local hospital. They're digging slugs out of coppers faster than you can pull radishes . . . '

'Wilture's been shot,' explained Riddle quietly.

'Sir, nobody . . . '

' . . . A bell, making more din than doom cracking, has been deafening everybody for miles around. Every surgeon north of the Wash is out of bed, mentally practising his own brand of knit-one-pearl-one . . . '

'Sergeant Boothby and one of the breakers have been injured.'

' . . . The local undertakers are rubbing their hands with glee at the prospect of business yet to come . . . '

'One of the breakers has been killed.'

' . . . *I* have been called out. Contrary to popular belief, I actually *sleep*, when possible. Superintendent Smeaton has been called out. Anything short of Armageddon, and you wouldn't get *him* past his front door. The chief constable has been dragged from his golden slumbers. Every weapon short of a Sherman tank has been drafted into the place. The town is over-run with police dogs. It is knee deep in fingerprint powder. It is bulging at its seams with police photographers. And – and – and . . . ' Barstow paused for breath then, in a whispered snarl, ended, 'And you want to know "*What scene?*".'

'It's not my fault, sir. Nobody tells me . . . '

'Fizz him, chief inspector.'

'Yes, sir.'

'Before you go off duty.'

'Of course.'

'Everything in the book, Riddle. From Idling and Gossiping to Neglect of Duty. Conduct Prejudicial to the Force. Check his uniform . . . nail him for being Improperly Dressed. The lot!'

'Yes, sir.'

'And *you*.' Barstow switched his attention back to Morrison. 'You disgusting character. Count yourself fortunate. A man less moderate than myself would have taught you a lesson.'

Barstow and Riddle left.

Morrison steadied himself against the edge of a desk. It was all well beyond the scope of his experience. Hindley had been

117

decidedly stroppy, yet Barstow had almost *approved*. He (Morrison) had not done or said a thing, and for that he was being crucified.

Without a shadow of a doubt, Barstow was certifiable.

Despite its clinically clean appearance, despite the floor to ceiling tiles, despite the gleaming sink and the glass-fronted cabinet of shining instruments, the hospital mortuary stank of death. The liberal use of disinfectant made no difference, the sweet stench of putrefaction was still there; the odour of a newly opened grave, but without the more healthy smell of freshly turned earth.

Chambers had been stripped and placed on the stainless steel post-mortem table. The attendant had just finished washing him down. The triple strip-lighting gave a harsh, shadowless glare and, via some horrific trick of illumination, made the corpse look even more dead than it was.

Martin wore gloves, heavy scarlet rubber gloves, borrowed from the morgue linen closet. He touched the terrible skull wound with the tips of his fingers, holding the body in a sitting position, the better to see. He parted the matted hair. He bent to peer at the contours of the shattered bone.

The girl, Patricia Fleming, would remember this night for the rest of her life.

As an only child and the daughter of a moderately affluent shopkeeper, she had been petted and spoiled when young; had been sent to a fairly expensive, local public school as a day pupil; had been expelled as a consistent trouble-maker; had thereafter run wild and refused even token parental discipline; had experimented with sex at the age of fourteen; had contracted syphilis at the age of fifteen, become pregnant at sixteen and had had an abortion before her seventeenth birthday.

She had left home in her late teens; lived anywhere with any male willing to support her on a day-to-day basis, then taken to the street and earned enough 'short time' money to rent a filthy, one-room apartment to which she returned whenever the night did not bring some other bed.

Had you asked her, she would have claimed that she had 'lived'; that she had 'seen the world'; that nothing – but *nothing* – could get through to her.

And yet she would remember this night.

It was no watershed. It was not going to change her lifestyle. Men, booze and drugs would dominate her life more and more. At forty she would be a physical wreck. She would be dead before she reached the half-century, and in those years prison, beatings, more pregnancies followed by more abortions and three more instances of venereal disease would punctuate her miserable existence.

All these things . . . but she would never forget this night.

'He's – he's dead,' she sniffled, and the tears from her eyes, and the dribble from her lips, mixed with the stream from her nostrils and stained Policewoman Nash's dress.

Fanny Nash did not give a damn about the dress. The dress could be dry-cleaned. Nor had she any misconceptions about Fleming; Fleming would either pull herself together or go from bad to worse, but that was not the immediate problem. What mattered now was the simple fact of a fellow-human being torn apart by fear, worry, misery and guilt, all compounded by witnessing a single, explosive act of violence.

'We don't know.' Nash tightened her ham-like arm across the trembling shoulders. 'We don't *know* he's dead.'

'He's dead.'

'Injured, perhaps. Maybe only injured.'

'You – you . . . ' Fleming swallowed and sniffed. 'You didn't see it.'

'Only a doctor knows,' soothed Nash. 'He's maybe okay. Badly injured, but okay. If he is, they'll fix him.'

'That sodding copper.'

'No, pet. You mustn't say those things.' Nash believed every word she spoke, and it put gentle urgency in her tone. 'You mustn't even think them. We don't *kill* people.'

✳ ✳ ✳

'It doesn't make sense,' said Kelly, 'Sitting there. Starkers. With a bloody great hard-on. And all he can say is, "She's French".'

'We see life,' agreed Bell with a grin.

'I think I should have shifted them.'

'Why?'

'Arsing around like that. It's not normal.'

'A spot of innocent enjoyment, mate,' soothed Bell. 'Nothing to do with us. If they like being kinky, let 'em get on with it. They were both over age.'

The comfortable gloom of the arcade encouraged lingering and friendly small-talk. It made for an exchange of confidences and a reluctance to move out and continue their solitary check of property on 'A' and 'D' Beats.

'A basinful of oral sex, old son.' Bell dropped the stub of his cigarette and squashed it into shreds with the sole of his shoe. 'That's all it was.'

'I don't get it.'

'Read much?' asked Bell.

'A bit. Magazines. Newspapers.'

'Books?'

'No . . . not too many,' confessed Kelly.

'I do,' said Bell. 'Light stuff, mainly. A lot of Westerns.'

'I can't see what . . . '

'Some of the good yarns. By people like Schaefer. People who know what they're talking about. Lots of it non-fiction stuff. Y'know . . . *good* stuff.'

'All right. But . . . '

'Those bar-room tarts.' Bell refused to be hurried. 'Frilly panties. High-kicking. Real old bags in real life. Poxed up to the eyeballs.'

'Look. I can't see what . . . '

'Listen, mate. Listen and learn. I'm trying to tell you something. The cowboys . . . real rough buggers. They got their money, then they made a bee-line for the nearest saloon. A combined boozer, doss-house, gambling joint and brothel, see? And the tarts – the floosies – one of 'em was always called

"Frenchie". Sometimes just "French". Sometimes more than one. It wasn't their *name*. Just a clue at what they specialised in . . . '

'Oh, bloody hell!'

' . . . The gob job, see? Very Continental. It wasn't, really, but the ignorant sods from the range didn't know any better . . . '

'Oh, my God!'

' . . . Anyway, the thing's stuck. Like Wellington boots. That sort of thing. So, them two in the car . . . '

'I *knew* I'd missed something,' breathed Kelly.

'What?' Bell paused in his potted history of sexual deviation in order to stare his puzzlement.

'When I – y'know – when I left; I had this feeling. I'd *seen* something.'

'Seen something?'

'*Missed* something.'

'Eh?'

'Y'know – missed something – something that should have jelled.'

'What for example?'

'The – er – the veil.'

'What about the veil?'

'I – y'know – I didn't shine my torch right at 'em.'

'Well – come *on*,' said Bell, impatiently.

'It was . . .' Kelly swallowed. 'It was Martha.'

'Who?'

'Martha. *Your* Martha.'

Morrison shambled to the stationery cupboard, slipped a document from its allotted place and gazed at it with an expression of great misery.

It was a Form Two-Five-Two.

It was always the same. Every force he knew, even the armed services, always used a Form Two-Five-Two. The Form Two-Five-Two was the universal Misconduct Form; the 'fizzer'. No doubt somebody with a very twisted sense of humour had once reached a decision. Most other forms differed from force to force – Statements Forms, Missing From Home Reports, Accident Reports, Sudden Death Reports – hundreds of different forms, and enough paper to sink a battleship. And every force gave the various forms a different number, a number peculiar to that force, until they reached Form Two-Five-Two. That was always the Misconduct Report.

(And, of course, the universal Annual Leave Form, the Form Two-Nine-Five . . . but *they* did not drop from trees like autumn leaves.)

Nevertheless, it was very odd. What the hell was so mystical about those two numbers? Why was it *always* Two-Five-Two and Two-Nine-Five? There had to *be* a reason. Somebody, somewhere, must have said . . .

'Are you busy?'

'Eh?'

Morrison dropped the Form Two-Five-Two back into its slot and turned to face the public counter.

'Busy?' repeated Blackburn.

'Not particularly.' Morrison walked slowly towards the slightly dishevelled stranger. 'Why?'

'A couple of young vandals. Tearing plants up and generally running wild.'

'Oh!'

'They must have done a hundred – more – quid's worth of damage.'

'Oh, aye?'

'I got their names and addresses.'

'Oh, aye?' repeated Morrison without undue enthusiasm.

'I have them here.'

Blackburn fished a used envelope from an inside pocket and placed it on the surface of the counter.

'They'll be false,' pronounced Morrison, without even looking at the scribbled names and addresses.

'No. They're not false.'

'You've checked, have you?'

'In my own way.'

'We'll have to contact the owner,' parried Morrison.

'Which owner?'

'The plants you're talking about.'

'The Parks Department,' said Blackburn.

'Oh!'

'It wasn't in somebody's garden.'

'We'll have to contact the Parks Department.'

'What about?'

'Whether they want to take action.'

'Hey, mister.' Blackburn's patience was wearing thin. 'I'm *from* the Parks Department. I *bedded* those plants.'

'Oh!'

'I didn't call here for a friendly natter. I want some action . . . from somebody.'

'Oh!'

'No coppers when you want one.'

'We've been rushed off our feet.'

' . . . And now you seem to be brushing it to one side . . . '

'I wouldn't say that.'

' . . . Well, not this time, you don't.'

'You'll have to make a statement,' sighed Morrison.

'That's all right. I'll make a statement.'

'Right. Just wait here.'

Morrison returned to the stationery cupboard for another form. This time he chose a Statement Form, a Form Twelve.

Then the telephone bell rang.

Having been made privy to a very private opinion, the attendant stood in the corridor outside the mortuary and listened to one half of a telephone conversation.

'Am I talking to the man who might be able to bottom it? . . .

'Good, because I'm not happy, squire. The post mortem might make me into a liar, but I doubt it. I can't find another mark on him . . .

'Agreed. But there'll be an inquest, and coroners tend to

want straightforward answers to very complicated questions
. . .

'Of course . . .

'Of course . . .

'Not at all, squire. I wouldn't dream of hanging a cat on what I've seen so far. Just pointers, but pointers you should know about . . .

'Not at all . . .

'As far as I'm concerned, he's a cadaver. What he was when he was alive doesn't concern me. He's dead. If I have any interest in him, it revolves around *why* he's dead . . .

'I understand he's on his way back there . . .

'Walking, I think . . .

'I'm obliged, squire. Just that I thought somebody should be informed.'

2 a.m. Consider this. Every square inch of the United Kingdom is part of some policeman's beat for every minute of every hour of every day of every year.

From Snowdonia to the Strand, from Blackpool's Golden Mile to the wild secrecy of Loch an Dherue, from Aintree on Grand National Day to the last storm-ripped rock necklacing out beyond Land's End; every square inch of land, to the shore's low-water mark and beyond, is the final responsibility of some ordinary flatfoot.

Chatterton took his time. Whatever he was doing, Chatterton never hurried; whatever he did, he always did it with great deliberation. Getting married had been a deliberate choice. Not having children had been a deliberate decision. Joining the force had been a deliberate resolution.

Sending the tearaway, Chambers, to where he belonged had, equally, been a deliberate intention.

Chatterton would have argued that there was far too much evil in this damn world; too many nut cases; too many do-gooders, and a lot too many people ready to listen to them.

Chatterton's father had copped it in Hitler's War. He had been blown to hell, and for what? Do not talk to men like

Chatterton about 'democracy'. Do not talk to them about 'freedom'. That was what Chatterton's father had believed in. At a guess, and when he realised he was dying, that was what he no doubt fooled himself into believing he was dying for.

Chatterton had no such illusions.

Chatterton turned into a darkened side street, fished pipe and pouch from his tunic pocket and packed the pipe with St Bruno. He struck a match, rested his backside on a low stone wall then smoked and rummaged around with might-have-beens.

He thought about Hitler. Hitler had not been bad. At the very least, Hitler had not been *all* bad.

As Chatterton understood things, Hitler would have made a separate peace with the UK and the Yanks, and that would have been a good thing. The wise thing would have been to shake hands all round, switch sides and smash the bloody Reds to pieces.

What a difference *that* would have made! It would have been a different Europe and a different world. Hitler would have been dead and buried by this time, there would be no Bolshevik bastards stirring up trouble in every corner of the globe and there would have been some discipline around.

Instead . . .

Half the hounds would not work. Thieving, mugging and God only knew what else was a way of life. Lunatics with big mouths and no brains had their fingers ready on the button, and any minute now the world would vanish in a puff of nuclear smoke . . . but, taking it all round, that might *not* be a bad thing. It was what the majority of mankind deserved.

Meanwhile, three cheers for terrorism. Curtsy to all the tinpot turds with the morals of hoodlums who ruled oil-heavy tinpot states peopled by flea-ridden yobs. Forget civilisation. Ignore simple decency. Spit upon basic pride.

Instead, wave encouragement to the gravy train and, if possible, climb aboard. It was impossible to starve, these days, so why work? Why give, when all you had to do was grab?

How did it go? Fill in the form, boys, go to the correct

counter, tell the required tale . . . after that, it's yours for the taking. You can holiday on some foreign coast. You're bottle-fed from cradle to grave. Luxury is yours for the asking, and you don't have to lift a bloody finger.

Hitler would not have worn *that*.

So . . . what was so wrong with Hitler?

Julie Kelly sat up in bed, with her knees tucked under her chin and her arms clasped around her shins. She looked strangely coy – strangely 'pure' – in the half-light thrown by street lamps, and with the sheet neck-high. Alongside her Wover's head was on the pillow and he was on the point of closing his eyes in exhausted sleep.

'You leave here tomorrow,' said Julie, gently.

'What?' The question was mumbled, because he had not heard the remark clearly enough to understand it.

'Tomorrow morning, first thing, you leave here.'

'What?' This time he did understand, and his eyes opened.

'You leave,' she said for the third time.

'Hey, what is this?' He hoisted himself on to one elbow. A look of surprised outrage accompanied the question.

'I'm getting it in first,' she said calmly.

'Getting what in?'

'The brush-off.'

'What the hell goes on in that little . . . '

'James, this thing isn't permanent. You know it. I know it. Let's not kid around.'

'Wedding bells.' He reached for cigarettes and the lighter. 'That was the subject of a very recent conversation as I remember.'

'You'll not be hearing wedding bells for a long time.'

'Did *I* say that?' He lit a cigarette.

'No.' She sighed. 'You said very little as I recall. You never do. Just noises. No promises you can't break.' She turned her head and smiled down at him. The smile was slow and sad. 'You're a bastard, James. An amusing bastard . . . but a bastard.'

'Okay, I'm an amusing bastard,' he admitted cheerfully. 'Why not have fun?'

'It's not "fun" any more.'

'Suddenly? Just like that?'

'Just like that.' She nodded.

'Hey, honey,' he argued. 'You have your freedom. You're a big girl now. You can sleep around.'

'Freedom?'

'That's what yesterday's po-faced pantomime was all about.'

She nodded. It was a very melancholy nod.

'Freedom,' he repeated.

'And for that,' she said softly, 'I traded in a meal ticket. I think the price is too high.'

'Since that fink telephoned.' There was petulance in his tone.

'He's a fink,' she agreed. 'Only a fink would have telephoned.'

'You don't want a creep like that.'

'A creep like *you*?' she countered.

'What about tonight? What about all the other nights? You don't think he's going to kiss and make up when he gets to know?'

'He'll get to know.'

'You bet your sweet little arse he'll get to know, honey. I'll make damn sure . . . '

'*I'll* tell him.'

'Crap.' He was so sure, he grinned. 'Even a fink like he is wouldn't . . . '

'We won't just turn a page,' she mused. 'We'll start a new book.'

'You'll blow it.' He inhaled cigarette smoke.

'Or *you'll* blow it?'

'You bet.'

'Either way it gets blown.'

'Sweetheart, you're not married to him any more.'

'That's odd.' She moved her head in a gentle shake. 'I still

127

feel married to him.'

'No way.'

'You wouldn't know.'

'No,' he agreed. 'I wouldn't know. And I'm not going to *get* to know . . . if it's confession time.'

'Not to you,' she muttered.

'Eh?'

'I wouldn't confess to you. To Freddie . . . '

'Darling Freddie.'

' . . . He just might understand . . . '

'That brand of confession?'

' . . . He's taken a lot from me . . . '

'He hasn't the balls to keep you in line.'

' . . . He might even take this . . . '

'You've lost your marbles, honey.'

' . . . If I promise to make it up to him . . . '

'Promises. Promises.'

' . . . Promise to be a good wife . . . '

'Honey, stop fooling yourself. You can't wear both. A chastity belt *and* itchy panties.'

'You're foul!' She turned on him, and the anger was real. It was anger aimed at him, but it had its roots deep in her own guilt. There was no make believe in the anger. 'What the hell I saw in you – what the hell I *ever* saw in you – I'll never know.'

'Trousers?' he suggested with a sneer. 'A standing tool that can give you more than that fink can ever give you?'

'On your way,' she raged. 'Out! Out of this bed. Out of this house. Out of my life. Move, you bastard. Don't wait till morning. Move, *now*! You aren't amusing any more. Find some other slut.'

'Get with it, kid. You're all sluts. Horizontal, you're *all* sluts.'

'Out, you bloody animal. *Out*!'

Policewoman Nash lied and knew she was lying.

'He's not dead. They'd have sent word by this time.'

Fanny, old girl, he's dead. Too true, he's dead. Johnny Adams has

128

*seen too many bodies. He wouldn't commit himself unless he was sure.
Whoever he is, he's dead.*

'Is he your boy friend?' she asked.

*You almost blew it then Fanny, girl. You almost used the past tense
and said, 'Was he your boy friend?' That's how sure you are.*

The sniffling face buried in WPC Nash's huge bosom moved
in a single shake of the head.

'Just a friend?'

Again a single shake of the head.

'Somebody you knew?'

This time a nod.

'Not to worry, pet. He'll be all right. It always looks worse
than it is.'

*And that's as far as you go, Fanny my girl. You didn't even see him,
so how do you know? This pathetic little madam did see him. She won't
thank you when she finds you've been feeding her a load of smooth talk.*

The cell door was pushed open, and Adams said, 'Instructions from Barstow, Fanny. Don't go off duty without letting
him know.'

Nash nodded and at the same time patted the thin shoulder
reassuringly.

*He's dead, my pet. Nothing surer. The big fella wants me around
when he interviews you. Get the tears out of your system while you're
able. Start being tough again. You're going to need it, if Barstow gets
into overdrive.*

Bell trespassed on to 'A' Beat, seeking the parked car Kelly
had told him about. Had he found it, he might have committed
assault, serious assault, but on the other hand . . .

It would seem that Martha was not quite the raw onion she
regularly cracked herself out to be. She was not quite the sweet
little angel everybody thought she was. On the quiet she
played mucky games in the back of motor cars with Army
officers.

Looked at any way you liked, she was a dirty little bitch, and
that was not the way she had been brought up. That was not
the way she had been brought up by a country mile. She had

always made a great song and dance about being trustworthy. *Trustworthy*! She was about as trustworthy as a she dog on heat.

On the other hand . . .

An Army officer would be able to keep her, and one thing led to another. And, if it ever got to that, an Army officer would not make such a bad son-in-law.

Meanwhile Bell wished he could find that bloody car.

He also wished young Kelly had been a bit more specific.

'We will,' said Barstow, 'take things very gently. We will indulge in no whoopee tactics. We will start with the reasonable assumption that Chatterton is an idiot . . . but not, necessarily, a homicidal idiot.'

'Your way,' sighed Riddle wearily.

'Most assuredly my way. I can think of no better way.'

They were in Riddle's office, but by the nature of things, and because Barstow was there, it was for the moment Barstow's office. Barstow sat in the desk chair. Barstow had swept the desk clean of all documents, and dropped them unceremoniously on to the seat of the only other comfortable chair in the room. Riddle's status, it seemed, was that of a superfluous intruder.

The chief inspector reached for his peaked cap, and said, 'I'll get some things organised.'

'Things?'

'At the moment, the town only has a two-man cover.'

'Simple mathematics, Riddle. Nothing too complicated. Nothing likely to bring on a brainstorm. Four beats. Two men. Double them up.'

'They each have a meal break.'

'Not tonight. Contact them. Suggest they get in touch with Oxfam if they get too hungry. You create problems, chief inspector. You end up with an Einstein equation where there is a simple how-many-beans-make-five question.'

'If you say so. There's also the matter of a section sergeant . . .'

'There's *you*.'

130

'Ah!'

'Paddle around until six. Be *visible*. That's all it requires. That exalted rank of yours should keep the proletariat in line.'

'As you wish,' said Riddle heavily.

'And for God's sake, sit down man. I want you around when I ask a few questions.' Then as Riddle lowered himself on to the remaining chair, 'This Chatterton? What's he like?'

'Quiet. Serious. A good officer.'

'He's just killed a man.'

Riddle nodded, and waited.

'Some clown called Martin, some highly decorative character from the world of medicine, seems worried. The staff landed on the *back* of Chambers's skull. No other marks on the body. Not *quite* in line with a plea of self-defence, wouldn't you agree?'

Riddle moved his shoulders.

'We aren't *paid* to kill people, Riddle,' drawled Barstow. 'The Constabulary Oath makes no mention of dotting people across the crust and sending them to Kingdom Come. For myself, I have no objections, but the rate-payers might not approve.'

'I think it might have been an accident.'

'Do you? Do you indeed?' Barstow cocked a sardonic eyebrow. 'And the human garbage stiffening in the morgue? Would *he* think it was an accident?'

'He might be mildly biased.' Riddle tried a watery smile.

'And this sawbones, this Martin character, who entertains grave doubts, is *he* biased?'

'I don't know him.'

'Nor do I, Riddle. But quacks tend to get stroppy when people snuff it ... unless, of course, they've killed 'em.' Barstow scowled his concentration. 'We start with Bulmer. Bulmer saw it happen.'

'He was there,' agreed Riddle.

Barstow raised his head questioningly.

'He was arresting the girl,' amplified Riddle.

'Riddle, he was *there*. At the scene. On the spot. He is a

police officer, supposedly. Eventually he will draw a fine, fat pension for *being* a police officer. At the moment he is drawing a fine, fat salary. For *seeing* things. For *hearing* things. For *observing* things.'

Riddle moved his shoulders again.

Barstow continued, 'We start with Bulmer. Whatever edifice we eventually erect, we use *him* as a base. Without him, we have nothing. With his help we can estimate the strength of the young tart simmering in a cell at the present moment.' Then, with a frown, 'Nash? What's *she* like?'

'Good.'

'Good what? A good copper? A good citizen? A good Christian lady?'

'The same thing, surely?'

'Riddle, you have been out in the rain far too long. That grey matter you mistake for a brain has fungus growing around its edges.'

'Chatterton?' said Riddle heavily.

'What about Chatterton?'

'He should be told. He should be warned.'

'When we know something. When *I* decide. Which means when we know enough to make educated guesses. Until then, I want him from under my feet. Not even here in the station. Outside, but readily available.'

'He has certain rights,' protested Riddle, mildly.

'He has the right to live, chief inspector. At the moment, he is exercising that right, which is more than can be said of the miserable character he hit with his truncheon.'

Ben Riddle was carefully packing a suitcase. Methodically, and with an almost exaggerated care, he was taking clothes from cupboards, drawers and the wardrobe, folding them and placing them in the case which was open on the bed.

Nobody had told him to leave . . . but nobody had asked him to *stay*. This packing was a prelude to a return to London . . . or it was merely a rather empty gesture of independence?

His ego had taken a bad pounding, first from Jenny, then

from Mary Barnes, then from Jenny again.

Dammit, women should not *say* those things. They should say things they were *supposed* to say.

He was not asking anybody to crawl, but a word in the right place would have done the trick. It was not that he was demanding too much of a fuss. He was a man, and he was capable of standing on his own two feet.

Just that . . . bloody *women*.

It was comforting to know that down there, *up* there in the Big City, he still had friends who knew his worth. Some of them were women. Some of them were widows and some of them were divorcees. *They* would not make him feel as if he had just crawled through a sewer. *They* would not have to be asked twice.

Just let him get back there. Just let him get his bearings. Let him get back to where men were men not milksops. Where men were not whining little runts with backbones like jellied eels.

On the other hand . . .

'There's a dead man in the hospital morgue,' said Barstow flatly.

'Yes, sir.'

'He shouldn't *be* dead.'

'No, sir.'

'He's on a slab, when he should be in a cell.'

'Yes, sir.'

Bulmer felt uncomfortable. He did not know Barstow too well. He knew him by reputation, but that was all. Top-drawer jacks did not mix, socially or professionally, with squad-car men. Nevertheless, the reputation was there. Very sarcastic – so he had been told. Not given to walking on eggs, that was what they said. And Jimmy Riddle's solemn expression was not encouraging. *And* Johnny Adams was in the background, scribbling notes. The whole set-up did not make for warm and comfortable feelings.

'That's what we're interested in,' said Barstow. 'The dead

man on the slab. And how he got there.'

'Yes, sir.'

'We need your invaluable assistance.'

Bulmer waited.

'You were there,' said Barstow.

'I arrested the girl, Fleming.'

'She's still alive.'

'Yes, sir.'

'The difference, you see.' Barstow's put-upon-patience was pure mockery. The words meant nothing. What was *behind* the words spelled trouble – T-R-O-U-B-L-E – with capital letters all the way. 'There'll be an enquiry. Not just the inquest, you understand. There'll be an inquest. The coroner will blow his usual froth and bubbles. He'll foam at the mouth a little, because that's expected of him. But after that, there'll be an *enquiry*. You take my meaning?'

'Yes, sir.'

'An enquiry as to why two arrests were made at the same time. At the same place. In identical circumstances. And why the subject of one arrest ended in a cell, whereas the subject of the other arrest ended on a slab.'

'Sir, I can't . . . '

'Hear me out, constable.' Something which might have been mistaken for a smile touched Barstow's lips. 'Before you commit yourself – before you burn enough boats to stage a re-run of Dunkirk – hear me out. Hear what I have to say. I remind you of certain basic facts. Facts you once learned, but which may have slipped your memory. Excusable Homicide. Justifiable Homicide. Unlawful Homicide. Manslaughter. Murder. Short of the corpse having suffered a sudden and very severe heart attack, it has to be one of *those*. There's a full pack, including the Joker. And you were *there*. You take my meaning?'

'Yes, sir,' breathed Bulmer.

'And?'

'I was arresting Fleming, sir.'

Barstow murmured, 'I'm not going to fix you, Bulmer.'

'No, sir.'

'I'm not going to "verbal" you, "frame" you, "drop" you –
use any of the lunatic expressions you prefer.'

'No, sir.'

'*Unless I have to.*'

It hit Bulmer like a house side. It stopped him and made
him blink. Suddenly he felt very lonely and very exposed.

'Did Chatterton kill him?' asked Barstow quietly.

'I – I think so.'

'Congratulations, Bulmer. We have that much in common.
How did he kill him?'

'He hit him with his staff, sir.'

'Of course.' Barstow nodded. 'But *why?*'

'Sir, I don't know.'

'I'm not suggesting you had a prolonged debate about it, or
that you took a vote. A simple question. I want a considered
opinion. Why did Chatterton kill Chambers?'

'Er – arresting him, sir – I suppose.'

'Rather more than "arresting" him, surely? He was *killing*
him.'

'I – I don't know, sir.'

'Careful,' warned Barstow.

'It was dark,' muttered Bulmer.

'No.' Barstow shook his head slowly.

'Sir, it was . . . '

'I was *there*. Remember? White sticks and guide dogs would
have been superfluous.'

'I was busy, sir. I was arresting Fleming.'

'Any difficulty?'

'Sir?'

'Arresting Fleming? Was she fighting?'

'Yes, sir.'

'Scratching?'

'Yes, sir.'

'Where?'

'Sir?' Bulmer looked puzzled.

'You should be marked,' said Barstow gently. 'Scratches.

Gouge marks. Bruises. Where are they?'

'I . . .' Bulmer enjoyed the luxury of a half-sigh. 'I haven't any, sir.'

'Therefore?'

'She's a woman.'

'Are you asking me or telling me?'

'Sir, it's just that . . .'

'I'll arrange for a strip search if you have any doubts.'

'No, sir. What I mean is . . .'

'What you mean,' said Barstow, 'is that you wish to be let off the hook. You are quietly peeing yourself, and with some cause, and you want out. That's not possible, Bulmer. We're fishing, and you're the only real worm we have. You're a poor thing, God knows, but you're the best we can find.' He leaned forward a little. 'Bulmer, if you're thinking of closing ranks, you've taken leave of what few senses you possess. This is far more serious than spitting on the pavement . . . *and you were there*. You were near enough to touch. Which means you were near enough to *prevent*. That, at least, is one line any good lawyer might favour. Certainly you were near enough to be what is laughingly called Second Degree Principal. Do you remember your law, Bulmer? Do you know what I'm talking about?'

Barstow paused, and Riddle murmured, 'Don't be blinded by misplaced loyalty, Bulmer.'

'No!' Barstow's gaze did not leave Bulmer. 'Let *him* decide, chief inspector. He'll be the one wearing a prison number if his house of cards tumbles.'

'Why this?' asked Chatterton, as he climbed into the front passenger seat.

'Riddle's orders.' Hindley fastened the seat belt. 'Charlie Bulmer's inside until he's made a full report. Then they let me know, and I bring you back.'

'Fun and games,' growled Chatterton.

Chatterton removed his helmet and threw it on to the back

seat. He, too, fastened his safety belt, while Hindley radioed in.

'Lima Ten to Foxtrot. Lima Ten to Foxtrot. Resuming patrol at Radholme.'

'Foxtrot to Lima Ten. Received and understood. Out.'

'Nip round 'B' Beat,' suggested Chatterton.

'Looking for more trouble?'

'Just making sure.'

'Okay. Then we'll call in and see how young Wilture's feeling.'

The squad car pulled away from Radholme Sub-Divisional Headquarters. Hindley had a new colleague and, in a vague sort of way, knew why. Chatterton also knew. Riding around in a squad car was not Chatterton's idea of policing, but he was wise enough to guess the reason for the switch.

2.30 a.m. Authors and scriptwriters try, but can never get it quite right. There are experiences beyond mere words, or even pictures; they have to be lived. To understand them, you have to be part of them and, thereafter, you cannot explain.

Police officers accept this mystical experience as part of the twenty-four hour cycle. It happens in the small hours on the streets. It is the gradual exhaustion of a community and the near-death of a whole town.

It is more than silence, and more tangible than silence. Silence is part of it . . . but never complete silence. It is a quietening down and a re-emphasis of lesser sounds. It includes the creak and flap of a flag pole, the soft, mechanical whir of a public clock before it strikes, footfalls heard from unseen streets, a snore from an open window, and the rising and falling hum of distant traffic.

It happens every night, from after midnight. It is like a slow lowering of a curtain, or the gradual closing of lids over eyes too tired to stay awake.

Police officers accept it as part of the routine of their work . . . but it can never be described.

'He had his truncheon out, when he went for Chambers?'

'Yes, sir. I think so.'

Bulmer felt like Judas, but he had no real choice.

'You only *think* so?' sneered Barstow.

'It was dark, sir.'

'You keep emphasising that point.'

'Yes, sir. But . . . '

'And *I* keep reminding you that I was there. There was enough light to read a party manifesto.'

'Yes, sir. But I was sideways on.'

'When Chatterton broke cover and went for Chambers?'

'No, sir. When he . . . '

'Shall we take it in small portions? A drop at a time?'

'Yes, sir.'

'Gastronomically speaking, let us not push meat, two veg *and* the pudding into the mouth all at the same time. Otherwise somebody might choke. Digest one small portion before we chew over the next. You are there, in the shadows.' Barstow stabbed the air with a forefinger. 'You are waiting. Fleming and Chambers are coming down the steps . . . '

'Fleming first,' interrupted Bulmer.

'Fleming first,' agreed Barstow flatly. 'Meanwhile, what are Bulmer and Chatterton doing? Are they facing each other?'

'Yes, sir. More or less.'

'Are they watching each other?'

'In a manner of speaking.'

'What, in God's name, does that mean? Which "manner" would you prefer?'

'Yes, sir,' sighed Bulmer. 'Facing each other. Watching each other.'

'Progress, at last. Then what?'

'When they reached the bottom of the fire escape we rushed them.'

'And Chatterton's staff?'

'It . . . ' Bulmer's voice became slightly hoarse. 'He had his staff in his hand, sir.'

'Actually *in his hand*?'

'Yes, sir.'

'It was out of its pocket?'

'If not, he was taking it from its pocket.'

'As you moved?'

'Yes, sir.'

'*Before* you moved?'

'That's asking too much,' cut in Riddle.

'Is it?' Barstow stared at Bulmer. '*Am* I asking too much, Bulmer? Are you as susceptible to my mannerisms as your chief inspector?'

'Sir, I don't give a damn about your mannerisms. The answer to your question: I don't know. On oath, I couldn't say whether Constable Chatterton had actually drawn his staff before we moved. But he was drawing it. And he *had* drawn it when we rushed Chambers and Fleming.'

'You see, Riddle.' Barstow glanced to his left. 'Get a man angry enough – tease him along and get him off balance – he'll tell you the truth, if only to prove to himself that he isn't afraid of you.'

The message came over the radio and Hindley said, 'That damn Jag. It's been playing tag all over the division for most of the night.'

'Slobs.' Chatterton was busy re-charging his pipe.

'Whoever's behind the wheel can drive.' There was reluctant admiration in Hindley's voice. 'He's given some damn good squad men a real run around.'

'Slobs,' repeated Chatterton.

Hindley flicked a look to his left, then said, 'There's one less slob after tonight.'

'No great loss.' Chatterton lit a match and spoke around the pipe's stem.

'It doesn't worry you?'

'No.'

'It would worry *me*.'

'Accidents happen.' Chatterton waved the flame of the

match out. 'People do daft things. They get hurt. Sometimes they get killed.'

'Anything said?' asked Barstow.

'Sir?'

'Anything said? Any conversation?'

'I'm sorry, sir. I don't know what you . . .'

'I'm not suggesting an Oxford Union Debate. I'm prepared to believe that whatever conversational exchange there might have been wasn't too scintillating.'

'No, sir.'

'I'll even accept that Chatterton forgot his manners, and didn't say "Excuse me" before crowning Chambers with his staff . . .'

'No, sir.'

'. . . Pushed a little, I might even believe . . .'

'*No, sir,*' shouted Bulmer.

'No, sir?'

'Nothing was said.'

'Nothing?'

'Nothing was said.' Bulmer lowered the volume. 'Neither Chatterton nor Chambers. Neither of them said a word.'

'Or made a noise?'

'Or made a noise,' agreed Bulmer.

'So . . .' Barstow's eyebrows highered fractionally. 'It wasn't a fight.'

'I . . .' Bulmer realised the cunning of the chief superintendent. In a tired voice, he said, 'I didn't see a fight, sir.'

'Or *hear* a fight?'

'Sir, the bell was kicking up such a . . .'

'Did you hear Chatterton and Chambers fighting?' pressed Barstow.

'No, sir. I didn't *hear* a fight.'

Barstow nodded slowly.

'The picture is taking shape,' he said quietly. 'A few more subtle brush strokes, and it might be recognisable.' He paused, then continued, 'I take it you agree that, had there been a fight

140

– had Chambers resisted arrest – you'd have seen something or heard something?'

Bulmer did not answer.

'There would have *been* a fight?'

'A scuffle, sir.'

'Bulmer,' sneered Barstow, 'you're like an old lady testing the temperature. Terrified that the water might be too hot. It is, Bulmer. It is *very* hot. It's scalding. And I hold the temperature gauge, and I stoke the boiler. And, however hot it is, eventually *you* have to take the plunge. That, too, is worth remembering.'

'He killed him, sir.' Then, in what was little more than a trembling whisper, 'Deliberately.'

'Who killed who?' insisted Barstow.

Very slowly, Bulmer said, 'Chatterton deliberately killed Chambers.'

'Take your time, Bulmer,' advised Riddle. Then to Adams, 'Bring Constable Bulmer a chair from one of the other offices.'

'And a statement form,' added Barstow. 'A statement form and follow-on-sheets.'

As Adams left the office, Riddle said, 'His own words.'

'I don't get your meaning, Riddle.'

'It's going to be Bulmer's statement.' Riddle's tone was respectful, but uncompromising. 'His own words. Exactly as he wants to tell it. Not your way. *His* way.'

'Wait outside, Bulmer.' Barstow's words were like feathers dipped in vitriolic acid. They were soft, but murderously scathing. 'Your chief inspector will let you know when it's safe for you to return.' Then, when Bulmer had left, and closed the door, 'Now, Riddle, you were saying?'

'You've gone far enough,' said Riddle calmly.

'A criticism?'

'No, sir. Advice.'

'I take it you approve of homicidal policemen,' mocked Barstow.

'That's an absurd remark to make, sir.'

'Riddle, you should be warned . . .'

'Chief Superintendent Barstow, I have a rank.'

'Oh, my word!'

'I have no objection to you calling me "mister", if you prefer. Otherwise, I'd be obliged if you use my rank.'

'You're treading dangerous ground, *Chief Inspector* Riddle.'

'I think not, sir.' Riddle smiled gently. 'I have a detective constable and a uniformed constable as witnesses.'

'Weak reeds, I assure you. They won't . . . '

'They *will*, because you've overstepped yourself, chief superintendent.'

'An opinion.'

'No more than that,' agreed Riddle. 'But firmly held on my part.'

'It doesn't matter that one of your constables has killed a man still technically innocent of crime?'

'It matters. It also matters that the constable is equally technically innocent.'

'You think he is? You think . . . '

'I'm not the jury, sir.'

'Good God, man! Can't you see . . . '

'I can see – I've *seen* – a good man, Bulmer, intimidated into saying exactly what you *wanted* him to say.'

'You must be . . . '

'And how you wanted him to say it.'

'I want the truth, chief inspector. If that makes me unusual, I'll *stay* unusual. If it makes me a museum piece, as far as the Police Service is concerned, I'll remain a museum piece. It's the coinage I deal in. The only coinage I know. The truth.'

'Or what you *think* is the truth?'

'Is one so different from the other?' Barstow frowned, but it was a frown without its usual contemptuous anger. 'If you're suggesting I want Bulmer to commit perjury . . . '

'That's what you'll get.'

'Let us assume I don't understand.'

'I could say, "With respect" . . . '

'You've left *that* qualification a little late.'

'. . . but it wouldn't mean a great deal. I respect the rank you carry. I don't particularly respect *you*.'

'At least the rank means something.'

'It means too much, sir. It gives you the right to browbeat. It gives you the right to bully. You've just exercised that right, over-exercised it. Bulmer knows what you want him to say. You've bullied him into saying it. If this thing reaches a Crown Court, however far it goes, Bulmer will continue to say what you want him to say ... whether or not it happens to be perjury.'

Martin stared at the Luger as if it, inanimate object that it was, represented all the evil in the world. Somebody had removed it from Nicco's waistband. It had not yet been collected by the police, and it had ended up on the desk in the Emergency Examination Room, along with all the other articles taken from Nicco's pockets.

The duty medic stretched out a hand as if to lift the pistol from the desk.

'Don't!' said Martin, and the medic pulled his hand away. Martin continued, 'No difference, squire. That and the atom bomb. Not a scrap of difference. The same justification, the same condemnation. Degree doesn't come into it.'

'Fingerprints?'

The medic gave a quick and timid smile. He could not understand Martin's outburst. Nor could he understand Martin's logic.

'They'll dust it,' agreed Martin. 'What is it they use these days? Aluminium powder?'

'And Sellotape to lift the print.'

'You know about these things?'

'I've seen detectives at work.'

'After the damn thing's been used to kill somebody. To maim somebody.'

'I'm – er – sorry.' The medic frowned non-understanding.

'These things, squire.' Martin moved his hand. 'To people like us they represent the final enemy. Or, if they don't, they *should*. We can't create life. We can only save life. They can give death. No sweat! The crook of a finger, the press of a button. What's the difference? You and me, squire. We belong to the foulest species on earth. What other animal uses mechanical means to kill its enemy? To kill its own kind?'

'Evolution, sir?' suggested the medic timidly.

'Evolution . . . *backwards*.' The sour grin sat awkwardly on the ruddy face. 'Think about it. We've just about licked 'em all. Even cancer, it's coming. We're making pain a thing of the past. We're dignifying age. We're making infirmity tolerable. Fine! Fine! We're also making those damn things. Those, and far more sophisticated gadgets for cancelling out progress. We'd do well to ease down a little, before we're back to living in caves.'

'Because of *that*?' The medic moved a hand towards the Luger, and sounded surprised.

'Because of the people who *make* that, and the people who make things *like* that. Because these things are available and, while they're available, some damn fool will use 'em. Always, squire. Always.

'You want proof? Consider Liechtenstein.'

'Liechtenstein?' The medic blinked.

'The only piece of the Holy Roman Empire left. Very civilised. No army. No army . . . next to no taxation. Unlike the rest of the world, Liechtenstein isn't gun-happy. Statistically the safest place on God's earth to live, the civilised world, that is. I have a soft spot for Liechtenstein.'

'Yes, sir,' smiled the medic. 'That's obvious.'

'Those damn things.' Martin nodded at the Luger. 'They're not ornamental. They only have one use and, eventually, they'll *be* used. Every last one of 'em. And whenever they *are* used, you and I can go home and forget everything we've ever learned. It's all been a waste. We might just as well have bought a guitar, joined a pop group and made *real* money.'

Barstow zipped up and waited for Riddle to finish at the wash basin.

'It's agreed then?' he said.

144

'I'm not pressing the point, sir.' Riddle allowed water from the hot tap to sluice the suds from his hands. 'The suggestion came from you.'

'Don't be modest, chief inspector. The suggestion that he's frightened of *me* came from *you*.'

'Not frightened, sir. Intimidated.'

'I'm surprised you have to suffer the inconvenience of having to shave. You're so skilled at splitting hairs.'

'Frightened? Intimidated? Not the same thing, sir.'

'The same result.'

'No, sir.' Riddle moved to the roller towel and Barstow stepped to the wash basin. 'Afraid of you, he'd have defied you, if only to prove something to himself. As it is, his loyalty is divided. To uphold the law? To give evidence against a fellow-officer? But *you*'re a fellow-officer, too . . . and the rank makes the difference.'

'To *please* me?'

'That's part of it, sir,' agreed Riddle.

'Back there in the office he kept his love of me a very closely guarded secret.'

Riddle smiled, and threaded an arm through one of the sleeves of his tunic.

'Psychology!' grunted Barstow.

'Not really. Knowing the men I command.'

'And I don't?' Barstow soaped his hands.

'How can you? The whole force? The number's are too great.'

Barstow sniffed.

'You question criminals,' said Riddle. 'Questioning police officers isn't quite the same thing.'

'And now, from your vantage point of high intellect, you're telling me my job.' Barstow lathered his hands with unnecessary violence. 'As a favour, Chief Inspector Riddle. I'm likely to be in your debt for the rest of my life. Don't crow. Don't be condescending. If you recall, they even nailed Christ to a tree.'

The motor-cyclist limped for the rest of his life. Nor was it the fault of the motor-cyclist. He was no ton-up kid. In his early twenties, he was making for his bed, having taken his fiancée home. He had enjoyed a late-night snack with his future in-laws and, as always, had promised his girl friend's mother to 'drive carefully'.

He had kept that promise. He had gone into the roundabout at little more than thirty, whereas the Jag had belted in at almost twice that speed, nudged the rear wheel, smashed into the side of the machine, then picked up the motor-cyclist and hurled him in an untidy, spinning heap at a traffic bollard.

The Jag did not even slow its speed.

More than twenty-four hours later, the motor-cyclist regained consciousness in the intensive care unit of Hagg-thorpe Infirmary. He never regained the memory of that last meal nor of the accident, and for the rest of his life he limped.

Nevertheless, he was lucky.

A local GP returning from a night call saw the accident and took the number of the Jag. He then quietly and efficiently saved the motor-cyclist's life.

'How's your bum?' asked Hindley.

Wilture twisted his head and grinned, before coming back with, 'Oh, shut up.'

'So is mine. It must be the weather.'

As a joke it was ancient and well worn, but neither of them could resist the opportunity. A low wattage bulb illuminated the side ward, and the ward contained two beds, one occupied by Wilture and the other empty, but made. Wilture was lying on his stomach, with a cage under the bedclothes keeping their weight from his injury.

Chatterton stood in the background. He was present, but not part of . . . nor, apparently, did he want to be.

'Anybody been to see you yet?' asked Hindley.

'Not yet.'

'They'll be here before morning. They won't be able to wait to view the battle scar.'

'It still hurts,' said Wilture, in a little-boy-lost voice.

'Bound to. Anything you want?'

'No, thanks. It feels as if I've been kicked by a bloody great cart-horse.'

'All the colours of the rainbow, mate. Fags?'

'No, thanks.'

'Something to read? Paperbacks? Magazines? What about a few girlie-girlie jobs? Elevate your mind to higher things?'

'No, thanks. Have you seen Sergeant Boothby yet?'

'No. Where is he?'

'Next ward, I think. Up the corridor somewhere.'

'We'll call in,' promised Hindley. He touched Wilture's shoulder. 'Take it easy, mate. Don't go riding bucking broncos for a while.'

They left without Chatterton having said a word.

'We do not deliberately *kill* people,' repeated Nash.

'Not unless you can sodding well get away with it.' The sniffling made the words sound as if Fleming had a bad head cold. 'But if you bloody well *can* . . . '

'That's enough!' Policewoman Nash fished a newly laundered handkerchief from her coat pocket and shook it out. 'Here. Use this. Blow your nose. And let's have no more of that sort of talk.'

Takes it easy, Fanny my girl. This one is a hard-boiled little madam. By tomorrow at this time she won't even remember the poor devil. That's how tough she is. But she'll need to be tough, once Barstow gets into overdrive.

Fleming blew her nose, noisily and messily, then made to hand the handkerchief back.

'Keep it. It's on the house.'

'Any chance of a benny?'

'You *what*?' Nash gaped.

'Any chance of a . . . '

'You have to be joking!' Even Nash was shocked. 'You're asking for benzedrine? Amphetamine tablets? Do you realise where you are, young lady?'

'In the bleeding nick. Where else?'

'Well . . . ' Nash swallowed. 'That's one thing that's *not* on the house.'

'Don't tell *me*.' Fleming's curling lips made her mouth ugly. 'What?'

'You get 'em. Sodding hell . . . think we don't *know*? You get 'em, you take 'em. Everybody who can get the bleeding things takes 'em.'

Hold your water, Fanny. Grab hold of yourself. This one is in a class of her own. She is a beaut and, when she nose-dives, she'll think the whole world has fallen on top of her. She needs some sort of understanding. Work at it, girl, work at it.

In a tight voice, Policewoman Nash said, 'You've gone far enough. Don't make more trouble for yourself.'

'Go get screwed, you fat cow.'

The duty medic met them at the door of the side ward. He was just leaving.

'Don't go in.' He closed the door firmly. 'If you see him now, he won't like it.' Then, after a pause, he added, 'He certainly won't like it later.'

Hindley looked a question.

'He's in traction,' said the medic flatly.

'I can't see what . . . '

'He's also weeping. Crying his eyes out. There's a nurse in there, trying to comfort him till his daughter arrives.'

'Look, if he's in that sort of pain . . . '

'It's not pain.'

'Oh!'

'Not *physical* pain. I think he might wish it was as simple as that.'

'Oh!' repeated Hindley.

The medic ushered them a few yards along the corridor and out of possible earshot of the side ward.

He asked, 'What do you know about Sergeant Boothby?'

'Just that one of the breakers jumped from an upstairs window and . . . '

'No, not that. I mean before tonight.' The medic ran fingers through his thinning hair. 'His daughter's been on the phone.

She's coming as soon as she can. She mentioned something about his wife being killed in a road accident. That might be part of it. That might be *all* of it.'

'Before he came to Radholme,' said Hindley, in a low voice, 'a bowser knocked his missus down. From what I hear, it killed her outright. *He* was sent to the accident.'

'Good God!'

'Rumours,' said Hindley carefully. 'Nobody asks, but it gets around. It shattered him.'

'That I believe.'

'He's supposed to have recovered, but he's . . . y'know, he *worries*. All the time. About little things. He's never quite sure of himself. It's hard to explain.'

'Who's his doctor?'

'I don't know.' Hindley turned to Chatterton, and asked, 'Do you know?' but Chatterton did not seem to hear the question.

The medic said, 'It doesn't matter. The daughter's coming in. She'll know.'

'So . . . ' Hindley looked slightly embarrassed. 'That's it, then?'

'I shouldn't go in.'

'No. Of course not. But tell him we called. Tell him we asked . . . when he's himself again, that is.'

The duty medic nodded and the two officers walked away.

As they crossed the car park towards the waiting squad car, Chatterton said, 'It's beyond me.'

'What's that?'

'A grown man crying.'

'A sign of weakness?' There was an edge to the question.

'What else?'

'It might show he's human.'

'It's beyond me.'

'Aye . . . it would be.'

To tell the old lady, or not to tell the old lady. That (as Hamlet might have soliloquised) was the question.

Not that the old lady would understand. At least, not at first

149

telling. He would damn near have to draw diagrams . . . and then she might not believe it of 'her' Martha.

And when – if – she was *made* to understand?

Bell knew his missus. The mote in his own eye did not prevent him from seeing the bloody great balk of timber lodged in *hers*. He could not vouch for other men's wives but, by hell, he knew his own. Some women (he was told) were very tranquil. Some women (he was reliably informed) did not give a toss. But *his* woman was not at all like that. Once the message was received, she would go stark, staring bonkers. That would be the first reaction. After that would come the sulks. Not a few hours of sulking, either. It would go on for days. Maybe even weeks.

There was something about wives.

Specifically, there was something about *his* wife.

When in doubt, blame the old man. If you cannot kick anybody else in the balls, aim one at his goolies. It is *his* fault. Or if, strictly speaking, it is not his fault, it damn soon will be, if you twist things around a bit. The Golden Rule being, do unto him what you'd like to do unto somebody else, but can't.

So, why tell the old lady?

The obvious answer was do *not* tell the old lady.

That left Martha.

Having a daughter like Martha, like he had *thought* Martha was, was bad enough; primping and mincing around the house, making believe she and her mother were a cut above everybody else. *That* was bad enough. But this other thing was going to be infinitely worse.

He could, of course, drop a hint.

She must have seen young Kelly. She must have recognised him. So what next?

A murmured, 'Constable Kelly tells me he saw you in a car last night.'

When the old lady was not around, of course. The less the old lady knew, the fewer questions she would ask. All it needed was a hint; a very innocent-sounding remark.

As he checked the property of 'D' Beat he muttered

150

variations of the words to himself. He tried putting the emphasis on different parts of the remark.

'Constable *Kelly* tells me he saw you in a car last night.'

That was wrong, of course. It made it sound as if coppers were standing in line to report sightings of her.

'Constable Kelly tells me he saw *you* in a car last night.'

That was damn near as bad. It hinted that young Kelly spent his life nosing around strange cars.

'Constable Kelly tells me he saw you in a *car* last night.'

That was more like it. It was not quite perfect. It was not quite subtle enough. There was not enough real innuendo. It was not . . .

Damnation! It was not just that she had been seen in a car. It was what she had been *doing* in the blasted car.

Come to that, what the hell *had* she been doing?

If Kelly was to be believed, she had been sitting there, all prim and proper. Not a hair out of place. She had even had her hat on.

All right, the clown alongside her had been starkers, but . . .

Bell blew out his cheeks in disgust.

She was just like her bloody mother. She was as crafty as they come. She would have an answer; some sort of answer. They always had an answer . . . so why waste grey hairs?

'Reminiscent of a vicarage tea party rather than a police enquiry,' grumbled Barstow. And it was.

Barstow, Riddle, Adams and Bulmer each had a cup of tea, and they shared a plateful of ginger nuts. Nor were they short of chairs; each had a chair and there was a spare chair which Adams and Bulmer used as a makeshift table upon which to rest their saucers. It was, therefore, rather like a tea party or, in view of the o'clock, rather like a forbidden feast in a school dormitory.

Riddle swallowed, sipped tea, then said, 'You understand the situation, Bulmer?'

'Yes, sir.'

'That the consensus of opinion suggests that you're terrified of *me*,' murmured Barstow mockingly.

'Not that, sir.'

'No?' The question almost called Bulmer a liar.

'Not you, sir. Not anybody.' Bulmer's tone was quietly determined. 'But, as you saw fit to remind me, if Constable Chatterton did what I think he did, it isn't just spitting on the pavement.'

'Bulmer, we need a statement. A starting point.' Riddle moved in, before Barstow could take over again. 'What we're doing is as tricky as it is unpleasant. We need as firm a statement as you can give.'

'I understand that, sir.'

'Therefore, we must be pessimistic. We must hope for the best, but assume the worst. And the worst means that you may be cross-examined at a Crown Court on what you say in the statement.'

'Let him get on with it, chief inspector,' complained Barstow. 'Don't waffle.'

Bulmer ignored the detective chief superintendent, and spoke directly to Riddle.

'I know my job, sir.'

'Quite. But *my* job insists that I remind you. Will you *make* a statement?'

'Good God, man! Of course he'll . . . '

'Yes, sir. I'll make a statement.'

'Will you write it yourself? Or would you prefer to dictate it to Detective Constable Adams?'

'I'll dictate it please, sir.'

'But carefully. What you *know* plus – and only if you wish – honestly held opinions. And the reasons for those opinions.'

Bulmer nodded.

Riddle glanced at Adams and Adams pulled his chair nearer to the desk, positioned the first sheet of the Statement Forms and wrote down Bulmer's rank, name and number.

Barstow tasted his tea and growled, 'In less polite company I'd be tempted to describe it as watered-down paint stripper.'

* * *

152

3 a.m. Those who can, do; those who can't, teach.

If this adage is true anywhere, it is true when equated with a Police Training College and what, of necessity, is taught there as opposed to street bobbying. Some of the instructors are good, practical men. Others have been shunted from under the feet of colleagues who wish to work unhampered by fools.

All are limited by textbook requirements.

From having a quiet word with a motorist who has broken some minor road traffic regulation, to dragging a fighting prisoner to the nearest cell – from escorting children across a busy thoroughfare to officiating at a post-mortem examination – the instructors must quote the book from cover to cover but, at the scene, the prisoner would escape and the pathologist would be working on his own while the 'coroner's officer' claimed the nearest toilet.

The first lonely pavement walked along in the small hours teaches the recruit more about basic policing than any instructor on earth.

Bell stopped the pedal cyclist.

The pedal cyclist was a middle-aged fool. He was a great one for knowing (and claiming) his 'rights'. These, it would seem, included the 'right' to race his clapped out machine along the pavement, without lights and with very dicey brakes.

Nor, it must be admitted, was Bell overflowing with the milk of human kindness at that moment.

'Hold it!'

The pedal cyclist dragged the soles of his shoes on the pavement, in order to assist the brakes.

'What's up?' The indignation was as real as the open-necked shirt, the rolled-up sleeves and the trouser cuffs tucked into the stockings.

'Guess,' growled Bell.

'Look, I'm in a hurry.'

'I won't keep you more than a couple of hours.'

'Eh?'

'So much of a hurry you forgot your front light and you forgot your rear light?'

'Oh . . . *that?*'

'So much of a hurry, you need the road *and* the pavement?'

'There's nobody about.'

'*I'm* about.'

'I'm not doing any harm.'

'You're breaking the law, Sunny Jim. Three laws. Front, rear and pavement.'

'Bloody hell! Haven't you got your quota of cases yet?'

'Not yet,' said Bell, coldly. 'But with loonies like you around it won't take me long.'

Bell slipped his pocket book from his tunic pocket.

'Bloody hell! You're not going to book me?'

'Don't bet money on it.'

'It's a pity you're not . . . '

'I know,' interrupted Bell. 'I've heard the aria so many times, I can sing it backwards. It's a pity I'm not out catching burglars. On the other hand, you might be a burglar.'

'Eh?'

'Not many knackered bikes in this district. And they can even afford bicycle clips.'

'Look, I'm on my way home.'

'Champion . . . where's "home"?'

'What?'

'Where you live. But I'll have your name, first.'

'I don't have to answer these questions. You've no right. Who the hell . . .'

'Bell,' said Bell, dangerously. 'That's who I am. Police Constable one-four-three-zero Bell. I'll spell it out for you if you lack the learning. Now, what's *your* name?'

'Go hump yourself.'

'Sunny Jim.' Bell moved a foot. The heel of his shoe rested on the pavement, while the sole put pressure on the spokes of the front wheel. Nor, while Bell gripped the handlebars, could the pedal cyclist ease the pressure on the spokes. Equally, there was no room for doubt in Bell's tone. 'I've taken all the drip I'm going to take. Any more, and you won't *ride* it home. You won't even *wheel* it home. You'll *carry* the bloody thing home.'

'You can't . . . '

'Don't push things!' Bell moved his face to within twelve inches of that of the angry cyclist. Then in a quieter, more deadly voice, 'Don't push things, Sunny Jim. Be warned. I might think horrible thoughts. I might have nasty suspicions. I want your name, I want your address, and I want proof that you aren't feeding me a load of old madam. If I don't get all those three things, I'm likely to suspect you've lifted this apology for a bicycle. Or I might suspect you're hurrying from a break-in . . . or even to a break-in. That's all it needs, and I have a very suspicious mind.' He paused for a moment, then growled, 'Put it another way. You're up to the nostrils in fertiliser, and sinking fast.'

'You know what?' breathed the pedal cyclist. 'You're a right bastard.'

'Of course. I wouldn't be talking to a pillock like you if I wasn't.'

Sally Boothby looked down at her father, then exchanged worried looks with the sympathetic nurse. The cat's cradle of the traction equipment kept Boothby rigid on the bed, but he stared at the ceiling with unseeing eyes and the tears ran down the sides of his face and soaked into the linen of the pillows.

'Dad,' she whispered, and bent down to touch his lips with hers. 'Dad . . . *please*!'

'He's . . . ' The nurse moved her shoulders in a tiny gesture of helplessness.

'I know.' Sally Boothby nodded, sadly. She pulled a chair closer to the bed, sat down and gripped one of her father's hands in hers. She murmured, 'I'm here, dad. You're going to be all right. Nobody's going to hurt you. You're not alone any more.'

There was a moment or two of awkward silence, then the door of the side ward opened and Martin and the duty medic entered. They walked slowly to the bed and, at a nod from the duty medic, the nurse left.

Martin touched the woman's shoulder and after hesitating,

then squeezing her father's hand in gentle assurance, Sally Boothby followed the stout medic into the corridor. They spoke in voices soft enough to be almost a whisper.

'Now then, old dear, how can you help us?'

'In what way?'

'It's not just his back. His neck. We can handle the pain. What else?'

'He had a crack-up. A bad nervous breakdown just over three years ago. Mother was killed in an accident and dad went to the scene. He didn't know it was mother till he got there.'

'That, more or less, is what we've been told. And today?'

'He takes Lentizol. Visits the doctor about once a month.'

'Uhuh.' Martin blew out his cheeks in a sad sigh. 'His physical injury will mend. No real problem. But . . . '

He broke off, and Sally Boothby gave a tiny, miserable nod.

'I'm biased,' she said gently. 'They were great parents. He still is. But, even taking that into consideration, it was obvious. They were very much in love. I don't mean they loved each other. It was more than that. They were *in love* . . . and he's never really come to terms with life without mother.'

'A hell of a situation.' The genuine sadness sat strangely on the apple-cheeked face. 'Strictly speaking, old dear, it's not in my field. But I know enough about it. He'll need more than Lentizol. He'll need a long, long time.' He paused, then added, 'This job of his. It carries heavy responsibilities. I'm sorry – I could be very wrong – but, at a guess, he'll never be quite up to it again.'

'We suspected,' she said heavily.

'We?'

'I have two brothers. We've all tried to drop hints.'

'And?'

'That business of responsibility. He feels he has another responsibility. As a father.' Then in a low, unhappy tone, 'He's a good father. He's a good *man*.'

'Look, old dear, it doesn't happen to *bad* men. It doesn't

156

happen to bad *people*. It's what makes them good that's part of it.'

'What can we do?' she pleaded.

'Help him get better,' he said simply. 'Help him get as well as he'll ever be. Show him he's wanted. The pills – the funny farmers – they'll do all they can, but he's his best doctor. Sadly, he won't be, unless he decides to be.'

'He's important to us,' she said quietly.

'I don't doubt it. But make *him* understand that.' He compressed his lips, and frowned. 'Somebody had better warn you, old darling. You're in for a rough time. He's likely to be a mental cripple all his life . . . and most of the time it won't show.

'We'll mend his neck. No real problem there. But the other thing? He has to be coaxed, without knowing he's being coaxed. He has to be convinced. He hasn't to be *allowed* to feel sorry for himself.

'Some damn fool will tell him to "pull himself together". They always do. Stamp on 'em. He's a lot more involved than a pair of curtains . . . remind 'em of that.

'Meanwhile, convince him. However you do it, *convince* him. His life did *not* end when your mother was killed. He's still important. Important to you. Important to his sons. Important to everybody who knows him. Get *that* across and he'll start getting better. The pills, the psychiatrists, they'll steady him. They'll help to make him receptive. At the moment – a personal opinion, of course – he de-values himself. Life isn't worth the trouble of living it, by which he means *his* life. He has to be convinced otherwise.'

She bit into her lower lip, and the word 'Suicide?' was a trembling, whispered question.

'Accept it as a very real possibility,' said Martin sombrely. 'It's a nasty by-product of his present state of mind. At the moment it wouldn't take much. But he won't – he *shouldn't* – if you can get through to him.' The quick smile was sad and compassionate. 'Not good news, old dear. But somebody had

157

to warn you. He's loved, that's obvious already. As I see things, he *deserves* to be loved. He has a hell of a lot more going for him than most people.'

James Wover's self-esteem had taken a battering. The prolonged argument with Julie Kelly had bruised his ego more than he cared to admit; the spitting insults, followed by the pushing and the threatening, then the final vase hurled at his head. The vase had missed its target, but at last Wover had grasped the general idea.

It had *not* been an out-for-kicks performance; a slanging match, followed by a bout of wrestling as a prelude to a panting sex session. The stupid little cow had *meant* it.

So . . . she would regret it.

Given time, she would come drooling back to him, begging for something only he could deliver. *Then* watch him put the pressure on. He would have her crawling. He would teach her a lesson she would remember for the rest of her life.

Meanwhile . . .

It was one hell of a time to be walking back to a cold and lonely bed.

It was nosh-time for the newest member of the Adams family.

Rosemary Adams suckled the child and, as a mental exercise, toyed with the possible activities of her absent husband.

John was a good man. Indeed, he was a *very* good man; a truly delighted father and a genuinely loving husband. She could find no serious fault in him. He was careful, without being tight-fisted. He was manly, without being aggressive. He was clean and tidy, without being ridiculously fastidious. He was quiet, without being sullen. In short, he was a thoughtful husband and a gentle lover . . . but above all else he was a friend. Being a pal was important. That, then, was what they were; husband and wife, but also buddies.

It was, she concluded, one of the strengths of their marriage. They could laugh with each other, even *at* each other, in the firm knowledge that there was no ridicule in the laughter.

Nevertheless, and despite all this, his profession worried her.

However hard she tried, she could not yet come to terms with policing. Of necessity she knew other officers, and the wives of those officers, and the menfolk had a certain arrogance, while the women accepted that arrogance with a timidity beyond the understanding of Rosemary Adams.

The babe gurgled and sucked. For the moment its mother's breast was its whole world, and a very satisfying world.

Meanwhile, worry about the babe's father nagged at the mother's mind.

She thought of the man with ultimate authority over her husband. She thought of Barstow. He was a chief superintendent, no less, but he was also a very obnoxious type. She had met him twice at social functions. He had, supposedly, been "off duty". But on both occasions he had quietly relished the power he wielded. He had demonstrated that power, not openly, but in a sly and cunning way. The snide remarks, the carefully chosen turns of phrase and the subtle tyranny with which he had brushed aside all offers of friendship had disgusted her.

That had been the time when she and John had had one of their few quarrels.

'He's a most obnoxious man.'

'Oh . . . come *on*. It's his way. That's all.'

'He's an animal.'

'Darling, he *handles* animals. It's what he's paid for, and he does it well.'

'You admire him?' She had been shocked at the realisation.

'He's a fine copper.'

'The sort of man you'd like to become?'

'If I ever get to be as good as him . . . '

'I'd have walked out on you years before,' she had snapped.

'Wha-at?'

'If you think I'd live with a man remotely like Barstow . . . '

Then had come the row, followed by two days of cold politeness. God, it had been awful. Inside she had been heartbroken. She knew that John felt as bad, but could hide it better.

Then had come the make-up, the kissing and the love-making. The quarrel had almost been worth it, but the subject had not been touched upon since.

Softly, she crooned her thoughts to the suckling babe.

'We mustn't let him, my sweet. There's two of us now. He's outnumbered. We'll look after him. Keep him as he is. As we want him. Not ambitious . . . not *too* ambitious. We'll keep him on the straight and narrow.'

Kelly tried to figure out how Bell might have handled the situation. Bell was both friend and mentor. Bell was the sort of copper he (Kelly) hoped he would become one day. Bell was on top of every situation, and never at a loss for either words or action.

'What's your name?' Kelly asked, and there was a slight shake in his voice.

'You *what*?' James Wover stared his disbelief.

'Your name?' repeated Kelly, tightly.

'You know damn well who I am.'

'Do I?'

'You saw me earlier today, in court.'

'Did I?'

'You know damn *well* who I am.'

'Where do you live?'

'Oh, go knot yourself.'

'Where do you live?' repeated Kelly, dangerously.

'For Christ's sake! You know that, too.'

'I'm on duty, mate.' Kelly clung to his rising temper. 'I'm in uniform, and I have a job to do. I'm doing it.'

'Go run up the nearest flag pole.'

'Don't walk away.' Kelly stopped Wover by grasping his upper arm. He used a very tight grip. 'I haven't finished asking you questions yet.'

'Take your hand off my arm, you useless jerk.'

'I want to know what you're doing walking the streets at this time in a morning.'

'You wouldn't enjoy being told,' sneered Wover.

'Nevertheless, you're going to tell me.'

'I'm going home. Now *take your grubby hand off my arm*.'

'Walking?'

'Is there a law against *that*, now?' Wover tried to pull his arm loose, but Kelly's grip tightened even harder.

'Why aren't you using your car?'

'Look, you miserable little jerk, if you don't . . . '

'Why not the car?' ground Kelly.

'Do you have to ask?'

'I'm *asking*.'

'We used *her* car.' The lips curled and the tone was a carefully studied insult.

'Don't . . . ' Kelly swallowed, then choked, 'Don't push it *too* far, mate.'

'No. I'm not pushing.' The soft, insulting laugh was a deliberate thrust. 'I'm not pushing at all, you useless creep. I haven't the strength to push. I've just climbed from on top of your wife. I've spent most of the night screwing her stupid.'

And that was when Kelly lost control.

It can be argued, with some force, that Kelly had guessed what Wover had been up to, and had forced the offensive remark from the man he loathed; that (albeit not consciously) he had sought an excuse for what happened. Equally, it can be argued that Kelly was, emotionally, a baby.

Physically, he was no baby. He was a grown man, in peak of condition, with slightly more than his fair share of muscle . . . and the thing switched from an emotional to a physical plane.

The balled fist of Kelly's left hand sliced across the grinning mouth. It burst the lips and loosened two teeth, and sent the spectacles flying. He released his grip on the arm, then stepped forward and buried his right fist wrist-deep in his tormentor's gut then, as the head came down, the left fist landed again; this time on the side of the head.

Wover sprawled on the pavement, holding his middle and spraying blood from his smashed mouth.

'Get up,' panted Kelly. 'Get up, you foul-mouthed bugger.'

'I'll – I'll get you for this. I'll . . . '

'Get up! I haven't even started.'

At which point Bell, having just handled one awkward customer, strolled round a corner, saw what was happening and hurried to Kelly's side.

'What the hell!'

'It's that mad sod.' Wover remained on the pavement. He felt safer there. 'The power-crazy bastard. He's . . . '

'He's – he's . . . ' Kelly danced around, fists still clenched, waiting for another chance to swing a punch.

'I know who he is,' said Bell.

'Look, he's just used physical violence on me. He punched me.'

'Did he?' The stone-wall question carried no hint of real interest.

'He thumped me.'

'Is that a fact?' Then in the same flat, unemotional tone, the question, 'What are you doing down there, lad?'

'Eh?'

'Bleeding all over the nice, clean pavement?'

Wover blinked disbelief.

'You fell,' said Bell calmly.

'Wha-at!'

'We've just come across you. Constable Kelly and I have just come across you. We're here to give you assistance, you dirty-minded little man.'

'What the Jesus Christ sort of . . . '

'We have,' continued Bell, flatly, 'been together for the past fifteen minutes. Our notebooks will verify that fact . . . eventually. We both saw you fall.'

'FALL!'

'When we came round the corner. Both of us. We saw you fall, and bash your face on the pavement. Check, the blood's making a right mess.'

'You – you can't . . . '

162

'Not another one.' Bell sighed mild, but exaggerated impatience. 'Everybody's telling coppers what they can't do tonight. It must be contagious. Take it from me lad, we saw you fall. We can prove we did. I doubt if you can prove we didn't. We ran to give you assistance. Like good little wooden tops, we *ran*. On the other hand, we thought you might be pissed.' Bell rubbed his chin meditatively. 'Maybe you *are* pissed. Are you?'

'I'm not drunk. This mad . . . '

'Good. Now show us both you're not drunk. Demonstrate why we shouldn't sling you inside for the night for being Drunk and Incapable. Get up and walk quietly home. Then we might believe you.'

'You've – you've got me, haven't you?' Wover gazed up at the stern-faced officers.

'By the short hairs.' Bell nodded solemn agreement. 'And you have about five seconds to show us why we shouldn't tighten the grip and send your voice up a couple of octaves.'

With the arrival of Bell, Kelly had cooled his rage, and he and Bell watched as Wover climbed unsteadily to his feet, retrieved his broken spectacles, wiped his still-bleeding mouth with the back of a hand, made as if to say something, changed his mind then staggered away, still holding his middle.

'Thanks,' muttered Kelly. 'He was . . . '

'I can guess.' Bell's voice was hard and unfriendly. 'Just don't do it again.'

'He said he'd . . . '

'I don't give a damn what he *said*. It's what you *did* that was bloody stupid.' Bell's tone melted slightly. 'Kelly, old son, they aren't worth it. None of 'em. You just damn near lost your job and your pension. You damn near lost me *my* job and my pension. I don't care if she's the Queen of bloody Sheba, she's not worth that. That horrible little turd could have pushed us both right up the pole. We were lucky. He hadn't the guts, and now he's left it too late.'

'I'm – y'know – I'm sorry.'

'We're all tempted at times, old son.' Bell grinned as his anger passed. 'This time we've got away with it. Put it down to experience, eh?'

The messages were coming over the squad car radio thick and fast. The stolen Jag was being sought, and every police vehicle in the area was being brought in on a saturation search.

Hindley unclipped the microphone from the dashboard.

'Lima Ten to Foxtrot. Lima Ten to Foxtrot.'

'Come in, Lima Ten.'

'That Jag might be making for the motorway. Shall we get there and wait, ready to cut it off?'

'Understood and agreed, Lima Ten. Lima Fifteen might be on to something. I'll link you up, and you can work in tandem.'

'Thank you, Foxtrot. Over and out.'

Hindley braked the squad car to a halt alongside the kerb.

He said, 'Into the back seat. Sit behind me.'

'Why?' The question was wrapped up in tobacco smoke.

'I'm not going to chase him. I'm going to *stop* him, if I get the chance. If necessary, I'll shunt him. That means hitting him with the nearside. So, get behind me, it gives us half a car's width to play with.' Then, as Chatterton began to open the door, 'And lose that pipe, otherwise it might come out of the back of your neck.'

'Satisfied?' asked Riddle.

'Yes, sir.' Having read what Adams had written, Bulmer dropped the sheets on to the top of the desk.

'Nothing you want altering?'

'No, sir.'

'Right. Sign it, please. Date it, and include the time you signed it. Then I'll witness your signature. Adams can certify it, then he can witness my signature.'

'Great balls of fire!' growled Barstow. 'He's not giving a receipt for the Crown Jewels. It's a statement, not a Death Warrant.'

164

'Sir.' Riddle's voice was gentle, but uncompromising. 'Not too long ago, those words could have boiled down to just *that*.'

3.30 a.m. Ask any honest policeman. Ask any copper with enough service behind him to know not to lick an indelible pencil.

If you press the point, you will be told that superintendents come in two distinct varieties. There are those who can. *There are also those who* cannot, *but who have the cunning to hide their shortcomings behind a surround of underlings who are reasonably efficient.*

The former live their lives on a perpetual limb, but are happy to do so and sleep deeply in the sound knowledge that no size-tens are likely to be aimed at the back of their necks. They know that when men and women salute them and say 'sir', those men and women mean it.

Sadly, the latter predominate.

They, the latter, have polished the art of string-pulling and can-passing. They would not be where they are otherwise. Their rank owes little to merit.

When these mildly useless officers move – when they are transferred or, as occasionally happens, when they attain chief-superintendentship – the strings become a veritable cat's cradle. Within weeks, their 'court' follows them. Chief inspectors, inspectors, sergeants and even constables suddenly, but not unexpectedly, find themselves faced with a 'proposed transfer'.

Thus, to move one of these superintendents is a very costly and a very inconvenient business.

The experience worries nobody. The ratepayers and the taxpayers foot the bill.

'We will,' said Barstow, with grim satisfaction, 'now allow the female lead to take stage centre. By this time she should have learned her lines, word perfect.'

Bulmer had left to take a belated snack. The statement had been studied by Barstow, and the next stage in the initial investigation was due to start.

'We'll need Policewoman Nash present,' said Riddle.

'But of course,' agreed Barstow, sardonically. 'Our betters have the minds of perverts. In any other walk of life, the male

165

and female work happily together. Alone and unchaperoned. But let the male be some miserable copper, and it matters not that the female might have a face like a cracked chamber pot and a figure to make the average door knocker look positively erotic, the vision of uninhibited rape immediately springs to mind. *And where the hell have YOU been?*'

Without knocking, Superintendent Smeaton had opened the door and stepped into the office. For a moment he stared at a scene he knew nothing about.

'I – I . . . '

'You disappoint me, Smeaton. You disappoint us all. We'd reached the firm and happy conclusion that you'd opted for early retirement.'

'I've – er – I've . . . next-of-kin. Your instructions were . . . '

'And, of course, they live in the Outer Urals?'

'No, sir. But . . . '

'They all collapsed with shock, and you've been bringing them all round. Is that it?'

'Sir, I . . . '

'Sit down, Superintendent Smeaton.' The blistering contempt, the deliberately sarcastic emphasis on the last two words, brought blood to Smeaton's face. Then as Smeaton made a move, 'No. Not in that chair. That one is reserved for a slut I'm about to have a long conversation with. Gather what energy you have left, Smeaton. Make a final effort. Tour the other offices, find another chair and carry it in here. After that, you can collapse and die in peace.'

Smeaton left the office, and Riddle glanced at his watch.

'I'll walk the streets for a while,' he said.

'Why?'

'The town is only on half-cover. There's no section sergeant. Somebody with authority should check things.'

'*I* think it's because Smeaton's arrived. I think *that's* the real reason.'

'No, sir. But if you press the point . . . '

'Assume it's being pressed, chief inspector.'

'I don't know this woman, Fleming. But a detective chief

166

superintendent, a uniformed superintendent, a detective constable and a policewoman. If this thing gets as far as a Crown Court . . . '

'Does Smeaton worry you?'

'Sir.' A gentle smile touched Riddle's lips. 'Oddly enough, *you* don't worry me, not any more.'

'I must be losing my touch.'

'But if Chatterton *is* charged, and if he *does* stand trial, and if Fleming *is* called as a major witness, a statement given in the presence of four – much less five – police officers will be God's gift to any reasonably competent defence barrister.'

'Point taken,' grunted Barstow. 'The same thing applies to Bulmer, of course.'

'Bulmer's a good police officer. He can ride the storm. The girl, Fleming, is an unknown quantity. At the best she, herself, will be facing serious charges.'

Barstow nodded reluctant agreement and, as Riddle stood up to reach for his peaked cap, said, 'Don't get lost, chief inspector. I'll feel lonely without you. I want to see you back here before I leave.'

'Lima Fifteen to Lima Ten.'

'Lima Ten, here.'

'He seems to be making for the motorway.'

'Lima Ten to Lima Fifteen. We're ready. Can you keep him in sight?'

'Will do. The bugger can drive. He's moving ahead on the straight, but we're making ground on the corners.'

'Lima Ten to Lima Fifteen. Keep him coming.'

'At a guess, he's making for the Cat and Fiddle junction.'

'We're waiting. A good half-mile south of the junction.'

'That's about right.'

'Keep him coming, mate. Jockey him into the southbound lanes. Tell us when . . . we'll bung a cork in his bottle.'

'Will do. Lima Fifteen, out.'

Hindley returned the microphone to its clip and, quite deliberately, relaxed in his seat.

The squad car was parked on the hard shoulder. All the lights were switched off, but the engine was ticking over and ready. This was what it was all about; not chasing them, but *stopping* them; out-foxing them.

The heavy stuff thundered past on their right. Some were high-loaded. Some were empty and rattling past; bouncing and shaking and with folded tarpaulin sheets on their boards.

They dipped and switched their lights and trafficators, communicating with each other in their own code.

Hindley watched, noted that the cars and vans were few and counted that as some small blessing.

From the rear seat, Chatterton growled, 'Interesting.'

'It could get *very* interesting.' Hindley's voice was not too friendly. 'You could end up with a Jag in the small of your back.'

Bulmer touched the side of the electric kettle with the back of his fingers. The bloody thing seemed to take longer and longer to boil these days. Something was wrong with it, but who paid for a new filament?

Up on the shelf, alongside the opened bag of sugar and the half-empty bottle of milk, the transistor spewed out non-conversation and non-music; crap which, supposedly, kept an army of night owls from closing their eyes in sheer boredom. It meant nothing. It was an audible extension of the foul taste which seemed to fill the mouth.

'Supper Time', it was called, and *that* was a joke in very dubious taste, too. A few minutes in which to munch sandwiches and taste tea brewed in the beaker; to sit in a not-very-comfortable armchair and give your feet a rest. And *this* was what the Branch Board had fought for, for years.

What a bloody victory!

Bulmer unwrapped his sandwiches. He unwrapped them slowly and without enthusiasm. Before he saw them, he knew they would be of mousetrap cheese and chutney. He was not going to be surprised. His taste buds were not going to do backflips.

It was a lousy snack for a lousy o'clock.

It was part of an all-round-lousy job.

'And *you* represent the species reputed to be more deadly than the male?' purred Barstow.

The girl, Fleming, looked puzzled. She looked puzzled and very annoyed. The tears had long since dried.

'The female of the species,' amplified Barstow mockingly. 'The ladies, God bless them . . . but not *all* of them. Or is it asking too much to hope that you might know your Kipling?'

'What's the crazy old git talking about?'

Fleming asked the question of Nash, but before Nash could speak Smeaton chipped in. 'You'd be well advised to keep a civil tongue in your head, young lady.'

'The "old git",' murmured Barstow, 'is talking about you. He is also talking to you. Nor does he think you look particularly deadly. More than a little brassy. More than slightly shop-soiled. Pathetic and very frightened . . . and with good reason. But, whatever else, not deadly.'

'If you think you can scare the shit out of . . . '

'The language,' warned Nash.

'Oh, no,' mocked Barstow. 'Let her use it. Let her bolster up her courage, what little courage she has left, by using lavatory phraseology. It won't shock anybody. We can match her, word for word, if necessary.' Then, directly to Fleming, 'Do you fancy a little warm up? A short swearing match, perhaps?'

'I don't know what the hell you're . . . '

'Of course you don't. You don't know what the hell I'm *talking* about. Miserable little creatures like you *never* know what a policeman's talking about. Perhaps they're too stupid. Or it could be part of their own obscure religion. It makes no odds. We accept it as an unhappy fact of life. So, I'll spell it out for you in very simple language.

'I'm talking about shop-breaking. About risking life and limb, crawling around on very high tiles. About making a hole in the roof of a chemist's shop and, thereafter, grubbing around with your filthy little fingers among things which are

169

not your property. I'm talking about carrying dangerous weapons around in public. Firearms. Shooting bullets at innocent policemen. *Hitting* innocent policemen on intimate parts of their anatomy. I'm talking about theft. About taking other people's property. Property to which you have . . .'

'What about Potty?' she spat.

'Who?'

'Potty.'

'Do we know anybody called "Potty"?' Barstow moved his head to encompass Nash, Smeaton and Adams. Then, 'Who is "Potty"?'

'Your bastard killed him, that's all.'

'You mean *Chambers*?' Barstow nodded slowly, as if gradual understanding had dawned. 'Ye-es. I have it on good authority that Chambers is dead.'

'Resisting arrest, was he?' The loathing made the words very ugly.

'I can't answer that question. I wasn't there.'

'*I* bloody well was.'

'In that case . . . ' began Smeaton.

Barstow snarled, 'Sit down, superintendent. Just sit down and *shut up*! That you're here is an unkind quirk of fate. Don't make things worse by being a damned nuisance.'

Sally Boothby smiled her thanks as she took the proffered cup of tea. She slipped one of the biscuits from the packet the nurse held, then glanced at her sleeping father.

'Dope?' she said, gently.

'Drugs.' The nurse corrected her with equal gentleness. 'A moderately mild sedative. It's wise. He needs sleep. We thought it best to let him see you first. Ease his mind as much as possible.'

Sally Boothby wondered whether this polite but brisk attitude was part of a nurse's training; this unflappabiiity; this no-panic manner. It helped, she supposed. Somebody had to keep their head at times like this. Somebody had to encourage *you* to hang on a little longer and be a little stronger.

Or perhaps they had seen so much. Perhaps they had seen *too* much, seen too much for it to register any more. All the pain, all the terror and all the sickness, day after day, year after year, must be something you had to learn to live with, and therefore must be something you had to accept as a normal part of your life.

'You feel like talking?'

It came as a slight surprise when the nurse asked the question then, without waiting for a reply, placed her own cup and the packet of biscuits on the bedside locker, pulled a chair nearer and sat down.

In a quiet voice, soft enough not to disturb the sleeping Sergeant Boothby, the nurse said, 'I usually have a break at about this time. I'll stay, if you don't mind.'

'Thanks.'

Sally Boothby estimated the nurse's age as being a good ten years older than herself. She was not old enough to be her mother, yet she was not of Sally's generation. She could have been an elder sister perhaps but, if so, a *very* elder sister.

The nurse glanced at the 'No Smoking' fastened to the wall, and said, 'Smoke, if you do. We can open a window when it comes light.'

'I . . .' Sally Boothby hesitated, then said, 'No. I'd better not.'

'Some people need to.'

'No. I've stopped it. I mustn't start again.'

'You're wise.' The nurse reached for her cup and biscuit. 'I take it that Martin has told you about your father?'

'Martin? You mean the fat gentleman? The specialist?'

'Martin,' agreed the nurse. 'One of the top men in the country.'

'He said his neck would mend.'

'Nothing to it.' The nurse almost chuckled.

'He seems to have doubts about his mind,' said Sally Boothby sadly.

'Easy, miss.' The nurse bit into a biscuit and chewed as she talked. 'He's no loony. Nor is he going to be. All he'll need is a little understanding, like all of us.'

'Full time.' The words came out on a sigh.

'And if so? It's been done a few thousand times before.'

'All right.' Sally Boothby suddenly wanted to yawn, and the need brought on a flash-feeling of guilt. She compressed her lips for a moment, swallowed, then said, 'Off the record – you can deny it the minute you get past that door – but what *will* it mean?'

'He's a policeman, so I'm told.'

'A uniformed sergeant.'

'That's out,' said the nurse firmly. 'The operative word, so far as your father is concerned, is "sedentary". No rush. No push. A very quiet life.'

'Nothing allowed to worry him. Is that what you're saying?'

'He'll worry. That's the big fallacy. People say, "Don't let him worry about things." That's stupid. It's not really what they mean. What they *really* mean is: he'll worry. He'll worry like crazy. He'll drive you up the wall worrying about things he *shouldn't* be worrying about. Stupid things. Unimportant things. But that's okay. That's part of his illness. Just don't give him anything *worth* worrying about, otherwise he won't be able to handle it. That's what it boils down to, but people can't quite grasp the truth. Not until it happens. Then they can't explain it.'

'I get the idea,' said Sally Boothby heavily.

Lines of temporary embarrassment touched the nurse's forehead, and she moved her eyes to Sally Boothby's left hand as she said, 'You're not married?'

'No.'

'Engaged?'

'No . . . not exactly.'

'Just living in hope?'

'Something like that.'

'Any sisters?'

'No. Two brothers.' Sally Boothby tasted the tea, then asked, 'Why are you asking me these personal questions?'

'Just that . . . ' The nurse stopped, took a deep breath, then said, 'No – dammit – why should I carry the whole can?

You're a sensible woman, and there's no easy way. Martin asked me. A woman-to-woman talk.'

'Go on,' said Sally Boothby, softly.

'We could all be wrong, of course. We could all be very wrong. These things – we make calculated guesses – that's as much as we're capable of.'

Sally Boothby waited.

The nurse drank tea, then continued, 'It's a possibility. That's all. Just a possibility. Something you should be warned about. He'll need somebody to look after him. Full time. For a year or so . . . maybe more.'

'Nurse him, you mean?'

'Not exactly *nurse* him.'

'Look after him?'

'Keep the world away from him. That's what it amounts to. In the old days . . .'

'I know,' interrupted Sally Boothby quietly. 'The daughter, usually the younger daughter, "looked after" the surviving parent. I have an aunt. *She* "looked after" her mother. She never married. It wouldn't have been "fair". Whatever that means. That's what she was told, and that's what she believed. When her mother died . . . ' For a moment, she looked as if she might break, and whispered, 'Oh God! Is that what you're trying to tell me?'

'It's not quite like that any more,' soothed the nurse. 'Age isn't looked upon as an illness any more. It's nothing like as bad as it used to be.'

'But that's what you're telling me? That's what the specialist has *told* you to tell me?'

'Psychiatrists perform miracles these days, miss.' The nurse retreated back into her professional shell. 'New drugs come on to the market every week. He's ill. He'll need looking after for a while.'

'Like for the rest of my life?'

'I didn't say that.'

'If it's necessary I'll do it,' said Sally Boothby, heavily. 'Of course I will. All this hinting and messing around wasn't necessary. He's been a smashing father, and I'm his daughter.

173

That's *still* what it all boils down to.'

'Sex isn't everything,' muttered the nurse. 'Having babies isn't *so* important.' She tasted tea, then continued in a more normal tone, 'I'm not married. I've no intention of getting married. That's for other women. I can lead a full life without having the same man dancing attendance all the time.'

Sally Boothby smiled, then said, 'Sure, but you made a deliberate choice.'

'Some bloody hope, eh?' Fleming turned her head and stared contempt at each officer. 'Some sodding hope.'

'I'm told it springs eternal,' drawled Barstow.

'You slimy git. You have all the answers, don't you?'

'No. I have all the *questions*. *You* have all the answers. Eventually you'll simmer down long enough to share them.'

'Does that mean something? Is that supposed to *mean* something?'

'Something. Nothing. It means whatever you want it to mean. It means we have all the time in the world. You have eternity at your disposal.'

'He killed him!' The rasped accusation was terrible in its bitter ferocity. '*I* know. *He* knows. What the hell else?'

'Too vague,' teased Barstow. 'Not even important. I don't know yet. When I do know . . . Then it *might* become important.'

'You want it like it happened? Like you say, you want it spelled out?'

Barstow moved his shoulders, as if he was not too interested.

The girl leaned forward in the chair and spat the words directly at the detective chief superintendent.

'The sodding wooden top. That's who. He went for Potty. Not a blind word. Not a word! Just jumped out behind him. That's all. Zap! Not one bleeding word. Opened the poor sod's head without even letting him see it coming. Nothing. *Nothing*! That's murder, mister whoever-you-are. That's bleeding *murder*.'

'Something along those lines,' agreed Barstow. 'If that's how it happened. If you're capable of telling the truth. If you can convince *me* you're telling the truth.'

Riddle walked the deserted streets and wished he was . . .

In the first place, he wished he was *not* Riddle. He wished he was not the sort of man he was, with the sort of name he had. Everybody called him 'Jimmy Riddle', that was an open secret, and the nickname was not based on popularity. He could not be popular. He knew that, too. Basically he was an introvert, and introverts were not given much space in which to manoeuvre in a profession top-heavy with extroverts.

In his own quiet, painstaking way, Riddle had long since reached certain conclusions. He could not be popular, therefore he tried to be just. He tried damned hard to be just; to be fair; to give everybody a fair crack.

Popularity was out, therefore he was not pulling for popularity. Indeed, and generally speaking, chief inspectors were *not* popular. Working coppers worth their salt did not take kindly to obeying too many orders. If they knew their job, they did their job in their own way, and each in his own individual way.

Therefore, they did not like chief inspectors.

A chief inspector was a cheap-rate superintendent, and yet he was *not* a superintendent and could never be a divisional officer. There was a demarcation line and, above that demarcation line, statutory powers were granted to police officers. A chief inspector held the highest rank *below* that demarcation line, therefore to the working PC the rank of chief inspector was a superfluous rank, and one more man from whom came unwanted orders.

Riddle had worked it all out, and was prepared to accept the burden of his rank without complaint.

If only . . .

If only he was *not* himself, and if only he did not carry the ridiculous name of 'Jimmy Riddle'. (*why's it so bad?*)

4 a.m. One day some academic egghead will write a treatise upon police canteens; police canteens in general, but with particular attention to police canteens when used during the after-midnight hours.

The project, if it is to have any validity, will take in the twenty-four hour, cafeteria-style, strip-lit caverns of huge, but compact forces, down to the three- or four-table cellars, with their serve-yourself, hot-drink dispensing machines, and will include the unhappy one-man rooms, which are sometimes merely annexes to offices, used by solitary coppers who drive vans through uninhabited night in the more remote areas of the United Kingdom.

Unfortunately, academics do not concern themselves with ethereal things, therefore, although sociological fundamentals and even atmospheres might be touched upon, the wraiths will be left strictly alone. They will be ignored and yet, ignored or not, they are there and always will be.

They represent generations of coppers who have chewed tasteless food and sipped tasteless drink, and called themselves fools for being what they are and where they are . . . and, in their complainings, they have left invisible marks of their passing.

Morrison needed boiling water with which to brew weak tea, therefore Morrison shambled his way into the tiny canteen. The electric kettle was empty and Morrison stared at Bulmer accusingly.

'You've taken all the water.'

Bulmer chewed at the mouthful of sandwich and grunted.

'I wish Barstow would go home.' Morrison held the kettle under the tap. 'I wish Smeaton and Riddle would go home. There's always trouble when they're around.'

'You don't know what trouble is.' Bulmer growled the remark through half-chewed sandwich.

'I'm on a fizzer.' Morrison re-lidded the kettle, then plugged it in. 'Barstow. There's no pleasing him.'

'Leave it.' Bulmer sipped tea, then added, 'I'll let you know when it boils.'

'I'll stay. Give myself a breather.'

'Leave it!' There was cold but controlled fury in Bulmer's tone. 'You're a pain, Morrison. A prolonged pain. You're the one person on God's earth I don't need. Get back to your bloody telephone. I'll let you know when the kettle boils.'

'I don't see what . . . '

'Get out of here. Take good advice when it's given; if

Barstow finds that switchboard unmanned, you'll be on *another* fizzer.'

'We're ahead of you, mate. Keep the roof flasher going.'

Hindley re-clipped the microphone, engaged first, then eased the squad car into the slow lane. He drove on dipped headlights, without any of the police signs illuminated. His eyes flicked constantly towards the rear-view and wing mirrors.

He said, 'Keep your eyes skinned for the blue flasher. They'll be coming up fast. With any luck before we leave this straight stretch.'

For a few long moments he allowed the other traffic to swing out and overtake him in the middle lane. A Volvo zipped past in the overtaking lane and, for one heart-stopping second, he thought he had boobed; he thought the Volvo was the Jag.

He could watch for only three things in the mirrors; headlights, speed and (hopefully) the following, blue-tinged sweep from Lima Fifteen.

He muttered, 'For Christ's sake, watch!'

As if in immediate answer to the remark, Chatterton said, 'They're here.'

It was there in the mirrors; the distant regular rise and fall of blue reflection, and ahead of it twin headlights slicing a path along the overtaking lane.

'Watch them.' Hindley increased the speed of the squad car and moved into the fast lane. 'Double check. Give me left or right – *our* left or right – to keep in front of them.'

As the Jag closed the gap the squad car moved right into the overtaking lane. Hindley switched on the police signs and the roof light. The Jag swung left, into the middle lane, to overtake on the nearside. Before Chatterton could call, 'Left,' Hindley was turning the wheel then, as the driver of the Jag played his bluff and turned right again, the squad car beat him to it and blocked the overtaking lane.

It was homicidal weave and counter-weave; bluff and counter-bluff at speeds in excess of eighty miles an hour.

The coloured youth could drive, but so could Hindley.

Hindley had the edge, in that Hindley knew his vehicle. The coloured youth took chances for the hell of it, but Hindley took *his* risks with a cold and calculated expertise learned at a Police Driving School. Nor did the situation help the Jag. The Jag had the legs, but other vehicles using the motorway prevented a straight run and, *always*, the rear bumper of the squad car was only yards ahead of the nose of the Jag.

The din matched the speed. Sirens howled; two sirens – Lima Fifteen had shortened the gap between itself and the Jag – and the demonic fugue warned other drivers that this was something special, and something not to become a part of.

The Jag swung left, spurted and used the slow lane to overtake an Austin. Hindley pushed down on the accelerator and, with an equal burst of speed, overtook the Austin via the overtaking lane, then crowded the Jag and forced a slight reduction in its speed.

Quite calmly, Hindley said, 'Hang on. He might brake and try to cut across behind us.'

But the Jag did not brake. Instead, the two cars raced forward, with inches between the nearside of the squad car and the offside of the Jag. And all the time, Lima Fifteen was coming up and closing in on the rear of the stolen vehicle.

The speed gradually dropped to below eighty . . . to seventy-five . . . to seventy . . .

'You've had it, you mad bastard,' breathed Hindley. 'We've *got* you.'

As if he had heard the remark, the coloured youth grinned and jerked the wheel of the Jag. The front offside mudguard of the stolen car screamed metallic protest as it smashed into the nearside panel of the squad car. Hindley held the steering wheel of Lima Ten rock steady against the impact. His foot didn't ease a hair's width from the accelerator but, as the Jag rebounded, the squad car moved even closer, until it was almost touching its quarry.

The nearside wheels of the Jag were now nudging the hard shoulder, Lima Fifteen was in position behind and they were coming up to the rear of a slow-moving lorry at a closing speed of almost fifty.

Hindley tensed his right leg, ready to slam on the brakes, and whispered, 'Now . . . get out of *that*!'

The only exit from the squad-car box was the hard shoulder, but hard shoulders are not made for Grand Prix-style driving and the hard shoulder was bordered by a grassed bank.

As the Jag turned left to overtake the lorry on the hard shoulder, Hindley snapped, 'Hang tight,' then spun the wheel and shot the squad car in a burst of speed to overtake the lorry via the fast lane. Lima Fifteen moved up to take the position left by Lima Ten and a terrified lorry driver trod hard on his brakes.

The coloured youth misjudged things. It was only a small misjudgment, but it was enough. The nearside wheel of the Jag mounted the banking, the Jag tilted, the coloured youth wrenched the steering wheel to the left to straighten up and centrifugal force, plus the angle of tilt, did the rest.

The Jag took all of twenty yards to slow to a halt, on its side and amid an uproar of shattering glass and tortured metal. Then, almost lazily, it turned turtle as the lorry shuddered to a standstill only feet away. Hindley braked the squad car in front of the over-turned Jag and Lima Fifteen stopped behind the stolen and now completely wrecked car. It was a perfect box-in, but it was not needed.

'How it's done,' observed Chatterton drily.

'It's easy, when you know how.'

Moments later, Hindley, one of the officers from Lima Fifteen and the driver of the lorry were helping the two young tearaways from the upside-down Jag. The youths were bleeding, but conscious and completely demoralised.

'Nice driving, mate,' grinned the Lima Fifteen driver.

'*He* helped.' Hindley smiled and nodded at the lorry driver. 'He did all the things I expected him to do.'

'Bloody right!' The lorry driver blew out his cheeks in mock disgust. 'I was nicked for speeding last week.'

'And, of course, you *weren't*.'

The officer from Lima Fifteen said, 'The breakdown and the blood wagon shouldn't be long. We've been on the blower.' Then he added, 'Your collar?'

'Yours,' said Hindley firmly. 'You were in charge. You herded him in. Put me down as witness.'

'Thanks.'

They were joined by Chatterton and the second officer from Lima Fifteen. In the distance, and coming nearer, they heard the rise and fall of other sirens.

The second Lima Fifteen officer said, 'Here comes the circus.'

'We'll need 'em. It's a two-lane closure for at least a couple of hours.'

Hindley eyed the side of Lima Ten, and said, 'Meanwhile, *I* have to explain why one of their beautiful motor cars has been dented . . . in triplicate.'

Later, as they strolled back to the squad car, Hindley murmured, 'Specific orders, Chatterton. To deliver you back to Radholme. Whole and undamaged. Nobody can accuse me of not trying.'

'Funny man,' grunted Chatterton.

Adams was taking it down. He was scribbling words on to foolscap – the questions, the remarks, the answers and the reactions – and it was not easy. His fingers were stiffening a little with cramp, and he was using his own make-do-and-mend shorthand. Eventually it would have to be deciphered, punctuated a little and typed out. It was going to be hell's own job, because nobody was talking at dictation speed.

'You don't believe me,' said Fleming bitterly.

'Not yet,' admitted Barstow.

'You'll *never* believe me. You sods never believe *anybody*.'

'I speak personally, of course.' Barstow's slow-paced conversation contrasted with the girl's high-pitched outbursts. 'I'm paid to disbelieve, and I do my job well. I also have this weakness. I believe *nothing* without proof.'

'You're all the bleeding same.'

'I assure you, I'm unique.'

'All of you.'

'Oh, no.'

'All the bleeding same.'

180

'You have it very wrong, young lady. The other people in this room are very gullible. I'm not.'

'You're bloody clever, eh?'

'I've never given it much thought.'

'Very smarmy?'

'No. I wouldn't describe myself as "smarmy".'

'What's a bleeding corpse, between friends?'

'I've already told her, sir . . . ' began Nash.

'You, too!' Barstow's voice was suddenly cold and hard. 'Just sit there and *keep quiet*.'

'Yes, sir.'

'Understand me well.' Barstow returned his attention to Fleming. This voice reverted back to its mocking drawl. 'I don't believe a thing. Nothing! I don't believe Chambers was murdered. Equally, I don't believe he was *not* murdered. I believe he's dead. And that's as far as my belief goes.' The quick smile carried utter disdain. 'I see before me a miserable little tart, anxious to avoid the consequences of her own crass behaviour. Somebody little more than a schoolgirl, who should have had a strap across her backside years ago. I see a creature eager to accuse anybody and everybody in a wild attempt to divert attention from herself.

'Do I credit that person with *recognising* the truth, even if it stepped forward to shake hands? In short, do I believe her? Or do I reach the obvious conclusion, that she's feeding me as much moonshine as possible? That's a neat problem. Fortunately, it is your problem. I shall not be going to prison. You will.'

'You're an evil sod,' breathed Fleming.

'You're entitled to hold that opinion. You're even entitled to express it. Just don't expect me to share it.'

'You're going to let him get away with it.'

'Oh, no.' The gentle shake of the head was a copper-bottomed warranty. 'Nobody gets away with *anything* while I'm around. Nobody! I pride myself on being something of a fanatic on that subject. You – everybody in this room – you're all liars until I believe otherwise.'

'He killed him. He murdered him.' There was a shake in

181

Fleming's voice.

'In that case, it shouldn't be too difficult; all you have to do is convince me.'

Riddle strolled along the frontage of the shops and, almost without conscious thought, checked the doors as he passed. It was a measure of the man in that he saw nothing undignified, or unbecoming to his rank, in checking property. He was a policeman, and that was what they *all* were. From cadet to chief constable, they all had the same basic job and the same basic responsibilities. The ranks differed and some were paid more than others but at the end of the day they were all police officers.

That was the trouble with men like Barstow. Barstow was no more important and no more necessary than (say) Bulmer, but Barstow would never accept that. Barstow would never admit that he was only one more policeman.

Barstow was a little like Riddle's father.

Great God, the Met was not the greatest force in the United Kingdom. It was only the *biggest*, and, some would argue, the most corrupt. But, corrupt or not, and however big it was, it was only another force.

Nor had the rank of desk sergeant been *so* extraordinary. It had been a rank beloved of the Met; a rank held out to elderly three-stripers whose street life was drawing to a close and who lacked the ability to make inspector. A supernumerary rank which, some few years ago, even the Met had recognised as unnecessary.

And yet his father was so damned sure. The finest force was the Met, and the finest rank in the Met had been the desk sergeant. He believed with all his heart that, much as the NCOs ran the Army, so the desk sergeants had run the Met.

Why, then, abolish the rank? Why, if his father was right, had other forces refused to acknowledge the rank? Why couldn't his father see the truth, accept the truth, leave it at that and take retirement as an end to one part of his life?

Thus the musings of Chief Inspector Riddle, when the man said, 'Hello. Can you get me back?'

Riddle pulled himself into the here-and-now and knew, instinctively, that the question was a prelude to more trouble.

'We require a statement,' said Barstow.

Suspicion narrowed Fleming's eyes.

Barstow continued, 'There is much legal waffle when it comes to taking a statement from moronic people like you. The policewoman will give it to you in the required jargon, but what it boils down to is this. Nobody is breaking your arm. Nobody gives a damn whether or not you make a statement. It might even be said we're doing you a personal favour by *allowing* you to make a statement. In short, who cares?

'But if you decide to make a statement, you must make it in your own unique brand of the English language. Say it – speak it – the policewoman will write it down. *She* will read it, *you* will read it, then you will sign it. Whether it is the truth, or not, is of supreme unimportance. If it is *not* the truth, *you* will be the unfortunate standing in the witness box, having your feet nailed to the floor by some unsympathetic barrister. It is also worth remembering that, if it *is* a pack of lies, you will collect a perjury charge to add to all the other baubles you've collected this busy night.' The hard smile came, and went. 'I will ask you once. Nobody will ask you a second time. Will you, or will you not, make a statement?'

Kelly licked his knuckles, where they had been slightly skinned in their contact with Wover's teeth.

Like Riddle, Kelly had a lot on his mind.

God, she couldn't wait!

His Julie had been in there, at it like knives, before the ink had had time to dry on the court papers. And, of course, Wover had been pleased to oblige.

Something would have to be done about it. There would have to be a lot of very straight talking. There might even have to be a trial run, to check that she *could* behave herself. *He* would set the pace and lay down very firm rules for a few months. Nor would there be any of this nights-out-on-your-own rubbish because that had started the rot.

'Freddie, I think we're getting a bit stale. I think we should each have an evening out, once a week, without the other.'

It had sounded very civilised and very sensible. There had been a tacit, but unspoken, assumption that she would spend the evenings with her girl friends, and he would spend his evenings with his mates. But it had not worked out like that.

Kelly doubted whether it ever *could* work out like that.

Julie had her cronies, and some of them were unmarried. Some of them were separated from their husbands, and a couple of them were divorced. They tended to spout feminist talk and sexual liberation crap, and Julie tended to listen. That (thought Kelly) had been half the trouble. Silly bitches spewing unwanted garbage into the ears of married women like Julie *had* to spawn problems.

Kelly's outrage was tempered with a growing glow of self-satisfaction.

He (Kelly) had gone out for a few jars with the boys, and that was *all* he had done. He had enjoyed a few games of darts and a few games of dominoes, and he had swopped a few dirty stories. Once or twice he had come home mildly drunk, but there had been no women. The idea of getting himself a woman had not so much as entered his head.

The self-satisfaction almost swamped the outrage.

Had they been asked, he supposed his friends would have described Julie as being a more emotionally stable person than *he* was. His friends *and* her friends would, no doubt, have made that assessment. They had even hinted as much.

Jesus Christ, emotionally stable!

Somebody, somewhere, was very wide of the mark.

Meanwhile, come daylight, James Wover would have a nice thick lip. For the moment, *that* bastard's good looks had been taken care of.

Nevertheless, it was a good job old Bell had arrived at the scene. Being a copper had certain hidden drawbacks. The bloody uniform was not at all helpful. Whatever they had done, and if you were in uniform, you could not take somebody round the nearest corner and knock hell out of them. It was not allowed. It was one of the things, one of the many things, you could *not* do.

In fact, this business of being a copper was not *quite* what the adverts made it out to be.

The man had that tell-tale, slightly-out-of-focus look of the eyes; that unnecessary half-smile of the lips; that hint of a frightened and worried frown about the expression.

He repeated his request.

'Can you get me back, mister?'

'Back to where?' asked Riddle.

'Back to . . . ' The man's mouth twitched into a quick, full smile, and he said, 'Back to Green Meadows.'

Riddle returned the smile and, in a gentle voice, asked, 'What's your name, old chap?'

'Fred.'

'You'd better come with me, Fred.'

'You're not going to thump me!' The man's expression switched to one of sudden apprehension. 'You aren't going to thump me, are you?'

'No, Fred. Nobody's going to thump you.'

The man's obvious concern, a concern touching terror, shocked Riddle. Green Meadows was a mental hospital on the outskirts of not-too-distant Haggthorpe. It was a large, walled-in institution, and had been built when young Victoria sat on the throne. It had once been a fearsome place with a terrifying reputation; more of a prison-cum-workhouse than a hospital, catering for unfortunates who were the end product of frightened ignorance. But today that old-fashioned, lock-them-away-and-forget-about-them attitude had changed. Today a broken mind was no more shameful than a broken limb, and the mind, also, could be repaired.

Or so it was claimed, so it was said whenever Green Meadows received media attention.

Riddle placed a protective arm across the thin shoulders for a moment, and repeated, 'Nobody's going to thump you, Fred, I promise.'

He was such a tiny man – not more than five foot six inches tall and skinny with it – and his clothes were obviously

185

'regulation issue'. He wore thick-soled, black boots; grey trousers of heavy flannel with deep cuffs and no hint of a crease; a well-worn, fawn-coloured pullover; an open-necked shirt with a frayed collar; a jacket which might have once been part of a tweed suit, but which was at least two sizes too big. A flat cap, placed squarely atop of wispy, greying hair completed the appearance of sorrowful inadequacy.

He trotted alongside Riddle, and kept up the conversation of a timid, frightened man trying to be brave. It was childish conversation, and he gave childish answers to Riddle's gentle probing.

'How did you get as far as Radholme, Fred?'

'I walked.'

'Really?'

'I like walking.'

'Won't they miss you?'

'I think they will.'

'Won't they be worried?'

'They'll wonder where I am.'

'I think they'll be worried,' insisted Riddle.

In his high, innocent voice, the man said, 'I was going to the pictures.'

'Really?'

'A Walt Disney picture.'

'They're nice pictures.'

'About an elephant.'

'*Dumbo.*'

'I've seen it before.'

'Oh?'

'I've seen it twice before.'

'A nice film, though.'

'Not when you've seen it before.'

'No, I suppose not.'

'So I came for a walk.'

'A nice night for walking,' observed Riddle.

'They let you walk from the main building to the concert hall,' explained the man.

'I see.'

'They don't mind.'

'No?'

'They don't take you.'

'I see.'

'So I walked out, instead.'

'That's rather naughty of you, Fred.'

'He uses his ears as wings.'

'What? Oh – er – yes. Dumbo.'

'I've seen it twice before.'

'We'll get you back,' promised Riddle. 'We'll get you back to your bed.'

'They'll thump me,' said the man sorrowfully.

'No, they won't.'

'They don't like me.'

'They'll not thump you. They'll understand.'

'I've seen it before, see? I didn't want to see it again.'

4.30 a.m. Somebody with a flair for the obvious once described war as long stretches of boredom, interrupted by highlights of terror. The same can be said of policing. Television and film scripts notwithstanding, a conscientious and even a keen copper can plod his way through thirty years of honourable service without once seeing the colour of a villain's blood.

Nevertheless, if it happens and when it happens . . . it happens.

Genuine tearaways – by which is meant men to whom violent blood-letting is a near-addiction – are comparatively rare away from the big cities. Indeed, many of them gravitate to the capital.

But however thinly they are spread, and because they are the exception in the provinces, the provincial copper stands a good chance of being caught on the hop. He tends to be without his truncheon, because the smack of a truncheon against his leg can in time become an irritation and, or so he thinks, it is never used. He sometimes does not read the signs correctly and, as a result, stands there like a lemon arguing sweet reason to an utterly unreasonable man to whom a bunched fist in the face is the only valid argument worthy of acknowledgement.

Thus are lessons learned.

Unfortunately thus also is the occasional rogue cop created.

* * *

Detective Constable John Adams walked into the canteen and flopped into a spare chair. He flexed his aching fingers, then held the hand to his mouth to kill a yawn.

'Knackered?' asked Bulmer.

'Christ, it's like writing a novel.' Adams moved his head, and added, 'Anything brewed?'

'Just this.' Bulmer touched his beaker, then continued, 'Help yourself, mate. The kettle's boiled. Morrison put it on.'

'Hard luck for Morrison.'

Adams stood up, flicked down the switch alongside the plug and, as the kettle began to sing, measured tea into a clean beaker.

'A sod of a night,' observed Bulmer gruffly.

'To put it mildly.'

'What the hell made Chatterton do it?'

'You were there. You saw what happened. *I* didn't.'

'That statement I made. It's quite true.'

'I don't doubt it.' The kettle began to boil and Adams knocked off the switch and poured bubbling water into the beaker. 'Barstow, Riddle and Smeaton. When *that* weight comes calling somebody's balls start blistering.' He poured milk into the dark tea, then spooned in sugar. 'I'm only pleased I'm not wearing Chatterton's number.'

'I'd no choice,' muttered Bulmer.

'No. Of course not.' Adams stirred the tea as he returned to the chair. 'Chatterton shouldn't have thumped him with his peg. That's all it amounts to.'

'I should have stayed at the front of the shops,' sighed Bulmer.

'He might have killed 'em both.'

'For Christ's sake! We're talking about Ernie Chatterton.'

'We're talking about a dead slob called Chambers.' Adams gingerly sipped the hot tea. 'Thanks to Chatterton, he's causing more trouble dead than ever he did when he was alive.'

'I think it must have been a mistake.'

'Balls! The girl's in there now. She's saying exactly what you said.'

'A statement?'

'Fanny Nash is taking it.'

'Oh, Jesus,' said Bulmer heavily. Then, 'Where's Ernie?'

'He's due in later. Barstow's giving himself time enough to twist the hemp into rope.'

'Barstow,' said Bulmer, with feeling, 'is a right swine.'

'And Chatterton isn't?'

'We don't know why,' mumbled Bulmer.

'Mate.' Adams sipped more tea. 'We don't have to know *why*. That he *did* is enough.'

'Just like that, eh? Screw the reason, the reason doesn't matter?'

'That's bobbying.' Adams voiced the solemn observation with a certain po-faced pomposity. He (Adams) was a jack, whereas Bulmer rode around in a squad car all day. 'It's what it's all about. It's why we have to keep our own doorstep clean.'

Policewoman Nash tried to keep the disgust from her tone and the sadness from her expression. She looked up from the statement she was writing.

'Just the facts, Fleming. We don't need any hearts-and-flowers stuff. What you saw and what you heard, that's all. We don't need your opinions. We'll reach our own conclusions.'

'The bastard killed him. *Murdered* him. I'm telling you that, aren't I?'

'Young lady,' said Nash tightly, 'I wouldn't take the time of day from you without consulting my own watch.'

'I'd be worried.'

Hindley drove the squad car at a very moderate speed back towards Radholme. Chatterton was once more in the front passenger seat, sucking calmly at a cold pipe.

'In your shoes,' insisted Hindley, 'I'd be *bloody* worried.'

'Maybe,' grunted Chatterton.

'You're not?'

'No.'

189

'They – er – they say you killed him.'

'*You* could have killed those two in the Jag.'

Hindley scowled, then in a tone carrying only part-conviction, said, 'Hardly the same thing.'

'They'd have been no less dead.'

'We were in immediate pursuit.'

'There would have been a similar enquiry.'

'They had a choice. They could have stopped the Jag.'

'Chambers had a choice.'

'I don't see how you can . . . '

'He needn't have broken into the shop.'

'Oh!'

In little more than a growled whisper, Chatterton said, 'Barstow's medal chasing.'

'For all that . . . ' Hindley shook his head slowly and, for a third time, said, 'I'd be worried.'

'That's it, then?' Having read Fleming's statement, Barstow dropped the sheets on to the desk top. 'The incident as you saw it. A highly illuminating insight into the strange workings of the criminal mind.' He continued, musingly, 'Your friend, Nicco, has some very fancy explaining to do, hasn't he? Banging away with pistols from an upper window. He'll no doubt send you a "Thank You" note for clearing up that small mystery.' His mood changed, and he stared, hard-eyed, at the girl. 'Nothing made up? Nothing gilded? A simple bash across the skull for no known reason.'

'He murdered him,' said Fleming harshly.

'You count it a great loss, do you?' Barstow mocked. 'An animal capable of heaving his pal through a window? What was *he* trying to do? Make friends and influence people?'

'He murdered him,' she repeated.

'Possibly. Eventually a jury might decide. Meanwhile some fatherly advice. Don't waste tears. Don't go mad and subscribe to a floral tribute. He wasn't worth it.'

'Of all the sodding . . . '

'You disgusting little creature, can't you understand that you have worries of your own? Take any more aboard and

190

you'll sink without trace. At the moment I'm interested in the latter part of this little lot . . . ' He touched the statement forms with the back of a finger. 'You might have to stand up in court and spout this, under oath. Is *that* clearly understood?'

'What the hell do you think I've . . . '

'Meanwhile.' He switched his gaze to Nash. 'Take this miserable wench back to the cells, constable. Give her the benefit of your legal expertise. Tell her what *she* is facing.' The curve of the lips was more sneer than smile. 'Impress the truth upon her. We handle no deals. We indulge in no you-scratch-my-back-I'll-scratch-yours tactics. What she's done, she pays for, and credit facilities are not available. I rather think that, when she fully grasps the situation some of the oil from her little lamp might evaporate, wouldn't you agree?'

Nash sighed, 'Yes, sir,' then stood up and touched Fleming's arm in a gesture indicating the end of the interview.

They met at the entrance to the police station; Riddle and the man called Fred, and Hindley and Chatterton who arrived having parked the squad car at the rear of the building.

Riddle spoke to Hindley.

'Have you anything in hand, constable?'

'I was thinking about a late meal, sir. I've been radioed to deliver Constable Chatterton. I thought I'd pick up Bulmer, if he's free, then . . . '

'Have your meal.' Riddle waved a hand. 'This gentleman is Fred.' Fred gave a quick, shy grin. 'He's from Green Meadows, and he's anxious to get home.'

'Take him back, sir?'

'Telephone Green Meadows. Get their ambulance to come and collect him. Meanwhile, if you can fix him up with a quick snack. He tells me he hasn't eaten since about five o'clock yesterday evening.'

'I'll fix it, sir.'

Fred was obviously delighted to find that he now had two uniformed friends. He happily followed Hindley to the stairs leading to the upper floor and the canteen.

'You, Chatterton.' Riddle turned his attention to the waiting officer. 'I think it likely that Chief Superintendent Barstow will want to see you in my office.'

'I haven't had *my* meal yet.'

'Arrange things with Mr Barstow.'

'I think I should . . . '

'Chatterton.' Riddle allowed his disgust to show a little. 'I have no intention of arguing. I haven't eaten either. At the moment, and as far as we two are concerned, food is of secondary importance.'

'I still think . . . '

'*I will not argue*. Into my office, if you please, Chatterton. Raise the matter with Detective Chief Superintendent Barstow.'

'You should have joined a force nearer home.'

'Mother!' pleaded Wilture.

'All the way from Leeds at this time in a morning. *And* we have to get back in time for your father to go to work.'

'Mother, I didn't *ask* them to . . . '

'When the sergeant knocked us up, and told us you'd been shot, we thought you were dead. What else were we supposed to think? It's upset us, Tony. You've no idea how much it's upset us.'

Wilture twisted his head and looked beyond his mother's shoulder to where his father stood, with one eyebrow ever so slightly cocked.

Pop knew the score. Pop had worked it out years ago, and now lived a very placid life. He was 'deaf'. The hell he was deaf! He very conveniently refused to hear what he did not want to hear, and that included most of the things mother gabbed on about.

'Isn't that right, Bert?' Mabel Wilture turned to her husband for moral support. 'Didn't it upset us?'

'What's that?' Bert Wilture inclined his head slightly.

'*We were upset*.' Mabel Wilture increased the volume. 'When we heard about Tony, *we were both very upset*.'

'Naturally.'

'Cool it, mother,' pleaded Wilture. 'You're in a hospital.

You'll awaken sick people.'

'You're sick, aren't you?'

'Well . . .'

'We thought you were dead. At least, *I* did. I don't think your father caught it, till the sergeant had had time to explain.'

'Mother.' Bert Wilture moved in to the rescue. 'We've forgot the treacle tart. We've left it in the car.'

'I thought *you* had it.'

'Eh?'

'You haven't brought me a treacle tart?' Wilture's self-image of a macho law-enforcement officer had taken some pounding during the last few hours. It was still being made to suffer. 'I mean . . .'

'You want some good food in you.'

'They'll *feed* me, mother. It'll be more substantial than rice pudding.'

'I wouldn't be too sure. You know as well as I do, it's one of the things you really enjoy. A homemade treacle tart. And we couldn't come empty handed. Then, as if reaching a great decision, she added, 'I'll go fetch it. Here, Bert, look after my handbag.'

Mabel Wilture handed a bulging monstrosity to her husband and left the tiny ward.

Wilture breathed, 'Bloody hell, mother!'

'Bide with her Tony, lad.' Bert Wilture should not have heard the remark, had it been six times as loud, and Wilture's long-held suspicion was justified. The older man went on, 'Your mother makes a lot of noise, but that doesn't mean she's an empty pot. She's a good lass, and she's had a shock.'

'I know, pop, but . . .'

'Put it this way, old son.' Wilture suddenly realised that this quietly spoken father of his was something of a droll, but very wise with it. 'She thinks the sun shines out of your arse, and that's the part you've been shot in.'

'Pop, I know, but . . .'

'She hurts when *you* hurt. Dammit, she hurts when *I* hurt. That's how good she is, and it's worth a lot.'

'You aren't deaf, are you?' accused Wilture.

'Hard of hearing.' Bert Wilture gave a quick grin. 'Stone deaf whenever your mother says anything I think she might regret. It makes it easier, all round.'

'And how do you know when?' Wilture returned the grin.

'What?'

'When she says it? That she might regret it?'

'*I* decide.' The grin came again, and this time it stayed. 'If I don't like it, I take it for granted that *she* might regret it . . . so, I don't hear it.'

'Happy families,' chuckled Wilture.

'Aren't we?'

'We are indeed, pop. I wouldn't belong to any other.'

'So, take the treacle tart, lad. Take it, and don't complain. You don't have to *eat* it.'

'I'll eat it. I'll even enjoy it.'

From the privacy of the canteen, Bulmer heard them coming upstairs. Adams had left and, watching through the slightly opened door, Bulmer saw Hindley and the strange little man approach across the landing and wished, with all his heart, that they would not arrive. He yearned for solitude in which to handle his conscience.

The canteen was a bolt hole. It was a hiding place, and somewhere in which to sit until the dejection left him.

Hindley and the little man entered the canteen and Hindley nodded a greeting to his colleague.

Bulmer grunted a return greeting.

You killed a man, Chatterton. Who cares that he was as twisted as a crummock. You killed him.

'Feel rough about it?' asked Hindley, gently.

'It shouldn't have happened,' muttered Bulmer. 'Hell's teeth, it shouldn't have happened.'

You murdered him, Chatterton. Without reason. Without so much as a hint of hesitation. Just, in there – wallop – murder!

'Don't get too upset about it, mate. It's not worrying Chatterton.'

'Who the hell knows what Ernie Chatterton is thinking? Who *ever* knew?'

And now, you hair-brained bastard, you've jockeyed me into this sweet corner. Evidence, if there's a trial. Copper against copper.

'This is Fred,' said Hindley. 'He's from Green Meadows. We have to get him back.'

Bulmer forced himself to give the little man a quick smile, and Fred returned the smile with the quick and meaningless lift of the lip corners of a puzzled loon.

As Hindley filled the electric kettle, he said, 'He's a quiet man. Chatterton, I mean. Some people might say too quiet.'

'Some people are too bloody noisy,' growled Bulmer. 'Too mouthy.'

'Some people,' agreed Hindley.

Good men versus good men, Chatterton, while the bad sods are laughing their rotten heads off.

Hindley continued with the preliminaries of snack-making as he said, 'Odd. I always figured him as a very handy guy to have around when your back was exposed. He wouldn't run. He wouldn't duck. He could be relied upon.'

'*Relied* upon!'

'That's what I thought.'

Sweet Jesus, Ernie! Why did you do it? Who needs enemies when your friends are as crazy as that? Who needs 'em, Ernie?

'Make yourself comfortable.' Barstow glanced at the chair across the desk from his own. 'I may be mistaken, but I suspect this is likely to take some considerable time.'

Riddle followed Chatterton into the office and said, 'Constable Chatterton suggests that he be allowed to have a meal before the interview.'

'Does he, indeed?'

Chatterton lowered himself on to the chair, and met the scornful gaze of the chief superintendent.

Very calmly, Chatterton said, 'I'm not asking favours.'

'Chatterton,' barked Smeaton, 'don't you ever salute your superior officers?'

'*Senior* officers,' Chatterton corrected him.

'Don't you ever *salute*?'

'Chief Superintendent Barstow isn't in uniform.'

'*I'm* in uniform.'

'You're not wearing a cap, sir.'

'That has nothing to do with . . . '

'It's the uniform, the complete uniform, that merits the salute. The rank, not the man.'

'That is insolence!'

'It's also correct, superintendent.' Riddle lowered himself on to one of the spare chairs. 'Saluting, when not necessary, is a form of lickspittle.'

'Lickspittle! Riddle, I don't call common courtesy . . . '

'Oh, for God's sake,' cut in Barstow, 'somebody give the man a salute. Genuflect in front of him. Burn incense under his nose. Anything! Just get him to stop bemoaning the fact that he isn't the lead horse in this particular team.' Adams tapped on the office door and entered. Barstow continued, 'Good. Adams, are you prepared to obey an order?'

'Er – yes, sir.'

'Without prolonged argument?'

'Of course, sir.'

'Excellent. Before you sit down, salute Superintendent Smeaton.'

'Er . . . sir?'

'Salute the superintendent, Adams.'

'Oh! Er . . . yes, sir.'

The mystified Adams brought his hand up in a very sloppy salute, then looked questioningly at Barstow.

'Beautiful,' mocked Barstow. 'My congratulations. Any self-respecting RSM would have shot himself on the spot.'

'Sir, I don't know what . . . '

'No, of course you don't, Adams. Nor is that important.' Barstow glared at Smeaton. 'Does that go some way towards taking the pressure from your self-esteem, superintendent?'

'I must object to . . . '

'Not at the moment, Smeaton. We haven't time for unimportant side issues.' Barstow switched his attention to Chatterton. 'Now, constable, you are claiming certain rights?'

'I'm entitled to a meal.'

'You're entitled to a meal,' agreed Barstow. 'I suggest you

contact Oxfam. You're not going to *get* a meal until I decide you're hungry.'

Nicco swam to the surface of consciousness on a tidal wave of foul language. He awakened every other patient in the ward, and brought the staff nurse running.

'Behave yourself,' she snapped. 'Remember where you are.'

Nicco did not know where he was. He asked for information, but the request lost itself in a thicket of swear words. Nor were they honest, Anglo-Saxon expressions. They were obscenities culled from paperback editions of tales of pornographically inclined 'tough guys'. By implication, they transformed the simple act of procreation into a bestial exhibition of foulness; they turned every aperture of the human body into a cesspit of filth, and every protuberance into high-relief indecency.

Even the staff nurse was shocked.

A nearby patient raised himself on to an elbow, squinted through the gloom and asked, 'Do we have to tolerate that?'

'Not,' said the staff nurse, grimly, 'while I'm strong enough to lift a hypodermic needle.'

Kelly had slipped into the police station to see what was happening. Like Chatterton, he was hungry and he sought a reason for not being allowed to eat.

Having been told, he hurried through the streets to find Bell and to pass on the information.

'On eggs,' he warned. 'There's enough weight in there to sink a dreadnought.'

Bell sniffed only mild interest. Bell had seen and heard it all before, and was well beyond surprise.

'Ernie Chatterton's killed a breaker,' explained Kelly.

'Oh, my word.'

'Guns.'

'Very nasty things, guns.'

'Wilture's stopped a bullet.'

Sudden concern puckered Bell's face.

'Not serious,' said Kelly, hurriedly. 'Across his backside.'

'Painful,' mused Bell, with relief.

'I wouldn't know about that, but Barstow's out. So is Smeaton. So is Riddle.'

'As you say . . . weight.'

'I just thought I'd warn you. That's all.'

'I should worry. *I* haven't shot anybody.'

'He's nasty,' moaned Morrison.

'He's nasty,' agreed WPC Nash.

Fanny Nash could not decide whether she felt more tired than she felt grubby, or more grubby than she felt tired. It certainly seemed an age since she had been called on duty, and the strange mist of dust which seemed to invade all cell areas, as always, had made her feel in immediate need of a hot shower.

'Nastiest person I've ever met,' expanded Morrison. 'Maybe that's why he's made chief superintendent. Y'know, because he's real nasty.'

'He has a job to do. He does it *his* way.'

Miss Nash felt peckish. She was not exactly hungry but, surprisingly for her, she felt a need for something hot to drink and something to nibble at.

Morrison pursued his theme.

'He could do it without being so nasty. I think he enjoys being nasty.'

'We're all nasty, Edgar. We're in a nasty profession.' She looked both sad and tired. 'It has that effect on us.'

'I wouldn't say *I'm* . . . '

'Who's in the canteen?' She was patient, she was remarkably long-suffering, but she did not want to spend too much time listening to a man like Morrison bolstering up his own petty ego. 'I could do with a fag and char, before I stagger off to bed.'

'Hindley's gone up.'

'Good.'

'And Bulmer. Bulmer went up some time back.'

'Good. I'll . . . '

'*I* never get time for a proper meal.'

'Wha-at?' She stared.

'Too busy. You people think this is a cushy number . . . '

'No, we don't.'

' . . . but it isn't.'

'We know damn well it's a cushy number.'

'That's what I mean. You're all so sure. You're all like Barstow.'

'God forbid!'

'Oh, you don't know it. You're all so . . . '

'You are a right moaning little man, aren't you?' Nash suddenly saw no reason to hide her detestation. She had had her off-duty evening ruined, Fleming had been a snotty little bitch, Barstow had been his usual self, Smeaton had been an even bigger pompous prat than ever and she (Policewoman Nash) was just about dead on her feet. Why, therefore, waste time on pretence? In a weary, heavy tone, she said, 'Edgar, you don't know what work *is*. You're like your kind the world over. You *talk* about it, but you never do it.'

'Look, I'm not going to . . . '

'Don't worry, Edgar. You're home and dry. You'll make Pension Day without losing a single drop of sweat.'

Hindley had been in touch with a night-duty official at Green Meadows. He dropped the receiver of the canteen telephone on to its rest and frowned his annoyance.

He turned to the little man, forced a smile, and said, 'Fred Ackroyd. Is that what they call you?'

The little man bobbed his head in acknowledgement.

'They aren't too suited at Green Meadows.' *pleased (yorkshire)*

'They'll thump me,' whispered Fred.

'No thumping, mate.' Hindley began to unwrap a small, but tidy parcel. 'You like buns, Fred?'

Fred nodded eagerly.

'With currants in?'

'Oh, aye.'

'Champion. That's what we've got. Sandwiches, then buns with currants in. Homemade, too.'

5 a.m. One of the things, indeed one of the thousand things, never

199

mentioned to a man when he first tries a police uniform for size . . .

The average copper spends two-thirds of his life grafting when most non-police people are not. He spends one-third of that life out on the streets in all weathers when, by the simple laws of nature, he should be tucked up in bed, and fast asleep.

Nor is that all. At those ridiculous times – at such impossible o'clocks – he has to have his wits about him because then, and arguably then more often than at any other time, the unexpected happens.

Thus, over the years, his life is turned inside out, back to front and upside down. He works the harder when other people play. He eats his meals at outrageous hours. His social life would make a sick parrot do handstands.

Contrary to popular belief, he does not suffer from flat feet. He suffers from ulcers. Nervous breakdowns are not unknown. Broken marriages are not too uncommon.

In short . . . it's a 'bobby's job'.

Secretly Barstow was rather pleased with himself. With a few well-delivered sentences he had done what he had wanted to do. He had upset Smeaton, he had flummoxed Adams, he had embarrassed Riddle and he had annoyed Chatterton. All this meant that he (Barstow) held the reins.

'You know why you're here?'

It was a half-question and it was addressed to Chatterton. They faced each other, and each knew that nobody else in the room mattered.

Chatterton said, 'Chambers is dead.'

'Quite. Unfortunately, he didn't die in bed.'

Chatterton held Barstow's eyes, but did not reply.

'He didn't die in bed,' repeated Barstow.

'If he had, I wouldn't be here.'

'For a man responsible for another man's death, you're taking it very coolly.'

'I'll sleep,' admitted Chatterton.

'Even though you've killed a man?'

'He tried to <u>break</u> arrest,' lied Chatterton.

'Balls.'   *resist?*

'He tried to break arrest.' Chatterton repeated the lie in a very controlled and deliberate tone.

'We will,' said Barstow softly and dangerously, 'clear some of the undergrowth. We will start by reaching firm ground, then we will establish a base-line. Chambers is dead. Do we agree upon that point?'

'He's dead.'

'You killed him.'

'I hit him with my staff.'

'And killed him.'

'Did I?'

'You surprise me, Chatterton,' said Barstow. 'For a man so sure of his own innocence, you're very cagey. Before long you'll be screaming the place down for a solicitor.'

'You say I killed him,' said Chatterton flatly.

'Are you saying you *didn't*?'

'I hit him with my staff and he's dead.'

'And?'

'It's possible I killed him. If so . . . ' Chatterton moved his shoulders.

'No more than that?'

'He's no great loss.'

'You knew him well, did you?'

'No.'

'Just a snap judgement? "He's no great loss." You're God, are you? You claim the authority to give or take life as you see fit?'

'He was breaking arrest.'

'Therefore, "He's no great loss."?'

'Sir.' Chatterton spoke quite calmly and a little slowly. 'Alive, he would have caused suffering. He was a tearaway. He would certainly have committed GBH. He might have committed murder, had he lived.'

'I see.' Barstow raised one eyebrow just enough to convey disdain. 'The proposition being that you killed Chambers on the problematic assumption that, had he lived, he *might* have committed murder?'

'He was breaking arrest.'

'Now you've retreated to a neutral corner,' smiled Barstow.

201

'A wise move.'

'He was breaking arrest,' repeated Chatterton.

'That's not what I've been told.'

'Oh yes, sir. *I'm* telling you.'

'He was . . .' Barstow lifted a statement form from the surface of the desk, and read, '"He was holding his truncheon ready, before he left his hiding place . . ." That's *you*. "He ran at Chambers . . ." That's you again.' Barstow looked up. 'That's what it says here, Chatterton. Black and white, and above a witnessed signature. No messing about. No room for doubt. No suggestion of "arresting". The word isn't even mentioned. The staff is ready, there in your hand, before you make a move. You were going to clobber him.'

'No.' Chatterton shook his head.

'You were merely eager to show him a police truncheon? Is that it?' mocked Barstow. 'You're convinced he's never seen a police truncheon in his life before? You're going to make his day?'

'No,' said Chatterton calmly.

'You surprise me. In that case, are we allowed to know *why* you were dancing around waving a police truncheon in the breeze?'

'It was the best I could do against guns.'

'Ah! *Guns*? Plural?'

'I didn't know how many. I still don't know how many.'

'Just the one. A Luger pistol.'

'It seemed wise not to waste too much time checking.'

'Did it? Did it also seem wise to eliminate the risk altogether by killing him?'

'Chief Superintendent Barstow, sir.' Chatterton's voice remained rock steady but life, in the shape of what might have been disgust, came to his eyes. 'When criminals carry guns, they have little cause for complaint if police officers use truncheons.'

'And apologise later?'

'My salary doesn't merit the risk of apologising before.'

'The rule, therefore, is "Hit first"?'

The corners of Chatterton's mouth lifted slightly, and he

said, 'He was breaking arrest.'

'You're the only one who says so.'

'I was the arresting officer. I'm the only one who *knows*.'

'Bulmer was there.'

'He had his hands full with the girl.'

'The girl was there.'

'She had her hands full with Bulmer.'

'I have statements,' purred Barstow. 'Very carefully worded statements. One from the girl, Fleming. One from your fellow-officer, Bulmer. Rest assured, Chatterton, I have proof.'

Chatterton's expression called Barstow a liar.

Barstow repeated, 'I have proof, Chatterton.'

Chatterton nodded, but the nod meant nothing.

'You had your truncheon out,' said Barstow. 'You were ready to hit him.'

'I thought he was armed.'

'You *hit* him.'

'He was breaking arrest.'

'Chatterton!' snapped Smeaton. 'Be *told*. Accept your responsibilities like a man.'

'How many?' asked Chatterton gently.

'How many what?' Barstow frowned.

'How many people asking questions?'

'Just me,' said Barstow, grimly. 'The others are onlookers. Ignore them. Answer *my* questions. Did you hit him on the head?'

'I aimed for the shoulder. He moved.'

'You aimed for the shoulder?'

'The book insists we should.'

'But you opened the *back* of his skull.'

'He was breaking arrest' Chatterton matched mockery with mockery.'He'd turned to run away.'

'You have it all worked out? An answer to everything?' sneered Barstow. 'You're a liar.'

The hint of a smile played around Chatterton's lips.

'You're hungry, Chatterton,' said Barstow gently. 'Go off duty to eat. Stay off duty until you're told otherwise. And, while you're eating, remember this. Chew it over with your food. Everybody in this office knows you killed Chambers, and killed him deliberately. The girl knows. Your colleague, Bulmer, knows. Medical evidence removes all doubt. You'll stand in a dock, my smart little friend. You'll hit the headlines. You'll spend the rest of your miserable life wishing you'd kept that truncheon tucked away in its pocket.'

'Am I suspended from duty?' asked Chatterton calmly.

'Of course.' Barstow's mouth curved into a tight but mirthless smile. 'But rest assured you're not going anywhere. It isn't a holiday. You'll be available, whenever we want you, and for whatever reason.'

The canteen seemed overcrowded. All three chairs were occupied and Hindley had hoisted one cheek of his rump on to the table and was letting his left leg swing freely. All four occupants of the room held beakers of tea. Bulmer and the man, Fred, held their beakers with the palms and fingers of both hands wrapped around the body of the beaker. Bulmer held his beaker steady, and stared with unseeing eyes at the inch or so of near-cold tea, while Fred raised and lowered his beaker to and from his lips in a slow, rhythmic movement and slurped noisily as he drank.

Policewoman Nash filled one of the ancient armchairs to overflowing and held her beaker in one hand and a smouldering cigarette in the other.

Despite the lack of a chair on which to sit, Hindley seemed the most relaxed person there. He sipped tea and chewed a sandwich in what was, outwardly, quiet contentment.

Fanny Nash raised the cigarette to her lips, inhaled, tilted her head, blew a plume of smoke at the ceiling then broke the silence.

'Not a very happy night,' she mused, quietly.

Nobody answered for a full thirty seconds then, without raising his eyes from the tea in his beaker, Bulmer muttered, 'Ernie Chatterton deserves to be shafted.'

'Chatterton doesn't give a damn.' Hindley bit into the half-eaten sandwich, and continued speaking as he chewed. 'It's all black and white to Chatterton. No greys. No mights.

No maybes. He's not even *concerned*.'

'Hell's teeth! He's *killed* a man.'

'We *think* he's killed a man.' Nash glanced meaningly at the little man. 'Nobody can be sure.'

'He's killed an unwanted animal. He's eliminated vermin.' Hindley drank tea to clear his mouth. 'That's Chatterton's belief and he has no regrets.'

'He's bloody mad.'

'We're all tired.' Nash drew on her cigarette again. 'I think even Barstow was feeling the strain.'

'Barstow,' said Hindley, 'is a man besotted by the sound of his own voice.'

'He likes to talk,' agreed Nash.

'Noise versus silence,' opined Hindley wisely. 'Silver versus gold. I know where *my* money goes.'

'You approve, do you?' Bulmer looked up. There was a nasty edge to his tone. 'You approve of a copper killing a man he's supposed to be arresting?'

'No . . . I *don't* approve.' Hindley's reply was measured and carefully spoken. 'I don't give a damn about Chambers. I don't know him, I don't even know his form, but I can guess. A clown who's capable of shop-breaking and shooting at coppers deserves all he gets. The Civil Liberties crowd might mourn Chambers . . . *I* won't. But Ernie Chatterton is due to be tarred as a right royal bastard, and every copper in this force will be tarred with him.

'That means the wrong people will be rooting for us. The wrong people will be rooting for *me*. People I can do without. That's extra mustard put on my plate – put there by Ernie Chatterton – and I can do without *that*, too. That's the bit I don't like. I can live with it, but I won't like it.'

For an off-the-cuff effort, it was quite a speech, and it was followed by the thoughtful silence it deserved. The silence stretched itself out until it wore a thin cloak of awkwardness. Fred Ackroyd continued to drink his tea with the noise of a badly trained child. Bulmer scowled his worry at the surface of the tea in his beaker. Nash enjoyed a few more lungsful of tobacco smoke, then squashed what was left of the cigarette into a tin ashtray before wearily pushing herself to her feet.

'A hot bath, then bed for Aunty Fanny,' she murmured.

'This little copper, too.' Hindley raised the hand holding what was left of the sandwich, and curtained a yawn with the back of his hand. 'Get Fred, here, home. That should just about see the shift through.'

Chatterton had left his helmet at the police station. He wore a loose-fitting, lightweight mac over his tunic. He strolled, rather than walked, and as he made his way home he puffed at his pipe.

His outward appearance was not one of bravado. Nobody was there to watch him, therefore he had no reason to be other than himself. Nor was he a strange man nor in any way an evil man. He was a man of his time, a police officer of his age and, although his kind were still thin on the ground, the numbers were growing.

He had stood at too many picket lines; been stoned too often and spat upon too much. Gradually it had become personal. The insults and abuse had been aimed at *him* rather than at what he represented. Then like the separation of water and oil in a shaken flask, beliefs and opinions had ossified. Where there had once been doubt, where there had been fluidity, there now remained hard crystallisation.

He would hear no arguments. He *knew*!

The bad were bad – but *bad* – and giving them a millimetre of leeway was a weakness they would exploit. Policing the bastards meant smashing them, or being crapped upon. Law enforcement was not a game. It was no longer even a profession. The law set the limits but, inside those limits, anything was permissible. It was naked warfare, and Patton had once voiced warfare's basic tenet.

'The object of war is not to die for your country. The object of war is to make damn sure the other sonofabitch dies for *his*.'

Chambers had died for his 'country' – assuming scum like Chambers knew the meaning of the word – so where was the gripe? He (Chatterton) had not introduced guns into the scheme of things but, once they had *been* introduced, any thought of pussyfooting had been pushed aside. Coppers had been given some very fancy funerals, coppers had been dumped in a wheelchair for life, because they had arsed around, waiting for the other guy to show his hand.

No way!

Chatterton paused in his stroll homewards, to stroke a match flame across the surface of ashed-up tobacco.

Suspension from duty did not worry him. The pay would come in, but he would not have to work for it. He could catch up on his sleep; catch up on his gardening; catch up on his reading.

Barstow did not worry Chatterton. Barstow was all wind and piss. Even assuming that Barstow's verbiage was based upon genuine outrage (which, of itself, was unproven) Barstow could not even raise a ripple. A good lawyer, twelve terrified nerks in a jury box and an accused who was not intimidated by the palaver of a Crown Court and Barstow was sunk before he had even set sail.

He (Chatterton) would walk out of court a free and much-maligned man, leaving Detective Chief Superintendent Barstow to crawl into the nearest dark corner with his tail between his legs.

It was going to be a breeze.

Chatterton waved out the match, tossed it into the gutter and resumed his journey home.

'We must nail him.' Smeaton made the pronouncement in a voice which suggested he had stumbled across a natural law capable of matching gravity. 'We must make an example of him. Good God, if the public hear of this . . .'

'If!' The impression was that Barstow spat the two-letter word out, then retrieved it in order to make a meal of it. 'Smeaton, you must have taken up permanent residence on Cloud Nine. "If" does not come into it. The public *will* hear of it. When bleary eyed John Doe crawls downstairs to enjoy his breakfast Cornflakes, when he turns on his transistor to verify that the world is continuing its normal, monotonous spin, he will hear nothing else. Every flannel-brained disc jockey will be feeding that topic to him, complete with opinions, discussions and inter-round summaries. The state of the national economy will be of no importance, by comparison. A naughty policeman has been wicked enough to slaughter a Persil-white tearaway. That's the best news since Goose Green.'

'I – I . . . ' Smeaton moved his hands in a helpless gesture.

'We will take what is humorously referred to as "appropriate action". Nobody will be satisfied. Short of public execution, nobody is *ever* satisfied. But . . . ' Barstow gave an exaggerated sigh. 'Our best is all we can do. All the public can ask of us.' There was a pause, then Barstow ended, 'Go home, Smeaton. Find what consolation you can between the sheets. You've had a busy night. Don't over-tax your mind.'

Policewoman Nash also walked home. It was not much of a distance, but she walked slowly and with bent shoulders. Her step lacked its usual spring. Her expression was without its normal cheerfulness.

In some strange way, she felt she had failed. She had done all that had been asked of her, but she had failed.

Barstow was part of it. Barstow had honed the verbal equivalent to the Chinese water torture into a fine art. To merely be in his company when he was at full spate resulted in a vague buzzing between the ears. The man was an oral mutation. He let loose a great Amazon of words, and they swept innocent and guilty alike ahead of them. If it was not directly aimed at you, a first hearing of his command of naked sarcasm brought on the giggles, touched with outright admiration, but that did not last. Soon, the realisation came that he was *not* being funny. He was *not* playing to the gallery. This drawn-out, blistering word play was his normal manner of conversation. Sardonic insinuation was more than a part of him and no temporary put-on.

To hear him speak was *always* to hear an outpouring of vituperation. Ergo, nobody could *ever* please him.

And not to please, not to be credited with doing her best, saddened Policewoman Nash. She was human enough to like praise, but realistic enough to know that praise had to be earned. Equally, she was honest enough to know that the night's work had been more than usually harrowing. The little cow, Fleming, could never truly mourn anybody but, after the initial shock of Chambers's death, she had wit enough to realise that, with the killing, she had a weapon of a sorts in her hand with which to goad the police. Barstow had quietened her – Barstow could quieten *anybody* – but, dammit, he had not seemed to have the sense to know that his task had been made easier by the way she (Nash) had handled things in the cell. Nor had it been too easy. A wrong word, even a wrong emphasis, might have ruined the case against . . .

And *there* was a thing!

On the face of it, Ernie Chatterton had committed simple, no-nonsense murder. The saints in heaven knew why. There had to *be* a reason, but that reason was well beyond the understanding of Fanny Nash.

Not – and without wisdom after the event – that Chatterton had ever been her favourite copper. There was something about him. There always had been. He was too – what was the best word? – too "controlled". Not wearing your heart on your sleeve was one thing, but denying you even *possessed* a heart was something else. The blokes did not seem to notice it but, maybe because she was a woman, Fanny Nash had long ago tumbled to the truth. Where normal people had emotions, Ernie Chatterton had something not too far removed from chilled steel.

She shook her head, as if to clear her mind of the after-effects of too much booze.

She muttered, 'Oh, shit!' in a very unladylike tone.

Then she concentrated upon bath and bed.

'Why?' asked Bulmer, and sullenness dropped his voice a few semi-tones.

'Reasons.' Hindley held the squad car door open, and spoke to the little man. 'Into the back, Fred. You're going home.'

Bulmer rounded the car and climbed into the front passenger seat. He waited until Hindley had strapped himself in, called control on the radio and was easing the car from the car park before he spoke again.

'Why not an ambulance?' he asked.

'They won't send an ambulance.' Hindley braked the car and checked that the road was clear. 'Some portentous clown at Green Meadows suggests we let him walk back. To teach him "good manners", that was the way he put it.'

From the back, Fred murmured, 'They'll thump me.'

'There'll be no thumping, old son,' promised Hindley.

The car gathered speed on the road and, ahead of them, the roof-line showed black against a slowly lightening sky.

'A lousy night,' muttered Bulmer.

'I've known better.'

'Why the hell Chatterton had to . . . '

'Drop it!' Hindley carefully timed the speed of the car to catch an approaching traffic light as it turned to green. 'Forget it, till it's time to remember it again.'

'Look, when a copper deliberately . . . '

'He's not a copper,' growled Hindley.

'Eh?'

'For Christ's sake, man. It takes more than the uniform to make a copper.' The growing impatience was there in Hindley's words. 'You, above all people, should know that. If you're right, when he lashed out with his truncheon – if he did what you *say* he did – that was him out. *Mister* bloody Chatterton, what the hell he wears. That's when he left the force. The rest is all whipped cream.'

'It's all right for you. But . . . '

'Charlie.' Hindley concentrated his eyes on the road ahead, but spoke with great sincerity. 'He's a bad bugger. He isn't worth a toss. If he hadn't the uniform, you wouldn't think twice. You'd be there, in the witness box, sending him to where he belongs. And that's *it*. That's where he *does* belong. That damn uniform doesn't turn a sod into a saint.'

Bell stretched his arms, and said, 'Roll on six o'clock.'

'Amen to that,' agreed Kelly.

The last hour of the night shift was ticking its way into

history and, as was their practice – as was the practice of just about every copper reaching the tail-end of an all-night stint – the tempo had slowed down to bare movement, and the time was being passed by the regurgitation of topics and opinions already soggy from mastication.

'You're sure it *was* Martha?' Bell lighted a cigarette as he asked the question. 'I mean – y'know – I can't see Martha messing around like that.'

'I'm pretty sure it was.'

'Aye. It's just that . . . y'know.'

'I'm pretty sure,' insisted Bell.

'Bloody women!'

Bell threw away the match, leaned more heavily against the shop-door upright and settled down to enjoy the last cigarette of the shift.

'About earlier,' began Kelly.

'What's that?'

'Wover. When I . . . '

'It didn't *happen*,' interrupted Bell.

'Ah, but it . . . '

'It didn't happen.' Bell tilted his head, and gazed with studied innocence at star patterns still visible in the pre-dawn sky. 'A thing doesn't happen, mate, you can't talk about it. Because it hasn't *happened*.'

'Oh!'

'So let's not . . . ' As the Rover turned the corner and braked to a sudden halt, Bell clutched his middle and bent forward.

'Hey, what . . . '

'*What are you two doing?*'

Smeaton bawled the question as he wound down the window.

Kelly's mouth opened and closed with the steady regularity of a goldfish taking ant eggs.

Bell tottered to the kerb edge, raised a hand as if to try a salute, seemed to become aware of the cigarette and dropped it on to the pavement.

He croaked, 'My stomach, sir. I must have eaten something.'

'Which beat are you responsible for, Bell?'

'"D" Beat, sir. I . . . I felt bad. I thought I'd better find Constable Kelly, before – y'know . . . '

'Before what?'

'I honestly thought I was going to flake out, sir.'

'Have you radioed in?'

'No, sir.'

'Why not?'

'I thought . . . ' Bell seemed to force a brave but wan smile. 'Everybody busy. I thought I'd stick it out until I was relieved.'

Smeaton scowled. He knew – or at least he was ninety per cent sure – he was being suckered. He glared his disbelief up at Bell.

Bell suddenly grabbed the roof of the Rover, clutched his gut with his free hand and made horrible, vomiting noises.

'For God's sake! Don't spew all over the car.'

'No, sir.' Bell straightened up. If his expression was to be believed, the effort was very painful. 'I'm sorry, sir. It's just that . . . '

'Kelly.'

Smeaton reached a decision. He had had enough for one night. First Barstow, now this. What matter that this miserable copper was putting on an Oscar-winning performance in order to dodge a well-deserved Misconduct Report? Who cared after a night like this? Who was to know?

Nevertheless Smeaton could not resist, 'You were smoking a cigarette, Bell.'

'Yes, sir.' Bell looked contrite. 'I – I thought it might help. I'm sorry, sir.'

Kelly joined the charade, and Smeaton said, 'Take Bell back to the station, Kelly.'

'Yes, sir.'

'Then resume your patrol.'

'Oh yes, sir. Of course, sir.'

Smeaton gave them a last, long stare, then wound up the window and drove the Rover along the road and towards his home.

212

The recovery was quite miraculous. Having given the Rover time to get well out of sight, plus time to be driven back to the scene via side streets, Bell straightened and grinned his victory.

'An early bed,' he said.

'Think he knew?'

'Of course he bloody well knew.' The impression was that Bell counted the question as being hardly worth an answer. 'We *all* knew. We'll have to walk on eggs for a few weeks, till he gets it out of his system . . . that's all.'

'Come on. Let's get you back to the nick, you crafty old devil.'

'The object,' explained Bell, 'is to grind the bastards into the dust. If they *know* they're being ground, that merely adds to the pleasure.'

5.30 a.m. The 'Laughing Policeman' and the 'Pantomime Bobby' may be creatures of pure fiction, but they are very necessary and very laudable creatures.

Nobody laughed at the Gestapo. Nobody laughs at the KGB.

To laugh at an institution while, at the same time, respecting that institution is a peculiarly British trait. The man in the street chuckles at the British bobby, but the guy on the sidewalk rarely chuckles at a member of 'New York's Finest'.

More than that even. The copper who can handle his job is prepared to be laughed at. He even joins in the fun.

Thus on marches, political rallies and protest get-togethers the coppers walk alongside or stroll amongst the protesters. They laugh and exchange jokes. It defuses situations and quietens anger better and faster than any baton charge or water cannon.

It licks the red-faced rabble rouser, every time.

How the hell can you inflame a mob against a handful of uniformed comedians the members of that mob have just been cracking jokes with?

It is so easy. It is so 'British'.

The cell area stank. The cell area always stank when prisoners had been bunked up for the night. The stench was unique to cells and cell areas. It seemed to be an objectional mix of stale urine and sweaty feet. It mattered not how clean the prisoners, nor how efficient the toilet arrangements, the smell was always there.

Morrison knew the smell from past experience. On permanent night duty, he was always 'bridewell' officer, and this *jail* necessitated an hourly check, through the peep hole in the *atten* door, to ensure that the 'guests' were still healthy and in their right senses.

There was, perhaps, a hint of voyeurism about this business of squinting at fellow-creatures; of watching them, when they did not know they were being watched. He would never have admitted it, but Morrison did derive some slight pleasure from this aspect of his duty. In the past, he had seen things. He had seen lips moving, as men talked to themselves. He had seen self-proclaimed 'tough guys' staring at the ceiling while tears ran, unheeded, down the sides of their face.

He had seen so many things.

He bent to look through one of the peep holes and saw Sammy Sutcliffe, huddled in a blanket and obviously fast asleep. The coarse brown blanket was pulled high, and half-covered his face. The expelled air, as he breathed, moved the wisp of hair which had fallen across his forehead.

Morrison moved to the other occupied cell. He peered inside, but only saw the dark blue of the screen material. WPC Nash had not forgotten. Fanny Nash never forgot those sort of things. A female prisoner had to be protected from the licentious gaze of raunchy policemen, therefore there was a screen provided in order to ensure privacy. Like all things 'official', it was bloody stupid, of course. Who the hell wanted to look? And if he (Morrison) wanted to do more than look he had the cell keys.

Morrison sniffed and moved from the cell area.

Fanny Nash was a great one for telling other people how little they worked. *She* could talk! Her job was to be here keeping an eye on the female prisoner. Until another WPC came on duty at nine anything could happen. And if it did . . .

'I'm away.'

'What? Oh!'

Morrison collided with Adams as he left the cell area.

'Home,' said Adams. He blew out his cheeks. 'I don't want another night like this in a hurry.'

'I've another hour of it,' complained Morrison

Adams glanced at the wall clock and corrected, 'Not quite.'

'Everybody else is going off duty.'

Again they almost collided with Bell and Kelly, as those two officers entered the Charge Office.

Bell was once again holding his stomach.

Bell said, 'I'm going off duty.'

'What the . . . '

'Upset stomach.' Then, exaggerating things a little, he added, 'Smeaton's orders.'

'Hey, steady on.' Something not far from panic quavered Morrison's tone. 'If many more go off duty, there'll only be me left.'

'Britain needn't tremble,' murmured Bell.

The late, and much loved, John Betjeman had a soft spot for Victorian architecture, but even the late, and much loved, John Betjeman would have been pushed to find anything pleasant about the lines of Green Meadows. The dark-red bricks, the high and sharply pitched roofs, the scores of poky windows and the arched, heavily doored entrance combined to give an air of threat to anybody approaching. The main pile seemed to scowl and glower. It gave promise of everlasting impatience; of subtle and never-ending petty denials; of a regime deliberately tailored to break the will of any man or woman sentenced to live there.

In a voice touched with sympathy, Hindley said, 'You're home, Fred.'

'They'll thump me,' whispered the little man.

Hindley braked the squad car to a halt, said 'Stay there,' then climbed out and walked to the main entrance.

He thumbed the brass bell push let into the stone lintel, then waited. He waited a full two minutes, but nothing happened. No approaching footsteps were heard. No extra light was switched on. He pushed the button of the bell a second time

215

and again waited. The result was the same, and Hindley began to look cross.

He growled, 'The buggers will come this time,' and rested a thumb on the bell push and kept it there.

It took almost another two minutes before the big man hurried around the corner, ready and eager to do battle. He was built like a bruiser, with a fleshy face and a head showing premature baldness. The thick-lipped mouth and the wide-spaced, button-dark eyes testified to an arrogance based upon petty authority. Hands with heavy fingers and muscular wrists poked from the sleeves of a cotton jacket which was at least two sizes too small. The anger was that of petulant outrage; the anger of a small tyrant whose domain had been trespassed.

'Who's making all the row?' he demanded.

'I am.' Hindley released the pressure on the bell push.

'What is it? What do you want?'

'Who's asking?' countered Hindley.

'I'm night-duty charge nurse. I was . . . '

'Asleep?'

'Of course I wasn't asleep.'

'Busy?'

'Look, what do you want?'

'I want whoever's in charge.'

'I'm in charge, until the day staff comes on duty.'

'Are you the lunatic I spoke to?' Hindley stepped nearer, and faced the charge nurse from a distance of less than a yard. 'Are you the clown who suggested I turn one of your inmates loose to walk back from Radholme under his own steam?'

'Oh!'

'*Was* it you?'

Instead of answering, the charge nurse stared dislike, and said, 'We don't use the front entrance. We use the tradesman's entrance.'

'If I ever become a tradesman, I'll remember that.'

Bulmer had left the squad car and was approaching. The little man accompanied him, behind his right shoulder, patently terrified.

'That's him,' said the charge nurse. 'That's the little

trouble-maker.'

'He hasn't given *us* any trouble,' said Hindley.

Bulmer arrived within easy speaking distance and added, 'He's frightened you'll thump him.'

The quick expression on the charge nurse's face left neither Bulmer nor Hindley in doubt. Bulmer unfastened the left breast pocket of his uniform.

'You *will* thump him, of course?' teased Hindley.

'Hey, mister . . .'

'Quiet, Fred. You – er – *will* thump him?'

'He'll be "reprimanded",' said the charge nurse with feeling.

Hindley nodded slowly, then asked, 'Who comes to visit him?'

'Nobody. They're all fed up with his ways.'

'Really?'

'He wets his bed.'

'Terrible.'

'He makes a nuisance of himself by pretending not to understand.'

Bulmer had taken a ballpoint from his pocket, and was scribbling on to an open page of his notebook.

'But he *should* understand . . . shouldn't he?' said Hindley gently.

'He's thick. Thicker than most.'

'My friend is taking all this down,' said Hindley with a smile. He gestured to the little man and said, 'Come here, Fred,' then, when the little man hesitated, 'Don't be scared, Fred. Nobody's going to thump you . . . ever again.'

Very slowly the little man approached.

'As from now he'll have a visitor,' explained Hindley, carefully. 'A regular visitor. I have, you see, now *another* friend.'

'And he,' added Bulmer, 'has *two* friends. Two regular visitors.'

'Would you like that, Fred?' Hindley spoke to the little man. 'If we visit you, regularly, will you be a good chap?'

'Oh yes, mister. That would be nice.'

'And you'll tell us if anybody thumps you?'

'Oh yes, mister. I'll tell you.'

'And you won't make them cross with you?'

'No mister.'

'Right. You stay here, old son. We'll talk things over with this gentleman.'

Hindley's fingers tightened on the charge nurse's arm, just above an elbow. The tightness of the grip made the charge nurse wince and, later, three tiny bruises showed where Hindley's fingertips had been.

He murmured, 'A word in your ear, my friend.'

When they were out of earshot of the little man, Hindley said, 'My colleague is not taking this down.'

'That *doesn't* mean that we aren't very serious,' added Bulmer.

'What the devil . . . '

'We'll ask him, and he'll tell us,' said Hindley grimly.

'Any more thumping and you're in the schnook,' growled Bulmer.

'Look, you've absolutely no right . . .'

'Of course we haven't,' agreed Hindley flatly. 'But we'll damn soon notify somebody who *has* the right.'

'Somebody from the Home Office,' added Bulmer.

'A few "investigative journalists",' suggested Hindley.

'You could end up very famous.'

'Or very notorious.'

'It's, it's not my policy,' mumbled the charge nurse.

'Change the policy.'

'I – I . . . '

'Change the policy,' repeated Hindley.

'I needed you.' Bulmer's voice was hard and tight. 'I needed somebody like you to prove I'm not quite the biggest bastard alive. You'll do, buster. You'll do nicely.'

'You get the gist?' The smile accompanying Hindley's question was neither friendly nor comforting.

'I'll – er – do my best.'

'Hope it's good enough.' Bulmer returned notebook and ballpoint to their pocket. 'Hope our friend thinks it's good enough.'

* * *

218

The men reporting in for the early shift drifted into Radholme Police Station. Seven men and a sergeant were due to take over the policing of the section at six o'clock, with a policewoman coming on duty at nine. Adams would remain on call, with other CID men available throughout the sub-division if necessary.

The men wandered in, singly, as they made their way from their respective homes. Some came by car, others who lived nearer walked. They all had that shiny, clean-shaven, newly washed look, and they all had that glaze about the eyes of men recently abed who have left their slumber reluctantly.

By this time Morrison had pieced the night activities together, and was able to pass on the information. Their reactions varied.

'Poor old Wilture. A bullet up the Khyber. What's it do? Diarrhoea or constipation?'

Or . . .

'Boothby? Oh, God! At a guess, that's Vic finished.'

Or . . .

'Barstow? Oh, my Christ! Let me initial the Information Sheet and get out of here.'

Only one man said, 'I'm not too surprised. Chatterton *would* do that.'

There had been a killing and there had been a suspension, there had been a breaking and two of their colleagues were in hospital, but none of the men on early shift showed undue concern. The night shift had handled its own problems and, in the next eight hours, new problems would arise and they in turn would have to be dealt with.

A new shift was dovetailing into an old shift, but although the joint was smooth and tight, one did not belong to the other. The men on night duty had handled things *their* way, but that was not necessarily the way of the men coming on duty.

It was a new shift, a new day and, as always, a new outlook.

Barstow and Riddle walked, side by side, towards where their respective cars were parked. They had left the building via the rear door and, as they approached the two vehicles, Riddle's expression showed mild disgust as he was reminded of the damage to the rear of his car.

It seemed a small lifetime since the bearded man had driven into the boot; since he (Riddle) had braked suddenly at the sight of Boothby in the entrance of Woolworth's store.

'Tired?'

The sudden question almost made Riddle start. Since the departure of Smeaton, Barstow had been uncommonly silent.

'It's been a long night,' he admitted.

'Smeaton?'

Again it was a single-word question, but this time it was not a simple question. It carried whole sentences, whole paragraphs, of innuendo.

'Superintendent Smeaton is my divisional officer,' said Riddle quietly.

'I didn't ask that.'

'He does his job in the best way he knows how.'

'Riddle,' drawled Barstow, 'you're not a ballet dancer. Wear clogs for a change. Smeaton is the modern substitute for the old-fashioned migraine. You know it. I know it. *I'm* prepared to air that knowledge.'

'I don't take sides, sir.'

'Wisdom or foolishness?' Barstow chuckled. 'I credit you with not being too scared.'

'Thank you, sir.'

'Equally, when you pass an opinion, it's been thought out.'

'I'm inclined not to pass opinion until I know most of the facts.'

'And you don't "know" Smeaton?' mocked Barstow.

'I know some of his idiosyncrasies,' smiled Riddle.

'Oh, very diplomatic. Very tactful.'

'I know some of *yours*,' murmured Riddle. 'I've learned a few more since I came on duty.'

'And?' challenged Barstow.

They had reached Barstow's car, but the detective chief superintendent made no move to unlock the door. They stood there in the cool of pre-dawn and Riddle sensed that this man-to-man conversation might determine much of his future.

He kept the delivery gentle, and as subjective as he was able, as he answered. 'You're proud of the reputation you've built up. Proud of it, but not too sure of it. That's why you over-egg the pudding. Talk a little too much. It's expected of you, and you deliver. When you don't deliver, when you *can't* deliver, you try to cover it by being particularly obstreperous.'

'"Obstreperous". That's a long word, short on meaning.'

'As now.'

'I'm being obstreperous?'

'You can't deliver,' said Riddle mildly. 'Chatterton won't break, therefore you can't deliver.'

'Chatterton will stand in a dock,' promised Barstow.

'He'll walk away.'

'He will have *been* there. He will have been crucified.'

'A crucifixion without nails. Chatterton won't mind that.'

'Chatterton,' said Barstow, 'is under the impression that he's fireproof. Nor, sadly, is he alone in that belief. The estimable Superintendent Smeaton is of a like opinion. Tell me, what are *your* thoughts on the subject?'

'I've already voiced them.'

'That he'll walk away from court?'

Riddle nodded.

'But thereafter?'

'If he is allowed to stay in the force . . . '

'He'll be allowed to stay on in the force,' said Barstow grimly.

'I see.'

'With boring regularity, I hear people who should know better mouth a certain phrase. "A community gets the police it deserves." One of those instant-wisdom phrases, beloved of politicians. It means damn-all, Riddle. Every man or woman who utters it is a hopeless fool.'

'I hope they get a *better* force than they deserve,' said Riddle quietly.

'They will. If I have anything to do with it, they certainly will.' Barstow turned slightly, rested his arm along the roof of the car and gently drummed with the tips of his fingers, as he spoke, as if tabulating already-reached decisions. 'Chatterton

221

is, at this moment, feeling very pleased with himself. He thinks, he *knows*, that unless he has the devil's own bad luck, he'll walk from a Crown Court a free man. He's also pretty sure he'll be given his job back. Not to do so would cause a stink with people who enjoy burning dirty rags under everybody's nostrils.

'So, he'll be given his job back.

'Meanwhile, I need somebody established here whom I can rely upon. The last person I want is Smeaton.'

'Superintendent Smeaton,' began Riddle, 'isn't quite . . . '

'Chief inspector, I don't want either loyalty or good manners to ditch what, at best, is a scheme riddled with doubts.'

'No, sir.'

'Smeaton will be offered a chief superintendentship. He'll accept it – of course he will. It will be sugared up to look like a plum job. What it will *really* be is a desk in some forgotten administrative corner where he'll do as little harm as possible. Where his monumental non-talent can be hidden from public view. When he moves, you'll take his chair. You will be promoted a rung, be made superintendent and become divisional officer.'

'You make it sound so easy,' smiled Riddle.

'From where I am, it *is* easy.' The sardonic tone left no doubt about Barstow's opinion of those at the head of the force. 'Once a man gets the words "chief constable" attached to his rank he becomes over-ambitious. The "assistants" and the "deputies" all have an eye on the golden office. Once in that office, they tend to toady to Whitehall. They haven't time to *police*. They all have a yen for the accolade. It's an ailment they all suffer.'

'I – er – I wouldn't know, sir.'

'I would,' growled Barstow. 'I'm surrounded by it. I therefore take full advantage of it. *I* – and, of course, my kind – run the force. We make the damn thing work. We're not too interested in police politics. We're stupid, but we prefer to be stupid. We "fix" things. I intend to arrange for Smeaton to be put out to pasture – unofficially, of course. I intend to arrange for *you* to take his place as divisional officer.'

'Thank you, sir.'

'Now, let me pick your brains, Riddle. The Crown Court. Chatterton faces a full-blooded charge of murder. We throw what little we have at him, but it's not enough. In your opinion, who's going to be the most unhappy man in that courtroom?'

'Not Chatterton.'

'Definitely not Chatterton,' agreed Barstow.

'I'd say Bulmer.'

'I, too, would say Bulmer.' Barstow nodded. 'We've jockeyed Bulmer into a position of twelfth disciple. The original hanged himself. Bulmer won't do that, hopefully. What he *will* do is hate the man who placed him in that position.'

'Chatterton.'

'He'll hate Chatterton.' Barstow's fingers drummed the roof of the car. 'His hatred of Chatterton should be matched by his respect for you. You opposed me on his behalf when things began to get rough.

'Chatterton will return to Radholme as a patrol constable. That should take a certain amount of starch from the tail of his shirt. No office job. No transfer. Back here where he's known.'

'He won't resign,' said Riddle.

'Of course he won't resign. I'm counting on him not resigning. If he resigned, he'd be out of my reach.'

'Bulmer might ask for a transfer.'

'Bulmer is going to be promoted to section sergeant. He'll take Boothby's place. Section sergeant over the man he hates. That should be very interesting.'

'And me?'

'You'll be there, quietly stirring the pot. Knowing that *I'm* keeping a distant eye on the temperature.'

'Will I?' said Riddle flatly.

'It's the name of the game, Riddle.' Barstow's tone left no doubt. It was *his* game, played according to *his* rules. 'We don't just clean the mess from our own doorstep. We scour the damn stone white. Chatterton will come back here. Not to gloat – to suffer. I want him wishing he *had* been sent down.'

'And if he goes too far?' asked Riddle, gently. 'He's obviously capable of terrible things.'

'I hope so.' Barstow's nod was without compassion. 'I hope he *commits* terrible things. Indeed, I think it very likely. He won't walk away twice.'

Riddle took a deep breath, then said, 'Sir, I did you an injustice.'

'Really?'

'I – er – I said you couldn't deliver. That, in effect, you'd lost control.'

'I never lose complete control, Riddle.' It was light enough for Riddle to see the old curl of the lips. 'A slight loosening of the reins, perhaps. To give a false sense of security. But I never lose *control*.'

There seemed little else to say and nothing worth the saying.

Riddle moved his shoulders in a gesture of resignation, turned and walked towards his own car. From behind his back he heard the sound of a quiet chuckle. In his own twisted way, Barstow was enjoying himself.

Well, it made a change that *somebody* was enjoying himself.

6 a.m. Radholme. Population, 25,000. A market town, not too far from the commercialised beauty of the Yorkshire Dales; not too far from the old Yorkshire/Lancashire border.

It was awakening to a new day with new stresses, new heartbreaks and new belly laughs. The population would increase and decrease, as babies were born and oldsters died. Friendships would be made and broken, love would blossom and wither, fresh hatreds would burst into flame.

It is known as 'life' . . . and it is the stuff of which policing is made.